Twilight
is the Barony of Traitc

First Night,
the Domain of Chance.

The Under-earth,
the Duchy of Treasures, Artists, and Smiths.

Fullmoon,
the Marquisate of Were-Creatures and Fools.

Second Night,
the County of Dreams and Dreamers.

The Hour of the Wolf,
the Kingdom of the Heart of the Night.

And finally,
Dawn, the Border of the Lost.

THE
SECRET
MARKET
OF THE
DEAD

THE SECRET MARKET OF THE DEAD

A Novel

GIOVANNI DE FEO

SAGA PRESS

LONDON **NEW YORK** TORONTO
AMSTERDAM/ANTWERP NEW DELHI SYDNEY/MELBOURNE

AN IMPRINT OF SIMON & SCHUSTER, LLC
1230 AVENUE OF THE AMERICAS, NEW YORK, NEW YORK 10020

For more than 100 years, Simon & Schuster has championed authors and the stories they create. By respecting the copyright of an author's intellectual property, you enable Simon & Schuster and the author to continue publishing exceptional books for years to come. We thank you for supporting the author's copyright by purchasing an authorized edition of this book.

No amount of this book may be reproduced or stored in any format, nor may it be uploaded to any website, database, language-learning model, or other repository, retrieval, or artificial intelligence system without express permission. All rights reserved. Inquiries may be directed to Simon & Schuster, 1230 Avenue of the Americas, New York, NY 10020 or permissions@simonandschuster.com.

This book is a work of fiction. Any references to historical events, real people, or real places are used fictitiously. Other names, characters, places, and events are products of the author's imagination, and any resemblance to actual events or places or persons, living or dead, is entirely coincidental.

Copyright © 2025 by Giovanni De Feo

All rights reserved, including the right to reproduce this book or portions thereof in any form whatsoever. For information, address Saga Press Subsidiary Rights Department, 1230 Avenue of the Americas, New York, NY 10020.

First Saga Press hardcover edition July 2025

SAGA PRESS and colophon are trademarks of Simon & Schuster, LLC

Simon & Schuster strongly believes in freedom of expression and stands against censorship in all its forms. For more information, visit BooksBelong.com.

For information about special discounts for bulk purchases, please contact Simon & Schuster Special Sales at 1-866-506-1949 or business@simonandschuster.com.

The Simon & Schuster Speakers Bureau can bring authors to your live event. For more information or to book an event, contact the Simon & Schuster Speakers Bureau at 1-866-248-3049 or visit our website at www.simonspeakers.com.

Interior design by Lewelin Polanco

Manufactured in the United States of America

10 9 8 7 6 5 4 3 2 1

Library of Congress Cataloging-in-Publication Data is available.

ISBN 978-1-6680-7736-8
ISBN 978-1-6680-7738-2 (ebook)

This book is dedicated to Elvira and Lillino.

Theirs were the first stories I've ever listened to.

THE
SECRET
MARKET
OF THE
DEAD

In the old church of Saint Francis, in Lucerìa, there is a statue of a young woman. Not many guides know about it, but if you ask the priest, he will lead you to a subterranean chapel under the main altar. The steps are slippery, the neon light defective, but the statue is well worth the trouble. It depicts a girl of about fifteen, life-size, with arms raised overhead, gripping a hammer. Her countenance, a fierce expression of will and defiance, is not easily forgotten. More striking are her cloak, woven from eyes, and complexion, black as ink. But when you ask the priest which saint she is, he will avert his eyes. For the young woman is no saint of the Day.

She is a Nocturnal.

In those days, it was understood that every town had a patron saint. Lucerìa's saints, though, were of a peculiar kind. Their statues, adorned with the usual halo and candles, always had something off about them, something twisted: a touch of the Night.

The Lucerini still worshipped the saints you can spot on any calendar, such as Saint Anthony or Saint Agatha. But their town was also home to seven Major Ones, seven Night Saints represented with the same statues and holy cards as their counterparts in the Day but after dawn, became someone else entirely.

For those seven were Nocturnals. Ogres, fairy queens, ghosts—you can find these aplenty in Naples. But Nocturnals belong only to Lucerìa and its woods, have resided in this land right at the heel of Italy's boot since long before it was finally made into one country. Before the Spanish reyes and before Napoleon, before Emperor Frederick of Hohenstaufen and his Muslim subjects, before the arrival of German hordes, before the Roman conquest of the Daunians, Nocturnals lived in the Night that is just on the other side of Lucerìa.

Sensing there is a tale to be told, you invite the priest for a glass of wine in Piazza Tribunali. He smiles thinly at your invitation and says he will tell you the story of the statue, but only if you promise not to believe a word of it. You think it must be your precarious understanding of Italian that makes you miss the joke, but the priest seems deadly serious. You mustn't believe a word, he says again, or repeat this story to a living soul, ever. And yet he seems eager to tell it himself.

You can't help but ask why you mustn't tell her story. In response, he stares at you with the same look he usually reserves for catechism students faltering over the Apostles' Creed. His hands shoot up.

She is a Nocturnal, he says. A story made flesh. They live on their telling and feast on belief. If you believe in them, they can come back. Kings and warriors, smiths and sailors, Wyrms, and Wiccae, and Garaudi, and Mazapegul, and Nuriae, Gale Riders and Pales, the whole lot, Minors and Majors, all the dead. And that's why you mustn't believe a word of it.

So you listen to the rest of the story and when it is finished your head is ringing. Maybe it is the three glasses of wine, maybe it isn't, but you shake hands with the priest, go back to your hotel, and when you arrive there, lay your head on your pillow. Just for a minute, you think, as you fall into a dark stupor, one so deep you cannot climb out of it.

You try to resist, for it is only seven o'clock, and if you sleep now, you will wake up in the middle of the night, here in Lucerìa, where the Night was born. But you can't resist, and so fall asleep, like a body slipping into dark waters.

And this is the dream you dream.

PART I

THE DREAMARQUISE OF CATS

ONE

During the first week of May 1747, as the saints' procession honoring the birth of King Don Carlos's heir made its way past Oriana's house, her twin brother Oriano suddenly dove in front of the cortege and was almost trampled to death. Nothing short of a miracle saved him, a miracle to which Oriana was the sole witness.

Oriana and Oriano spent almost the entire night before the parade in games and whispered expectations. The twins' bedroom, a narrow attic space, also served as a drying room for the festoons of oregano and dried peppers that hung from the rafters. Two glass jars full of fireflies emanated a greenish glow that barely lit the game they were playing. Their corn husk–stuffed mattress swished every time they moved to turn over a card. On a patched blanket, holy cards smudged by use were arranged in four rows of five. The eight-year-old twins sat across from each other and stared at them in concentration.

"My turn," said Oriana.

"That one," replied her twin, pointing at a card.

"Right. That's . . . Saint Barbara, protector of miners, prayed to for protection against lightning, and her day is the . . . third, no, the fourth of December. Turn it!"

Oriano turned over the card and held it close to the jar to

reveal a young girl crowned in gold, a tower being struck by a lightning bolt in the background. The little boy slapped his knee.

"You're cheating! I know you are. Just tell me how you do it!"

"I am not. I just have a good memory. Now, that's six against one. Your turn. That one," she said, pointing at a card on the edge of the bed.

"Can I have a peek first?"

"Of course not. You know what Papà says. It's no use agreeing to something if you break your word after."

"Well, I haven't agreed to lose six to one!"

"Just play your turn, Oriano."

"All right, then. That's . . . I think Saint Simon, patron of the leather people—"

"That would be the tanners."

"Tanners, that's what I said. Prayed to for . . . chicken, I mean, when you want to eat chicken, or have your chickens get fat. Am I right?"

"Go on."

"And his day . . . his day is . . . can I have a hint?"

"Oh, I should think not."

"You are the worst! His celebration day is . . . ah!" he said, suddenly beaming. "I know it! It's the day Mamma and Papà married! I know because it's coming in two Sundays, so it's the fifteenth of May! Turn it over!"

Oriana turned over the card: an old man with a flame in his hand and a piglet at his feet stared at them with hollow eyes.

"Saint Anthony, protector of all smiths," said Oriana, "sorry."

"I'm done. I don't want to play your stupid game anymore," he said, and shook the coverlet, showering all the cards on the floor.

"Oriano! Those are Mamma's holy cards! If they get filthy, she'll only feed us bread and water for a week!"

"I don't care. You cheated, you just won't admit it!"

"I did not!"

"Yes, you did!"

A thump interrupted their quarrel. The twins jumped and stared at the trapdoor.

"I'm hearing a ruckus," sounded Donna Lena's muffled voice, "when I should be hearing prayers or silence. Need I come up?"

"Sorry, Mamma," said Oriana. "We were just about to go to sleep."

"You'd better. You still want to see the saints' procession tomorrow, don't you?"

"Yes!" the twins replied in unison.

"Then you must be on your best behavior. And if you lose one of my holy cards, I'll shave your heads to shame you both. Do I make myself clear?"

"Yes, Mamma," they sang together.

"Buonanotte."

Quickly, the twins collected the cards from the floor, draped a black cloth over the firefly lanterns—leaving one alight so they could see a bit—and slipped under the sheets. In that cozy half darkness, the siblings breathed face-to-face, their foreheads touching. Oriana was the taller of the two, and slightly stockier, but both had the thick eyebrows of the Siliceo family, unruly brown hair, and their mother's mischievous green-gray eyes.

"Do you think Papà will finally get a commission?" Oriano asked.

"I heard Mamma pray to Saint Anthony for it, so maybe he will."

"Will the statue of Saint Anthony be there tomorrow?"

"Why? Are you still thinking about your spinning top?"

"Well," he sniffed, "I wouldn't have to ask Saint Anthony for it if Papà had bought me a new one."

"If he could have, he would have."

"And why shouldn't I ask Saint Anthony? Or perhaps I could call the Night-One, the Duke of Under-earth, to come in his stead!"

While no one had seen the Duke manifest in nearly a hundred years, as patron of smiths and craftsmen and the earthliest of the seven Major Ones, his mere presence was said to grant gifts. Oriana stuck her head out of the blanket, as if to make sure they were still alone, then dove under again. She brought her forehead against her brother's.

"You know Mother would *kill you* if she heard you speak their names."

Being from Naples, their mother found the whole concept of Night Saints blasphemous, and hated all their silly rites. The only time she seemed to bear the idea was during Vigils, and even there she would pointedly make the sign of the cross. Luckily, Oriana's Aunt Ciccerella thought otherwise. The girl remembered well how her aunt lay in bed with her on New Year's Eve, whispering of the Night.

All Nocturnals were Diurnals once, the way all those who are now alive, one day will die. Some of the dead are told, and those who are sometimes come back, but with something of the Night, something wild and old.

Aunt Ciccerella told her that Nocturnals only existed when Diurnals told stories about them, especially at Night. She then listed the seven Major Ones, each an earl of their own domain, a part of the immortal darkness.

Should you need to call for their help, these are their names. Ossifrago, Baron of Twilight and Jester of the Night King. Uriene, Earl of the First Night, prophet, and dice master. The Emistuchivio, Duke of the dark that lies Under-earth.

Briace, Marquise of Fullmoon and Lord of were-creatures and lunatics. Serapide, Countess of Second Night, she-warrior, and bringer of dreams. The Grim King himself, Lord ruler of the Hour of the Wolf and of all Night. And finally his spouse, Queen of Dawn and our Lady of sorrows.

Few adults she knew would dare utter their names at night, even for protection. And yet calling out to them, daring them to respond, made Oriana feel safer, stronger. All her life she imagined seeing Nocturnals out of the corner of her eye. When at dusk the branch of a pine tree quivered overhead, she imagined the spiny face of a Mazapegul. And when the railing of a staircase shifted under the moonlight, Oriana thought it a Wyrm slithering over the palazzo to get a better look at her. Sometimes at night she heard songs in the wind. She could never remember their words, only a tingling sensation, like her whole body was on fire. Was that the Night? Though she had called out to it several times, she received an answer only once—the year prior, after Oriano returned from the spring market in Foggia.

In hindsight, she wasn't so sure that it hadn't been a dream. Not that sleep would have made it any less real, for the Night-Ones come out of dreams like swallows from chimneys. She remembered lying with her eyes wide open until she felt the dark pressing in on her from all sides. And when she stood up to open the small window above her bed, the sky was ablaze with stars. She stared at them for so long she forgot herself completely; she wasn't a little girl looking at the Night, she was the Night looking at a little girl.

Then, she saw it. A cloud of stars descended onto the roof and took the shape of a man. Had it been summer, Oriana would have thought them fireflies, but it was still too cold.

And if you see fireflies in early spring or winter, be careful. Garaudi wear cloaks made of eyes—stolen from vagrants—that glint in the dark. For they were makers of sublime beauty but refused to see it until it was too late. And so the Duke of the Under-earth punished them by turning them blind.

It seemed like the creature was looking in Oriana's direction, though she couldn't know for certain. She ought to have felt scared under its gaze but didn't. It was blind, after all, slave to the Under-earth and its master. Poor, poor Garaude. The creature came ablaze, its cloak-eyes opening. Right in the middle of its form, she could make out a hood, and in that blackness, she imagined salty lips, soundlessly forming an O.

She had said its name. Was it saying hers?

She wanted to tell Oriano straightaway, of course. But even then, Oriana felt that the experience was meant for her and her alone. He had gone to the spring market without her, hadn't he? When her mother caught a fever, it was she who had to stay behind and help her in the house. He had the Day, and so she would claim the Night. Also, if she told him, sooner or later he would tell Mamma.

"If the Duke came," Oriano whispered under the bed covers, "I could ask him for a spinning top made of darkness, fire, stars, or wind. Can you imagine? Me spinning my top in front of our house and all the hats in Lucerìa flying high!"

"The Emistuchivio," she hissed, drawing closer, "will not come for a little boy. And anyway, you have nothing to offer him."

"But I do!" He beamed.

He emerged from underneath the blanket and walked over to a hole in the wall of their room. Carefully, by the fireflies' low glow, the boy retrieved a ball of cotton and unwrapped it to reveal two teeth. Sitting up, Oriana frowned at her twin.

"Don't the Tellers say," he began, cheeks flushed, "that the Duke sows children's teeth in the ground to grow his bone soldiers?"

"Who on earth did you hear that from?"

"From Aunt Ciccerella, at the Vigil of the Dead last year."

"And you've kept your baby teeth hidden in that wall for, what . . . months?"

"Think about it, two teeth, two Boons from the Duke!"

"That's greedy."

"I wanted you to have one. Isn't there anything you want?"

She bit her lip. There *was* something she wanted. It was the very reason she had felt such disappointment when Oriano was allowed to go to the spring market in Foggia and she had to stay home. But she didn't even dare think it, much less say it aloud.

"Oriano, if Mother sees this, she'll bring Hell upon us. You won't get to go to the spring market, and neither will I."

"I'll keep them hidden."

"Promise me, then. Swear."

He swore. They slid back under the blanket, whispering about secret keys that led to secret chests, which held all the treasures of the Under-earth. And even though at times Oriana tried to stifle her brother's excitement, she was no longer able to quench her own. That night, they slept little, if at all.

The Day surprised them with a fullness of light that spelled disaster. Their father was still not back from his errand, and neither was their mother. She had gone to spin at Mamma Eba's workshop with an old companion from Caserta, and the twins were expected to be clean and ready to go when she returned. Oriano was still too excited to be of any real help, so Oriana had to get the water from the public fountain in the piazza herself.

On her way home she caught a glimpse of her father's workshop, just three houses down the street. For a moment, the little girl was transfixed. She breathed in its scent: coal, iron, sawdust. Despite her enthrallment, she wouldn't take a single step toward it; an old superstition in Lucerìa warned against a smith's children entering his workshop before they came of age. But the smithy's deep oak door was slightly ajar, and Oriana could glimpse inside from where she stood. By the forge's light, she spotted the square anvil and her father's hammer resting atop it. It was an old, ugly beast, dented and blackened by use. And yet in her father's hands, it could create wonders.

A draft made the smithy's door creak shut and the girl hurried home, careful not to spill the water. In a flurry of legs and arms, brother and sister washed in the tin tub. While Oriano splashed around in unabashed mirth, his twin trying to scrub the both of them as fast as she could, they heard the distant drums. The procession was about to begin. They were still frantically rubbing each other's heads when Donna Lena entered the kitchen, the baby Tato asleep in her arms. The twins froze, water still trickling from their wet hair.

Donna Lena was a robin of a woman, not small, but bent by the everyday labor she took on to make ends meet since her husband's lack of commissions. At twenty-six her beauty was fading, her luscious hair tamed, braided flat on the nape of her neck. Fatigue was her default state. Still, as she adjusted her shawl, she couldn't help but smile at her children.

"If you don't have your good clothes on," she said quietly, green-gray eyes narrowing, "by the time I finish two Hail Marys, I'll go without you."

Oriana and Oriano jumped out of the tub and bolted to their room.

The muddy street—surrounded on both sides by low white houses and crowned by rows of balconies—was a mass of heads swaying like sunflowers in the wind. All of Lucerìa's craftsmen were there: carvers and tanners, smiths, farmers in their straw hats and women dressed in black, each waiting for the statue of Saint Anthony, patron saint of their contrada.

Oriana, her mother, and her two brothers stood just outside their house, watching for the approaching statue. They had already seen the lily-adorned Madonna, Saint Sebastian pierced by arrows so realistic that his wounds seemed to ooze real blood, and Santa Barbara with her golden crown and the martyr's palm in her hands.

"Look, Harp-tooth, the Duke is farting stars!" someone shouted.

It was mad Totò, the scrawny cemetery guardian, talking to the old cat on his shoulder. A few people in the crowd tittered in response, though most ignored him. The approaching statue wasn't exactly farting, but a pungent cloud hung over it all the same. Fireworks shot from the thin metal ring around its head. Just like the illustration on the holy card the twins had studied the night before, the statue depicted Saint Anthony's customary halo, white beard, brown cassock, and plaster pig. Yet he was different from any other you might see in a neighboring town. He looked quite short—older, wilder—the pig at his feet vaguely misshapen as if it weren't a pig at all.

As the statue approached, cloaked in sparkling fire and enshrouded by smoke and the beating of drums, soft hymns could be heard from the rows of women. Some were holding tallow candles, so that by their light, the statue could help them find what they had lost. But a few carried strange crowns of dried flowers, barking puppies, or squealing piglets in offering—not to Saint Anthony, but to that other one, the Emistuchivio, Duke of Under-earth and Lord of the darkness that lives below the ground.

Oriana glanced at her twin. He held his left fist behind his back, lips moving in silent prayer. Oriana took his other hand and squeezed it, hard, in warning. She was still nettled by missing last year's spring market. She'd waited patiently for an entire year, twelve long, dreary months, and would not lose her chance once more. But as the procession approached,

Oriana felt her own excitement rise. She knew Night Saints were real and allowed herself to briefly fantasize about the Duke showing himself and granting her a Boon. At least their mother had not noticed, too lost in her own reverie. Even after ten years, she missed Naples bitterly. Sometimes Oriana thought her mother would always see herself as an outsider.

"It's almost like in Via Reale, when Don Carlos came," Donna Lena sighed. "The whole avenue was alive with carriages and there were fireworks on the sea."

As Oriana watched it move closer, the statue itself caught her attention, particularly the metal arch where its fireworks sparked. Oriana tugged at Donna Lena's arm, insistent.

"Mamma? Did Papà work on the statue's arch?"

Donna Lena shushed her, rocking the newborn in her arms, and watched as Don Giacomino—from his bay horse—reached into his bag to retrieve a handful of almond biscuits shaped like doubloons. At once, a throng of children screamed, hands shooting up to catch them. The priest laughed as he showered them with biscuits, his youthful face flushed. The children surrounded him, catching biscuits in midair or scurrying to pick them off the ground. All but one. A boy stood in front of the horse, left fist held high, offering something not to the priest, but to the statue behind him. Oriana had barely noticed her brother slip away.

"Oriano!"

Donna Lena's scream pierced even the roar of fireworks. Yet few heard her, and none saw the wide-eyed child on the road. Certainly not Don Giacomino, proudly trotting along at a steady pace. The horse's hooves would snap Oriano's bones before anyone would notice.

Oriana didn't scream, didn't run to her brother's aid.

Instead, she looked up at the statue.

"Please," she whispered.

The statue tilted its head, mouth agape.

She heard a soft snap, nearly drowned out by the surrounding noise. Then the statue raised its wooden leg and kicked the first porter in the back of the head.

At once, the young man stumbled and fell.

The statue and its metal framework followed, fireworks showering the crowd. The people scattered, shrieking, as the priest reined in his frothing horse. While the women wailed at the bad omen, Donna Lena scooped up Oriano and hurried off. As the chaos dissipated, the Lucerini found their culprit in the stunned porter, a beefy apprentice of seventeen, who was seized and carried away.

Oriana wanted to shout that it wasn't his fault. But then, whose was it? The Saint's? The Duke's? Or her own?

TWO

As soon as Donna Lena put Tato in the hammock and shushed him to sleep, she turned to her other children with eyes of furious emerald.

"You will go to your room and be very quiet about it."

"But Mamma—" began Oriana.

"Now."

Even half a century later, Oriana would remember the taste of injustice with bitter clarity. She and her brother scampered up the wooden ladder and through the trapdoor to their room. The chains of garlic and bunches of drying herbs hanging from the ceiling swayed in the sudden draft.

"I didn't show the teeth, Oriana, like I promised! Just my fist! You'll see, Papà will bring us both to Foggia."

"Shut up."

As her brother dove face-first into their corn husk mattress, Oriana sat on the edge of the bed. Was he sleeping already? He always had a talent for dozing off on command. She peered at her twin. Awake, he was as different from her as a sunflower from an artichoke. But when Oriano slept, his face better reflected the flesh and blood they shared, one the mirror of the other, like Day is to Night. Was she jealous of Oriano? How could she be? They were of the same, even if her brother was allowed to go to the spring market in Foggia last year and she wasn't. Though, truth be told, she wasn't thinking about that at all anymore.

Had anyone else seen the statue move?

She was certain that the Emistuchivio had listened to her plea. There was a word for people who had dealings with Nocturnals. *Night-touched.* Like Totò Ciotola, the mad cemetery keeper. A sudden noise made her start, one that would have wakened her from the sleep of Death: her father's hammer. Her back stiffened. That sound meant Mastro Peppo had finally returned from his errand. Soon he would finish his work at the smithy and come home, expecting to find the table set and the children in their seats.

"Come down, both of you!"

Her mother's voice startled her. But when Oriana turned, she saw with alarm that her brother was lying face down on the trapdoor, blocking her from opening it.

"What are you doing? Get up!" she commanded.

"It's no use, Mamma thinks it's all my fault, and so do you."

"Oriano, just—"

"No! It's no use! No use!"

She knew it was impossible to reason with him while he was in this state, so she grabbed him by the shoulder. At once, her twin turned his head and bit her. Oriana screamed. Before she could blink, they were wrestling on the floor, biting, scratching, and pulling each other's hair. She took his blows until she could grab hold of his arm and bite him fiercely just above the elbow. Her brother collapsed, sobbing hard against the floor.

Donna Lena was calling again, her voice impatient. Oriana waited for her breath to slow and then opened her mouth to respond sensibly, like she always did. But then, impulsively, she turned to her brother.

"Do you know what he's working on?" she asked. "I think he is welding the links of a chain. A chain so long it can wrap around Mount Vesuvius seven times, so strong it can hold back seven hundred horses at full gallop, so hard it can only be melted by the fire of seven Wyrms, and yet so thin, so light, and so soft you could wear it around your neck like a silk scarf."

Her brother gave no sign he was listening. Still, she went on.

The twins had played this game since infancy, but this time, it was as if her palate was an anvil and her tongue a hammer.

"He is also working on the seventy-times-folded-mansion, a palace made of layers of iron so thin that, when folded, it looks like a kerchief. But when you unfold it, not once, not twice, but seventy times, the cloth appears as what it really is: a huge iron palace with sixty-three doors and one little window, right at the top."

"Another," murmured Oriano, his face still buried in his arm.

Their mother called again, but this time, they both ignored her.

"What could it be . . ." she mused, sitting on the bed. "It's hard to tell by the sound of the hammer alone. Is it an armored hat, which protects its wearer with cannonball-proof steel? Or maybe a mechanical snake that moves when your name is sung in reverse? A portable staircase? Or an infinitely bottomless cup? Which would you have?"

At last, Oriano sat up. He was still flushed, but his eyes had dried.

"I think I'd take the mansion. So that I could hide there, and Mamma would never ever find me."

The table was set, the bottle filled to the brim, and bread on the cutting board.

When their father entered, the twins stood up. Mastro Peppo was still wearing the yellow garment of his trade and smelled of burnt wood. He was short, stocky, and balding, with the large face and curly beard of a tanned Neptune. Under the lush bushes of his brows, his eyes were the color of unwrought iron. He took small, pensive steps as he approached and, unsmiling, sat down. His family followed.

Donna Lena poured the wine, and her husband filled their wooden bowls with steaming maccheroni. Each finished their pasta in silence. Oriana thought it part of their punishment for what happened at the procession. But Mastro Peppo had not uttered a single word, and his wife seemed as concerned as the children. Something was wrong. The smith hadn't touched his wine, instead staring vacantly at the bottle. Oriana had seen him like this only once before, after his own father died.

When at last Mastro Peppo spoke, his voice had the crackling sound of an old fire.

"The other night," he said, "all the door handles in Villa Mezzacasa were found twisted and changed."

It was well known in their town that two centuries ago, the Mezzacasa family had trapped Ossifrago, the Baron of Twilight, and used him to make their fortune. And sometimes, even centuries later, Nocturnals visited their home to play tricks on them. Donna Lena's face drained to the color of sourdough. She hated any mention of Nocturnals.

Finally, Oriana gathered her courage and asked, "Changed into what?"

The blacksmith wet his lips.

"Thorny vines," he said. "Tree branches. Leaves. The family said the leaves acted as tongues that whispered their dread, the thorns grabbed their cloaks to tell them their desire, and the branches grew eyes that saw directly into them. They axed everything down this morning and burned it all. I was there."

Oriana blinked. She could feel her brother's excitement like hot waves of perspiration. And her mother's contempt for the Night Saints like an icy draft.

"Papà, that's a lot of work for you, isn't it?" Oriana blurted.

Finally, Mastro Peppo smiled, showing off his beloved wrinkles.

"Seventy-two door handles," he said, "in silver. Paid upfront."

"I'll make the coffee," Donna Lena said.

She stood up, a hand over her mouth, unable to contain her pride. Oriana had scarcely an idea of how much coin that would be. Could they afford a new spinning top with it? Or even—the forbidden thought came to her in a flash—a book? By the stove, she caught her mother's sideways smirk, the one she made when secretly pleased with herself. Wearing that thin smile, she carried the steaming pot to the table. The smell of coffee filled the room like the perfume of orange blossom at Easter, the very scent of happiness.

As he drank from his cup, the Mastro said, "If you two behave, tomorrow you can both come with me to the fair in Foggia."

Oriano kicked her under the table, the *I told you so* in his green-gray eyes, but Oriana didn't speak. Her heart was so ripe, she was afraid it would grow into an apple and drop out of her mouth.

"Not Oriana," Donna Lena said.

The girl put a hand over her cheek.

"Why?" asked Mastro Peppo, putting his cup down.

"Because she flung herself in front of the Saints' procession and almost caused a mortal accident. It was a miracle Oriano got away with his life."

Oriana could hear her own heart thundering in her throat. She stared at her mother. Donna Lena had always been strict, but never cruel. And yet now, Oriana had the choking feeling her mother didn't see her at all, like she was nothing.

"Is this true?" her father inquired.

Wide-eyed, Oriano opened his mouth, but no sound came out.

Finally, the boy nodded.

Oriana heard her chair scratching against the floor before

she registered that she had stood up. It was her moment to speak. But her fear, confusion, and fury were like tumultuous winds, each blowing her in a different direction. Would her version—one that included the favor of the Duke—even be believed? Offering it would accuse her mother of being a liar and her brother of being a coward. She was still struggling when she met her father's sad eyes. His decision was already made.

"Next year," he assented, "she will have learned to behave."

Oriana turned around and climbed the shaky ladder to their room, slamming the trapdoor shut so hard the oregano's festoons billowed as if from a storm. She felt such a storm ripping her to bits from the inside, all lightning and thunder. To leave the table unexcused like that was unheard of, and of course her parents immediately called her back.

But the trapdoor never opened to show her mother's furious face, and she didn't hear the sound of her father bellowing her name. Instead, the conversation downstairs resumed, stilted at first, and then in more cheerful tones, until she heard her brother burst out laughing, a sound of unfettered joy. It was right then that Oriana decided that her rebellion would not stop at cutting the meal short.

She would go to Foggia for the spring market, with or without her parents' consent.

THREE

Mastro Peppo and Oriano set off after dawn on a coach bound for the plains of Foggia, eight miles away.

Oriana was counting on her mother to leave her in peace for one morning, and she did. As soon as she heard Donna Lena leave for Mamma Eba's seamstress workshop, Oriana bolted from her bed and groped about for her shoes. Walking at a good pace, grown-ups could make the trip to Foggia in less than four hours. She would probably need five, maybe six. The real challenge would be staying hidden from the neighbors. For that purpose, Oriana donned her father's straw hat and his walking stick. On the road to Foggia, she'd be mistaken for one of the many child shepherds running errands for their masters.

She sat by the window and listened. Only when she heard the sheep's festive bells and bleating lamentations did she open the door. In the early days of May, most shepherds went back to their mountains in the Abruzzi. And as they were not from town, none would care for her presence unless she spoke to them. Keeping her face down, Oriana joined the woolly tide, the shouts of the shepherds right behind her. They would escort her up to Porta Foggia, one of the four town gates, and from there she would find the tratturi, the thin chalk road, to take her to the market.

When she reached the orchards, hours later, the sun was scorching her nape. Summer was close, and in Apulia, the heat baked the grass until it was terra-cotta. The olive trees were in full bloom, though, twisted old men with white rows of flowers like teeth biting the hot syrup air. She had not brought any water, which she bitterly regretted. She didn't dare ask the shepherds, for fear that they would inquire about her, so by the time she saw the brown haze of Foggia on the horizon, her temples were pulsing in a vicious vice.

A forest of noise approached just behind the crumbling city gates, sounds both human and inhuman, animal and mechanical, natural and artificial: oxen bellowing, sheep bleating, goats clanging their bells, drivers shouting, dogs barking, hawkers crying, and sudden bursts of firecrackers. As she crossed the gate, vision caught up with sound: a stream of colors running into one another—the black cassocks of priests, the red scarves of the fish vendors, the wool jackets of the smiths, and the ragged variety of the stalls' awnings.

Oriana splashed her head into the cattle fountain, drinking avidly.

At last, she breathed, water streaming down her face, revitalized. Despite the pain in her legs, joy was riding the hot tempest of her heart. She had to find her father. If she were alone with him, without her mother, she was certain he would look at her disobedience with a forgiving eye and maybe even a few coins for what her heart most desired.

It was a little after noon and the market was at its peak. She looked around. The fair was divided into sections. There was the animal market with its high-fenced pens, where the steam rising from the oxen formed a mist that hung about them like ghosts. Then the meat markets with their long stalls, adorned with ribbons of assorted colors, fluttering in the wind. Among them a flock of sturdy women, crowned with wicker baskets, were talking with such gesticulating alacrity that Oriana could understand them even at a distance.

Then she saw Bruno, her father's apprentice. Seventeen years old, short, shaggy haired, and scoundrel eyed, he was offering an apricot to the youngest of the basket women. She laughed in response, covering her mouth and slowly shaking her head. At once, Oriana tipped down her hat. She had never liked Bruno, though she couldn't say why. He was polite enough, yet somehow he gave the impression that he didn't care for them at all. It was vital he didn't see her, or he would tell her father before she had the chance to speak to him first.

"What are *you* doing here? They told you not to come."

She swirled around, her mouth dry.

But it was not Bruno or Mastro Peppo. She almost hadn't recognized Oriano in his Sunday best and small straw hat. Her twin yelped when she took him by the elbow and dragged him under the shadow of a large tent.

"Quiet," she said. "Do you have coin?"

Oriano blinked, pale faced.

"Well, no. I mean, yes, but it's mine!"

"I reckon you owe me, though, don't you think?"

Staring at her outstretched hand, the boy sighed.

"I suppose," he said, and put a hand to his waist pocket. "But I wanted to buy a flaming apple. Maybe . . . we can share one?"

A few stalls ahead, a stand displayed candy apples. They were coated in sugar, then dipped in blue spirit and set alight by the vendor.

"Just one, Oriana, please! We'll take one bite each—no one will know."

"A spirit-soaked apple? Have you lost your mind? Now, scamper off before I tell Papà what really happened at the procession."

She wouldn't, but Oriano didn't need to know that. Also, she was not sure what had happened herself. As soon as Oriano handed her the coins, he turned and ran.

"And don't you dare tell Bruno! Or Father!" she yelled after him.

Her brother couldn't be trusted to keep her presence a secret, but Oriana just needed an hour. She weighed the coins in her hand. Six carlini. Would it be enough? She had no idea. She spotted Bruno again. He had found the marionette theater and was eating a cone of salted chickpeas. She glanced at him, but the young apprentice was laughing so hard at the puppets' antics that he didn't even look her way. Finally, she could seek out what she had come to the spring market for: a book stall. It was the secret she held close to her heart. Unlike the rest of her family, she could read. She had learned at church, listening to Don Giacomino and then studying the pages of the Good Book. For Oriana remembered all that was said to her, sometimes word for word. Mass after Mass, she had figured out the secret of letters. So far, the only one who knew her secret was the priest.

Don Giacomino had shown her a book about the history of Lucerìa. She couldn't believe that an object so little could contain so many lives—all the lives of people before her, saints and crusaders, explorers and scientists! She would stay behind after every Mass just to read a page or two. She couldn't read particularly well, but she wanted to. What she saw in the priest's eyes as she read—surprise, respect, even awe—fueled her desire. And there was something else too. Books told very different stories than the ones she heard at the Vigils. Not strange tales about nocturnal monstrosities, but real accounts of real lives. There was no way she could acquire a book in Lucerìa without her mother finding out. But she could buy one at the Foggia market and hide it under her blouse to read later. Five hours under the scourge of the May sun was well worth it if she could bring one home.

"Excuse me, good sir, would you know where I might buy a book?"

Vendors and buyers passed her by without a glance. Oriana blushed to her ears. Was this what a big city was like? To think that at her age, her mother had been a flower seller in Naples. No wonder she had grown to be so overprotective of them. Oriana's impatience turned into a haze as she passed stall after stall. They were selling every kind of good, from old keys to chamber pots, but no books. She was beginning to despair when an empty stall caught her attention.

In fact, it was like she had sensed it in the very corner of her eyes, a vacuum of stillness in the busy fabric of the market. It was odd. No customers, no merchandise, just an empty timber plank. Behind it was a wooden shed, and hanging from its eave were a hat, a scarf, and a handkerchief. Oriana frowned. Had the owner forgotten them there, or were they for sale?

A creature crawled onto the plank, feet dangling. A monkey? If it were—and what else could it be?—it was the ugliest monkey she had ever seen. Stout as a bulldog, furless, neckless, disgustingly pale, and with claws one would be repulsed to call hands. Worse was its head. Oversized, with thin hair, and a horrible grin stamped on a face like dough. It mocked everyone who passed by with uncanny precision. In an instant its clammy face assumed their stupor, their hurriedness, their frown. As soon as each passerby saw themselves mirrored in that ghoulish flesh, their eyes widened in horror. The hairless beast mimicked that, too, until finally they hurried away, cursing or spitting on the ground, sometimes even making the sign to ward off evil. Not a great way to attract customers, Oriana thought. She glanced at the wooden shed. Had the monkey's owner known how poorly his creature served him, he would have beaten it senseless.

Oriana looked back at the creature—and her heart froze. Her fright was reflected in that hideous face. Instinctively, her body turned to flee, but she gritted her teeth and rooted her feet. She had seen a Garaude over the rooftops of Lucerìa and had asked for the help of the Emistuchivio; she would not be scared of an ugly monkey. Instead, she hissed back at it like their cat Marfisio did when he was in a mood. Screeching, the monkey fell from the plank and dashed to the shed, disappearing inside.

Alone with the strange merchandise Oriana looked up at the hat hanging from the eave. She blinked. Something about its material was not quite right. She looked around, perplexed. The hat was made from many concentric strips of cloth, yet it was impossible to tell if it was concave or convex, hollow or full. Every time she looked at it, she felt queasy, as if its mere existence changed the shape of things. Indeed, when Oriana looked back at her hands, for a moment they seemed not to be solid shapes but a hollow space in the air, a finger-shaped emptiness.

The scarf was even more unsettling. If you looked at it long enough, you could make out its strange pattern of branching roots. But as soon as you noticed it, they seemed to multiply, until you were standing in a forest of root patterns, of scarves within scarves within scarves. She felt that if she didn't look away, she would grow old in that very spot, and they would find her there in a century, a mummified child staring at the empty air. Oriana closed her eyes. She was scared to look up again, but as if of their own accord, her eyes opened.

The handkerchief was the most bizarre item of all. As soon as she decided the silk was shaped like a square, she counted five sides. And if she kept counting, its sides grew—six, then ten, then fifty—until the square became a circle. And just when she was sure it was round, she realized it had been a square all along.

Oriana looked away from the handkerchief for a bit of relief, only to realize that nothing she saw made sense. All the tents, the stalls, the farmers, had lost their numerical logic: People had six or seven heads, ten or two hundred hands, each with a thousand fingers. Oriana staggered forward and doubled over, retching.

Her father created physical objects that either were or were not. To her, this ambiguity was blasphemy. And yet some part of her yearned to understand how this trick worked. With effort, she lifted her head. The marionette play was still in its first act, and her brother showed no sign of returning. Oriana turned again to the shed and quietly walked toward it. She knocked twice.

Hearing no answer, she turned the handle, pushed open the creaking door, and entered.

FOUR

The interior was small, but not as cramped as she had expected.

The furniture was old and quite odd. There were yellow fungi growing from the chair legs, half the bookcase was covered in moss, and lichen grew out of two fat tomes. Dark shapes darted about, too fast for the eye to catch. She turned in time to see a gray tail slip away. Geckos, she thought.

Oriana took three little steps forward.

The owner of the stall was working at his table and didn't turn around when she entered. He was dressed like a smith, a simple goat's wool jacket and a low black cap. He was a sturdy, barrel-chested man with a bushy beard and two powerful arms ending in gigantic hands. His arms were in fact so large that the man appeared deformed, as if his limbs had been taken from a giant and attached to the body of a dwarf, or someone dwarfed by some inhuman pressure.

The monkey-creature sneered at her. It was helping its master repair an exquisite porcelain music box. From what she could see, its tiny dancer had come apart, her arms torn from her torso. The latter was made of raw bone. The child frowned, wondering if it was human bone that made up the trunk of the small ballerina. Was its torso a human phalanx? The man's own fingers were thick, yet he reattached the statuette's arms with flawless precision. The creature smirked and wound the music box; it played with such melodic perfection that Oriana sighed audibly. The man finally turned and stared at her.

"Do you like it?" he asked in a deep voice.

Oriana nodded, even though she didn't know if he meant the music, the box, or the stall's interior generally. It didn't matter; she liked it all.

"So you are here to buy," he said.

"I—I..." she stammered.

"Gobbo! Fetch the merchandise!"

Gobbo sneered again and dashed out of the stall. When he came back, he held the long scarf, the hat, and the handkerchief.

"Here, on the table," instructed his master, pushing his tools away with a shove of his huge hand. With exaggerated care, the creature put the three objects on the table as if they were made of crystal.

"Now, which one," asked the smith, "is the most precious?"

Oriana frowned. It felt like one of those games adults played with children before turning nasty when they didn't perform as expected. And yet she was not so sure that the man was an adult at all. Instinctively she raised her arm and pointed at the long silvery scarf.

"Very good," he said. "That is indeed the most precious, or at least it would be to most men. But is that the one you would buy?"

Oriana looked around, at a loss. Even Gobbo, that wretched creature, was eyeing her with a shade of compassion.

"Can I touch them?" she finally asked.

"Of course not. If you touch one, it's yours. Eyes are the windows of Desire, at Night as well as during the Day. Use them."

She looked at the table again. The shivering beauty of the scarf. The strange convex-concave appearance of the hat. But once more it was the shape-shifting handkerchief that drew her attention. Under the lamp its surface was uneven. It took her a while before she understood why—the silk cloth was folded. She stretched out her hand and touched it.

"Yes," said the stall's owner, "that's the one. Unfold it."

She began unfolding it. Once, twice, six times. And the more she unfolded it, the more it grew, not just two-dimensionally but upward. In seconds it was taller than Oriana; very soon it would be taller than the shed, erupting from it and visible from every part of the fair—a huge mansion with iron towers and iron rooftops and iron doors.

"Stop," the man said, and she stopped.

Oriana had to pause a minute before she was able to breathe again. The iron mansion had not disappeared. On the table it sat, small but to scale, so she could see how big it could become. Bigger than her house in Lucerìa.

"What is it?" the man-dwarf asked her.

"I-it's the seventy-times-folded-mansion, the one with sixty-three doors and just one tiny window at the top."

"Good. And this one?"

"It's the armor-hat. When you put it on it casts iron circles all over your body, to protect you from head to toe."

"Excellent. And the scarf?"

"It's a chain so long it can wrap around Mount Vesuvius seven times, so strong it can hold seven hundred horses, so resistant it can be broken only by seven Wyrms' fires."

"Indeed," the man said, nodding.

"But how can that be?" she said. "I made them up!"

"You did. And so I made them."

For a long time the child stared at him.

"You don't look like your statue at all," she said at last.

"I do not. Diurnals made it, not I."

"Why did you help me and my brother at the procession?"

"Because it pleased me. That was without price. This one is not."

The girl took out the six coins from her pocket and put them on the desk with a slight tremble of her fingers. The Emistuchivio nodded.

"This is very welcome. Gobbo, thank the young lady here."

The creature jumped on the table, opened its mouth, and produced a most horrible grating sound.

"*Grrrrazie.*"

Before it finished its utterance, the creature snatched the coins from the desk and, howling, ran out of the shed on all fours.

"He doesn't see much coin nowadays," the man said.

"But I thought the coins were for you!"

"Me? You think you can buy the seventy-times-folded-mansion with six carlini? Well, that would be surprising, wouldn't it?"

"Then how can I repay you?"

"Oh, that's simple. Bring me the secret ores that flow from the mountains of Kush, the invisible key to the hidden vault of Mu, the fire-ring of the sky shamans, the diamond eyes of the lizard kings. Get me any of those, and I will be satisfied and ask for nothing in return."

Shaking her head, Oriana stepped back.

"I can't."

"Then you owe me," he said, his eyes glimmering deep red.

"I don't want it, then! Take your mansion back! Take it!"

"I will not. I said that if you touched it, it was yours. You owe me."

Oriana could hardly hold in her tears. She was scared and dispirited, but also furious. Fists clenched, she sucked her breath in.

"What is it that you want from me," she croaked at last.

"Now we're talking. Tokai!" he said, clapping his hands.

One of the shadows in the back of the shed darted. Oriana saw the flick of a lizard's tail and lo! on the table was now a blue crystal bottle of Tokai. The odd little man poured two tiny cups and offered her one.

"But I'm eight years old! I don't drink!" she said.

"Because you were told not to. Now, drink."

She drank. Oriana was expecting something disgusting, but it was delicious. It tasted like blueberries should by the way they look, but never do. She no longer felt like crying. She was becoming a bit light-headed, yet her mind was getting sharper, clearer.

"Now," he said, "listen carefully, for I will say this only once. I am looking for my most precious tool. This is what I need you to get back for me." He paused. "A hammer."

"A hammer," she repeated. Her tongue felt like pins and needles.

"Not just any hammer. The Deep Red Hammer. The Dreamarquise of cats has it. You will have to get it back from him."

The silence was so absolute she could hear the lizards moving about.

"You want me to steal a hammer. From a pussycat."

Lighting his clay pipe—a dreadful white thing that looked like a long, gnarled bone—the Emistuchivio frowned.

"The Dreamarquise of cats is not to be jested about. He used to be a good friend of mine, before he stole my Hammer. I just want it back. Now, here comes the hard part. The Hammer has been changed; that's why my people can't find it. Also, the Dreamarquise carries it with him at all times. But he is such a braggart that in six months' time he's going to show it off, at the Secret Market of the Dead."

"Markets don't have dead," she said. Why did she feel she was getting smarter and yet her words sounded dumber than ever?

"They do, actually. Some, at least. Some of the dead. The ones whose stories have been told, but not enough to turn them into Nocturnals. They are stuck, the poor creatures. Hybrids. Half stories, half oblivion. They want to buy their way out of a nameless eternity."

"Where is this th-thingy thing, then," she stammered, all flushed.

"In the Second Night, the Night that belongs to dreams, storms, and the unquiet dead, the Night that is Serapide's. My sister is angry at me for something she believes I have done. We don't need to go into that, her grudges last millennia. Anyway, she won't let me in. She is also the protector of cats. That's why I need an external agent, an outsider."

"H-how do I g-get there?" Talking was becoming impossible.

"I will send one of my men to fetch you, six months from now. You won't have to do much really, just go out in the eleventh hour, infiltrate the dead, watch the Dreamarquise do his stunt, snatch my Hammer from him, and get out of the market. Alive, if possible. If you do all this, I will give you your precious mansion. And so no one will dare say I'm not generous, I'll throw in an extra Boon. What do you say?"

By now Oriana was unable to speak. She didn't fully understand what the blue Tokai was doing to her. She could comprehend the Duke's words perfectly (in fact, she could have sung them in reverse), but she couldn't say a word in response. She stepped forward, pointed at her chest, and shook her head.

"No?" he replied. "Do you really want to know what will happen, then?"

She hesitated for a moment, then nodded.

"All right. If you don't get me my Hammer, I'll take your name and spin a tale around you, and when I'm finished, no one will ever know you existed, not your mother, not your father, not your brothers. Then I'll put a sign on you and change you into a rock. I'll wield one of my hammers and smash you to bits, then I'll melt you and cool you and mold you. I'll turn you into a thing, an object to be desired, craved, lusted after, a ring, maybe, or a crown or a statue. You won't be destroyed for centuries to come, yet in all that time, a spark of your consciousness will live on, voiceless, unable to die. This is what I will do to you."

Oriana felt a tear cut her cheek.

She was about to brush it off when the man-dwarf, leaning over, caught it. Between his thick, dirty fingers the tear had become a crystal. He looked at it with professional interest, then crushed it between his thumb and forefinger.

"Or," he said, "I could always turn you into a companion for Gobbo. He's so lonely at times. You should hear him sing, it breaks your heart."

Stepping forward, Oriana slapped her chest twice, eyes wild. He looked at her unblinkingly, breathing out low, white puffs of smoke.

"Why did I choose you, Oriana Siliceo?" he said. "I chose you because you are made of sterner stuff than most and because you're not easily scared. You're practical enough to understand the value of tools, yet imaginative enough to see what can only exist in the Night. You will serve me well, smith's daughter, one way or another."

Then the Duke of Under-earth gestured a brisk goodbye, and Oriana felt the whole shed moving away from her.

Before she could blink, she was outside, staring at the closed door. Instinctively she made for the handle, but there was none to be found. The door was perfectly smooth.

A shout behind her. She turned around.

It was Bruno, his shaggy hair looking wilder than his eyes, her brother standing pale-faced by his side.

"So it was true," Bruno hissed. "You are here. I thought Oriano had made it up as an excuse. We've been looking for you for hours!"

Oriana saw that the marionette stand was gone and many of the other stalls were closing, too; the sun was so low it made long shadows of the passing farmers.

"Well? Why are you here? And what did you do with Oriano's coin?"

But try as she might, she couldn't utter a word. She opened

her mouth to force the words out, and Oriano stared. Her tongue was all blue.

"She bought a spirit apple," he gasped, "and ate it all by herself! I told you! It wasn't me. I didn't lose my carlini! She took it! She took all my coins!"

"You vile child," Bruno spat at her. But his face betrayed a smile, as if he had expected no less from her. "You are no better than a common thief!"

At that, Oriana dropped to the ground and burst out crying.

Not for fear of punishment, or shame, but for the sheer injustice of suffering such an accusation and not even being able to protest.

FIVE

Thus began the loneliest months of Oriana's childhood. From mid-May to the end of August she wasn't allowed to leave the house. The reason for her punishment was kept secret from the neighbors, which only made her seclusion worse. It was said that she had a contagious disease. In those days, that was more than enough. She spent her days either assisting her mother in the kitchen or sitting alone in her room. What's worse, Donna Lena ignored her even when she was helping around the house, like she wasn't even there. They seldom had visits from relatives, and when they did, her cousins clustered together, staring at her from a distance.

Every time Oriana opened her mouth to speak the truth of her predicament, her tongue went all prickly and she could do nothing but shut it again. It happened for the first time when Angia came to visit her. Though Donna Lena spread word of Oriana's convulsive fever, there was no stopping her friend from bursting into her house. Redheaded, pale, and, tall and thin like a candle, Angia was the seventh daughter of the butcher in Via del Gesù, who had asked the Queen of Dawn for a male heir and gotten six more daughters in return, all loud and red haired. Oriana never quite understood Angia's boundless affection for her—maybe Oriana was the quiet sister she never had—but in the early weeks of Oriana's imprisonment, Angia had evaded Donna Lena's watch and slipped into her room. After hugging her friend tight, she produced a dead frog from her apron. Holding it by its right leg, she instructed Oriana to crush it and smear its green blood on her head.

"What for?" Oriana blinked.

"So your fits cease and never come back, silly."

Oriana laughed so hard she almost fell over.

"I am fine, really," she said at last.

Angia frowned.

"Why did your mother lock you up, then?" she said.

"She believes I stole my father's coin to buy spirit."

"Really! And how did it taste?"

"Of course I didn't actually buy spirit! And anyway, it tasted delightful."

Oriana slapped both hands on her mouth. Her friend shrieked in joy.

"I want to know *everything*!"

Oriana sighed, more than a little relieved. But when, ignoring the funny feeling in her mouth, she tried to tell the tale, Angia started giggling.

"How are you doing that?" she asked, pointing at her face.

"Doing what?" asked Oriana, her words slurry.

"Your tongue, it's all blue! You have to teach me the trick!"

Oriana turned to the foggy glass she used as a mirror.

It wasn't just her tongue, but her lips and her cheeks, too, and then her hair and her nails. They were all turning the color of sapphire.

"How? What did you—" her friend stuttered, shakily standing up.

For Oriana hadn't stopped changing. All the veins in her body were turning into turquoise corals, her flesh an opaque cloud, and her eyes the same color as the Tokai, the blue of spirit and spirits.

Stunned, Angia opened her mouth to say something, but

her own tongue began to go numb too. In horror, she raised a hand. Her nails were turning the same blue. And like her friend, she couldn't speak of it to save her life.

Angia bolted downstairs. Oriana never saw her after that.

It wasn't just that Oriana couldn't talk about the Duke and her debt to him. Ever since that day in Foggia she felt as if a thick glass barrier had grown between her and the world. This feeling of separateness never left her entirely. Even during the Day, while cutting onions or peeling potatoes, she felt the presence of the Night. For Lucerìa stood on one side of the world, and now, having been to the other, Oriana knew life was hollow.

The only way to cope with it was to bridge that loss with her imagination. So when she saw an old man seeking shelter from the rain, she thought, *What if you had a hat that as soon as it got wet became a house?* Or that couple, blowing kisses by a window: *What if you had twin enchanted cups, so that even at a distance, if one of you drank from one, the other would feel your lips?* Sometimes Oriana felt guilty for this daydreaming. After all, being a blacksmith was as practical as it got. And yet she wondered what she would do in the smithy, when she became her father's apprentice. Would she call for the Duke's benediction, as some smiths in Lucerìa did? Would she dare to make some of her fancies real?

The only one she could talk to was Marfisio, the big tomcat her father had found in the gutter, half-dead and missing an eye. He had been tortured for hours by the street urchins who lived across from the Church of the Annunziata. Marfisio took months to recover. Nowadays, he spent most of his time sleeping and had grown quite fat. But Oriana was fond of him, his gentle purring, and the way he sometimes woke her with a raspy lick. She loved him even more now since she'd discovered she could talk to him freely about her encounters with the Night Saints without her tongue turning blue.

"Do you know this market, Marfisio? The dead haven't got desires, so what could they trade with? And what about this Dreamarquise? Have you ever met him?"

Usually the cat didn't seem very interested in what Oriana had to say and went on sleeping, snoring softly. But one evening, as she was asking the cat her usual questions about the market, the stout widow her mother had recently hired to help around the house, Cetta, looked up from her sewing and crossed her heart.

"*Santa vergine*, don't speak of it when Twilight is nigh!"

Cetta's work had been a blessing for the household. Since she had been hired, the Siliceo house seemed brighter and smelled of freshly cut flowers. Cetta herself was a small-town woman who had lost her husband and three sons to an earthquake. That tragedy had left her with several quirks, the most irksome of which was a fondness for proverbs. "*A shoe of silver makes iron soft,*" she would comment, eying the new furnishings in the house. Or, when helping Oriana get dressed, "Yours is fine as is. You know what they say: *Comb your hair every day and you'll go the Emerald Dame way*!" And when looking at a newly bought mirror, "As the proverb goes, *An old woman's mirror must be empty*!"

Presently, the old maid stared at Oriana as if she held the Grim King right between her teeth.

"Speak of what, Cetta?" the girl said, unabashed.

"You know what, miss."

"The Market of the Dead? What about it? Oh, come on! Twilight is still an hour away and *they* can't hear us. No one will know."

"It isn't good to talk about them either way. It *feeds* them."

"Well, then I hope they feed until they choke! If it hadn't

been for—for . . ." But Oriana went quiet, for her tongue was getting funny again.

Cetta shook her head and said, very quietly, "I will tell you, but you must promise never to ask me about it again."

"I swear, by the East Wind and the Dark Sun."

"Good, then," the widow sighed. "They say that on the Day of the Dead some of the departed hold a market in the Night."

"A market after dark? How come I've never heard about it?"

"Because it's held in the Second Night. The night of storms, dreamers, and the unquiet dead."

Oriana bit her lip.

The Second Night was Serapide's reign, just as the Duke had said.

"Not just the dead attend it," the maid continued. "They say that the dreams of men and animals go there, too, to trade with them."

"What do they trade?"

"No one knows. They say that if you know what currency powers the market, you could use it to bribe Nocturnals, even the Major Ones. That's why the Grim King doesn't approve of it."

"But what do people get out of it?"

"Now, that's a good question. Some Tellers say that the Market of the Dead sells Moira, destinies. People can get filthy rich, find their lifelong sweetheart, or become great poets or generals if they buy the right trinket."

"So it's a good thing, to find it."

"Not really. For those who buy anything there are often cursed."

"Cursed?! How?"

"They say that buying a Moira makes the dreamer turn . . . bad. That whatever they spend on their new Moira burns them. Turns them into parodies of what they once were."

"I see," Oriana said, "and where in the Second Night is it? How does one find the market?"

"No one knows for sure. They say the dead move it every year so the Grim King can't find it. There are those who have looked for it all their lives and never come upon a trace of it. But miss, to trade with the dead is not what life is about. Only people who are desperate—the extremely old or the extremely foolish, the ill or the damned—only they go to the market. You are a pretty little birdie, and you mustn't trouble yourself with it."

Oriana smelled the summer's arrival in her brother's musky odor when he came to bed, a scent of freshly cut grass. She became so jealous of him that every time he tried to tell her his outdoor adventures, Oriana turned her back to him.

There always had been a subtle difference in the way the Siliceo siblings were treated by their parents, and that gap was getting wider. One late June day, after her brother came back from the First Communion of their cousin Salvo, Aunt Ciccerella's second son, she found herself looking at him with discomfort. There was something new that hung around him like a halo. She stared at him trying to figure it out before realizing. Oriano's hair had been cut a bit shorter than hers.

His haircut was only the beginning. As he settled into his changed appearance, Oriano became bolder and louder.

Her mother bought him new clothes: a real shirt and waistcoat. That night, after the horse race to commemorate the night Serapide saved the town from the Visigoths, Oriana heard his laughter coming from the street. She peeked from her window and saw Oriano talking with Angia. Seeing them together, Oriana's face flushed.

Was she jealous of him?

In truth, Oriana missed her twin. Their tickling games under the blankets, their long runs in the cornfields, the sound of his laughter when she told him some mad story about the smithy. Oriana wondered if he missed her too. He never said as much, and Oriana suspected that guilt played no little part in his silence. But one cold stormy night while she was shivering in their bed, she felt someone put a blanket on top of her. She thought it was her father, but when she looked up, she was stunned to see Oriano. He said nothing and retreated in his own shy way, but she would long remember the affectionate gleam in his eyes.

Oriano's new clothes were just one example of the changes that swept through Mastro Peppo's household. The Mezzacasa commission had gone so well that word of his craftsmanship spread quickly, and other noblemen began to shower him with jobs.

In his youth, Mastro Peppo was an ambitious apprentice; he had even traveled to Naples to work on the construction of the San Carlo, the biggest opera house in Europe. It was in Naples that he met Donna Lena, who at the time sold paper flowers to theatergoers. He won her over with the grace of his big hands, unfolding a paper bird and refolding it into the shape of a rose. Then the death of his elder brother called him back to Lucerìa, where he was to take charge of the old family smithy.

They still had that rose, though, in a glass case on the mantelpiece. Donna Lena was very protective of it and polished the glass every day before brushing her hair. Recently, Oriana's mother had taken to brushing her hair twice a day in front of the mirror, singing an old song from Naples.

Luck is on its way
She has come to stay
She has come to stay

Oriana didn't dare ask her mother about the song. She still wasn't allowed out of the house and resented her mother for it. But Donna Lena didn't seem angry with her anymore. In fact, she had asked Don Giacomino to teach her daughter to read. Oriana's wish had come true, just not in the way she had hoped. It was indeed as if the Duke had heard her secret desire and made it happen. She didn't have a library of her own, but she did have free time and real books she could read.

Strangely, the one who took the most pride in her progress was her mother, who boasted about it with the local gossips. In front of strangers she bragged openly about her daughter's intelligence as if she hoped the East Wind would pick up her words and spread them all over Lucerìa. Oriana didn't care, as long as she had a steady supply of something new to read. In this she was lucky. Don Giacomino was something of a liberal, with some sympathy for Enlightenment thinkers, so he gave her Diderot's *Encyclopaedia*, freshly shipped from Venice. She was particularly fond of the fascicle on ironmaking, and spent hours looking at its illustrations, repeating the French names of the tools. And all the while, in the back of her mind, bloomed the desire that one day she would help her father, Mastro Peppo, in the forge.

On her birthday, as the late August heat wave turned to rain, Oriana's punishment finally ended. Summer was almost over, and dark clouds rolled over the infinite cut of the hills. She tasted the first raindrops with arms spread wide, her tongue sticking out, before Cetta hurried her indoors.

To celebrate her birthday, Donna Lena prepared a luscious breakfast and invited all Oriana's friends from the contrada. She delivered the invitations herself, going from house to house to speak with their mothers—the cobbler's wife, the tanner's, the butcher's—and tell them that the doctor had declared Oriana fully recovered. Donna Lena had outdone herself. And Oriana couldn't have been more surprised or more grateful. It was like she had her old mother back.

Meanwhile, the smell of freshly baked pasticciotti was so tempting that Oriano had to be threatened with a stick so he wouldn't eat them before the company arrived. The twins helped with the verbena festoons as their mother taught them a new song, one she'd heard in the San Carlo. Oriano struggled with the melody, and his pitchiness cracked Oriana and her mother up. Laughter lifted ten years from Donna Lena's face, small childish snorts that Oriana loved her very much for. After the laughter and song subsided, and the festoons were done and the food was set on the table, they waited.

They waited for the better part of the morning, Oriano visibly restless while Oriana grew quieter and quieter as if freezing from the inside out. They waited until the church bell tolled noon.

"Can we eat now?" asked Oriano.

After a pause, Donna Lena nodded.

Oriana watched her brother eat the pasticciotti but said nothing. When he was finished, she asked her mother if she could go to her room to read.

"Of course, titilla," her mother said, her eyes gleaming.

Oriana was doleful for a month afterward and couldn't bear to look down at other children playing in the streets. Something had hardened in her in all those months of isolation. Even after her punishment ended, she didn't ask to go out more than necessary. Instead, whenever Cetta spared her a chore, she locked herself in her room and read about the history of Lucerìa, the Byzantine empire, the Mohammedan years when the German emperor peopled her town with his Muslim subjects, and everything else she could lay her hands on. She was so taken by her books that she almost didn't notice the first signs of autumn. And so fall snuck up behind her back, and when it finally sprang on her she found she was unable to defend herself.

On a quiet early October afternoon, Oriana was home alone. Her family had all gone to visit Aunt Ciccerella, who had been ill with fever, before joining in the street celebrations. Oriana was rereading the glass-making fascicle when a large gecko fell onto her page. She wasn't squeamish. In fact, she liked geckos, but she resented the interruption. Oriana took the creature by the tail and placed it back on the mantelpiece. The gecko climbed across the wall with a drunken gait. No wonder he had fallen; it was getting too cold for him. But Oriana noticed something odd. With every step, the creature was leaving behind a letter on the plaster wall. She looked down at the page she was reading. All its letters were scrambled, scattered over the thick paper. Wild-eyed, she looked up again. The gecko's letters formed words that stood out in shiny black against the white plaster.

"'On-the-Night-of-the-Dead...'" she read.

The message was a coiled arabesque. The more she read it, the more the October chill took hold of her, until she was shaking as if standing naked out in the cold.

On the Night of the Dead, go to bed with a pair of shoes and a cloak. When the church bell tolls eleven, leave the house and look for my agent. He will bring you to the market.

Oriana stared at the words until they started to fade. She looked around frantically, searching for a witness. But the only other presence in the room was the gecko. It peered at her with squinting eyes and a queer little smile, then, with surprising agility, wriggled out the window and was gone.

SIX

The Day of the Dead in Lucerìa was a time of Vigils, for telling stories about the dead could change them into Nocturnals, over time. After the sun had set, pumpkins decorated as purgatory skulls, cocce priatorie, burned in the windows across the hills by the dozens, amber fires in the dark, each fire a lantern, each lantern a Teller, each Teller a crowd of faces beckoning the recently departed to visit.

In Oriana's house, chestnuts crackled in the pan, a circle of chairs around it. As soon as her father's relatives arrived, Oriana noticed a glint of envy as they eyed the new mirrors and tablecloths. Donna Lena beamed at them. Never had Oriana seen their house filled with so many people, uncles and cousins she didn't know she had, but who seemed to know everything about her. Oriana felt a cold stab to her heart when she saw that Aunt Ciccerella wasn't there. Uncle Nino assured her it was just the grippe, but something in his eyes didn't quite convince her, and Oriana took her seat with a sense of unease.

"Is it true that you're rabid?" a little one whispered to her.

"Of course," she replied, "and I also eat children's ears."

The boy covered them with his hands and squealed away. It offered her grim satisfaction to overplay her reputation. Usually Oriano was the center of attention. As soon as all the adults were seated, Oriana grabbed a handful of wood shavings and threw them into the fire. And so the Vigil began.

First, Riddles were asked of the little ones—*What has a*

neck but no head?—then a song sung about the Nuriae, the ghostly washerwomen of Twilight, which took the form of a lullaby as creepy as it was wistful. To change the mood, fat cousin Gratiano, the tanner, told a playful anecdote about his mother, who had died three years ago in June. The adults drank wine, smoked pipes, laughed out loud, ate roast meat, and went on telling story after story, not all of them fit for a child's ear.

Someone told a story about Fullmoon, that portion of the Night that came only once a month. It was the tale of how poor Totò Ciotola, the cemetery guardian, had lost his sanity. Looking for mushrooms so that his children could survive famine, he strayed into a wood within Fullmoon. A mysterious old lady with a mushroom face—all lumps and tumefaction—gave him a bowl filled with exquisite porcini mushrooms, enough to feed all his children. And he did. For every Fullmoon afterward, the mushrooms grew out of his bald head, feeding his family for years. Totò was never quite the same, though, as the mushrooms grew inside his head too.

"This is what the gifts of the Night do to the likes of us," finished Uncle Nino. "They grow and grow, without peace."

"What about Serapide?" asked Oriana. "Do you have a story about her?"

Uncle Giacomino did. It was about the Farmacia della Pioggia, the infamously Night-touched rain pharmacy, where even in the Day you could hear a ghostly dripping of running water. In the Second Night, however, when the pharmacy's doors were shut, these drips grew into a forest of sounds: thunder, hailstones, and the roar of rain.

Seventy years ago, Guido dell'Oglio, the first pharmacist in Lucerìa, was challenged by Nanni Vasari, the horse doctor. The latter told the apothecary of a specific plant that grew in the Second Night, a night dandelion that was black like midnight and flourished only during Serapide's fire festival. Its seedheads wavered at approaching storms and could even pollinate dreams. Dell'Oglio, who hailed from Foggia, didn't believe a word. So when Vasari invited him to come to the festival and gather a few specimens for himself, he derided him. That night, as Dell'Oglio was taking inventory, he heard a violent thunderstorm. At once, he scampered outside to retrieve the dispensary booth. To his surprise, while the streets were busy with the festivities, its night skies were clear. And when the pharmacist returned inside, he almost pissed himself, for a mighty storm raged over the majolica jars, flooding his shop. Because he hadn't gone to the dandelions, the dandelions had come for him. They grew by dozens over the walnut shelves, their seedheads bending at the impossible storm. After that, his pharmacy was named della Pioggia, and for as long it remained open, it always had dark dandelions populating its shelves.

As the kids begged for another story, Oriana stared at the flames. She, like Totò and the rain pharmacy, had been Night-touched. Would the same happen to her? Would she go mad or become so odd that she would no longer fit in the Day? Lost in thought, Oriana looked up with a start when she heard someone talking about the Duke. It was Uncle Tonno, telling a story about the Emistuchivio himself, sovereign of the Under-earth.

"And so," Uncle Tonno recounted, "the Duke looked at the weaver and asked him, 'Weaver, where are your siblings?' And the weaver replied that they were asleep in their rooms. Then the Emistuchivio took him by the hand, like a small boy, and brought him to the rooms where their swollen corpses lay, hand in hand. When the weaver wailed in despair, the Duke asked, 'Where was your compassion when your kin was dying of thirst? You were too enthralled by your own creation to notice. Didn't I warn you not to care only about your own art? This was your greed. And so your art belongs to me, as do the eyes which saw no beauty other than what you created.' Then the Duke of the Under-earth extended his hands and plucked out the weaver's eyes, turning the best craftsman ever to have graced the court of Emperor Frederick II into a Garaude. And still today he stalks the Night, nameless, asking Riddles of unwary travelers so he can steal their eyes."

The tale still echoed loudly in Oriana's mind—she could *see* the weaver's bleeding eyes whenever she closed her own—by the time she realized everyone was getting up and the Vigil had ended. She stood and began helping Cetta with the coats. As they were leaving, each one of her aunts stopped to kiss her, one after another. Oriana was exhausted. Still, when her mother kissed her goodnight as she climbed up to her room, she felt a foretaste of triumph. The next time she saw her she'd be able to speak the truth. But the Night was long, and her wait had just begun. Downstairs she heard Cetta and her mother moving about and talking softly, preparing the house for the dead. After that, the house was quiet.

Her shoes rested on her stomach, but Oriana wasn't afraid of falling asleep anytime soon, she was far too excited for that. Her brother had been sleeping for what felt like hours when she heard the church bell strike nine. The Second Night was still so distant, a faraway country. And yet as the hours waned, she began to see it, a misty island slowly approaching her half-closed eyes . . .

She opened them wide.

How long had she been asleep? She'd had a nightmare of Gobbo entering through the open skylight and crawling into her bed, his teeth glinting in the dark. Thank God she had woken up. Only . . . what was that smell? A musty odor, pungent and wild, like wet fur. Oriana glanced up. A small pale hand appeared, followed by the monkey's misshapen head. It peered down at her, crooked teeth flashing.

A scream froze in her heart; then the church bell tolled. Nine, ten, eleven. The Second Night had just begun. Gobbo descended on her like living lightning, sat on her chest, and screeched loudly. Oriana's blood curdled. He'd wake up the entire household! But her brother, lying within arm's reach, had not even stirred. Maybe she *was* dreaming. She certainly felt wide awake, and very afraid. Gobbo opened her hand and pushed something soft into her palm. Then the monkey laughed madly, scuttled away, and darted downstairs through the trapdoor. Oriana drew a long breath. She already knew what the monkey had given her. She stowed it in her waist pocket, pulled on her shoes, then her shawl and wool coat, and climbed down from her room.

On the ground floor her parents were sleeping, motionless in their bed by the fireplace. Even little Tato didn't stir. The kitchen table was still set—plates and forks, bread and wine—for the dead. There was no trace of Gobbo, but she saw the shadow of a woman, sitting on a chair and staring at the flickering embers. Oriana inhaled sharply. Slowly, the dark figure turned her head.

"Auntie?" whispered Oriana.

It was indeed Aunt Ciccerella, with her beloved arched nose and deep dimples. Oriana waited for a response, and when she received none, took note of her aunt's sullen eyes, that distance no human word can hope to bridge.

"Auntie, I'm so sorry," she said, and began to weep.

The shadow rose from her chair. Oriana felt a cold hand caress her neck and heard a voice that was more sigh than whisper.

"Beware the Emerald Dame."

Oriana turned around. She was alone now, her parents and Tato pale and motionless as if calcified by the moonlight. Well, not completely alone. The front door opened, and there, in the pale radiance, a black patch of fur grinned.

Gobbo gestured to her.

"Coming," she said, brushing her tears away.

SEVEN

With a quick step she followed the monkey through the crooked alleyways, hushed piazzas, and abandoned courtyards. As she moved through the night, Gobbo ran ahead to climb on a wall and mock her with his ghastly mimicry. When Oriana fell behind, the creature would at once begin hammering his head on the wall, each bang a wail. It would have been funny, had its screeches not reverberated through the empty streets with an ominous echo. Each time, as soon as the girl caught up, the creature hopped down and scuttled ahead to wait for her on another wall, in another street.

Oriana should have recognized the streets, but the essence of the Second Night permeated them. All the buildings, all the palazzos, all the piazzas in Lucerìa, looked as if they had traveled to strange lands and come back stranger. Sometimes it was the odd leaning window or the railings on the balconies, shivering as if made of leaves, or the changing towers, growing taller ever so quietly under the moonlight.

She found her way more from memory than from sight, but still she stumbled. It seemed as if the entire town was moving around her. More than once she came across a street that was supposed to be elsewhere, equestrian statues she had never seen before, or marble arches where there had once been buildings.

Oriana knew that there were boundaries between the seven regions of the Night. Some were obvious, like Fullmoon, Underearth, and Twilight; but others were tricky, like the Hour of the Wolf, which was both a certain hour and a disposition of the soul. Few in Lucerìa were brave enough—or foolish enough—to walk about at night. They could never know for certain if they'd trespassed from night to Night. But also, they could be swept away by the Night's currents and end up stranded in a different region from the one which they entered, drifting ashore to another Twilight or another Dawn.

Oriana remembered what Aunt Ciccerella said about the Second Night. One could reach it only in dreams, remaining awake though the journey only if following a Nocturnal and forgetting about their visit when they woke. She stopped. Thirty steps ahead, Gobbo halted at the foot of a stooped, hooded statue. The statue stood inside a niche in the wall of the palace of justice, a grim, sandstone building. The monkey was looking at the statue with an expression of such longing it made Oriana cringe. But when she inquisitively stepped forward, the statue knelt down before her. She blinked.

It was a man, dressed in a cloak as black as soot, with leather sandals on his feet, and a swarthy face she could not quite make out. The man caressed Gobbo, who in turn purred, his mad eyes rolling like moonstone marbles. Oriana stepped forward to speak, and his cloak lit up. Its black fabric was made from radiant, interwoven eyes; they opened and closed in synchronous waves, pulsing to their own rhythm.

Oriana took a deep breath. The man before her was not just any Garaude, but the same one she had seen from her window a year and a half ago.

The creature stepped out of the niche and his hood fell back. He had a squared-jawed face with a short beard and curly black hair. He was younger than her father and his skin was far darker. More importantly, he didn't have eyes. Not even sockets; nothing at all. Oriana stepped back. At that, the man's cloak blinked, each of the eyes at once. The Garaude stretched out a gloved hand.

"I mean no harm," he said.

She quivered. His voice was so soft, like a page turning.

"Are you my guide?"

"Indeed I am, milady."

"Good. I thought it was Gobbo and I didn't like that one bit."

The monkey growled and hid behind the Nocturnal.

"Poor Gobbo," said the Garaude, caressing its head. "He wears the face of a sin that few men would be able to bear."

"But he is mad! And spiteful!"

"That might be, milady, but that is not by his choice. Few Nocturnals have endured what this poor creature has."

"Don't call me that."

"Call you how, milady?"

"*That!*"

"Ah, but I must. In my time it was the custom for addressing people of rank, whatever their age."

"But I have no rank!"

"Maybe not in the Day. But we are in the Night now. Here, bloodline and riches count for nothing. Do you think a Major One would ask something of a Diurnal if she didn't show some gold?"

"My father works iron, bronze, and silver, but no gold."

He burst out laughing. The sound was strangely out of place, like a firecracker in a basilica. She darted a shy glance at him, then looked away. She would never grow accustomed to his eyeless face.

"But your father and your mother did work with gold, Oriana Siliceo, or we wouldn't know about you and your stories."

"How do you know about them?" she asked, curious.

"The Dreamarquise of cats told us."

"The thief. The one who stole the whatsitsname."

"He did so, yes. But before, he was a good friend of my master."

"So he said. Shall we go to . . . wherever we have to go?"

"We shall, milady. Follow me."

He headed straight to Saint Francis. Oriana followed. Under a half-moon the church was impressive. With its tall towers it looked a bit like a huge stone hand bidding her and her companions to stop. The bell tower—the longest finger of the hand—was by far the tallest in Lucerìa, even taller than the Duomo's. On a night like this, its doors had been left open for the dead. As they entered, all the candles adorning the statues of the seven saints of Lucerìa blazed. Gobbo screeched in mockery, but Oriana was awed.

"Did you do that?" she asked her guide.

"The Night did, and the Grim King. The temples of Christians love our kind, even if their priests sometimes don't."

Oriana frowned. "You aren't a Christian."

"I wasn't, when I was alive."

"You came here with the German emperor, from Sicily."

"You know many a thing, for your age."

"Oh, I could do nothing else but read this spring and summer and fall. Thanks to you and your master!"

The Nocturnal lowered his head.

"I am not my master, milady. And he does what pleases him."

"You are not free, then?"

The Garaude shuddered, shaking his head.

"I never was, milady. Neither alive nor dead. Such is the servitude of beauty. But lo, we must make haste, for the Second Night will not last long and we must catch the Secret Market before it blooms."

He gestured for her to follow him, and she did.

They climbed up a steep stairway. Even Gobbo began to show signs of fatigue, and Oriana was dripping in sweat. Only the eyeless gentleman seemed fresh as an idle boy. After a while, the creature stopped and turned his eyeless face down at her.

"May I help you, milady?"

"You ask me *now*? After two hundred steps!?"

"To help you I'd have to touch you. It might not be pleasant."

"I don't care! Help me, help away!"

The man stretched out his gloved hand and in one motion lifted her up on his shoulders. His touch was dry and inhuman in a way she couldn't easily put into words. Not that his hand lacked warmth, exactly, it simply didn't have the quality of life. Oriana shivered, but her sacrifice was well repaid, for now the Nocturnal quickened his step. He wasn't running, but it was as if the tower was unwinding under his feet. Up on the Nocturnal's shoulders, Oriana closed her eyes, her face flushed in delight. Then the sweet smell of the November night whipped against her face.

She opened her eyes. They were so high that she could see all the rooftops of Lucerìa stretched out before her. A lunar garden of impossible beauty: hundreds of terraces, patios, balconies, verandas, towers, belfries, all frosted with the thinnest moonlight. Oriana could see the Duomo, the bishop's palace, the market square, and even the brown city walls. And yet she still had the impression of being in another city, for even from above things were not as they should have been. The Duomo, for example, was supposed to have only one belfry, but from it rose two towers, minarets. And now that her eyes had adjusted to the feeble light, she could see that the whole city was continuously shifting. Entire buildings withered like flowers, only to bloom again in different shapes, Romanesque palazzos grew tall spires, which then dwindled into small houses and shortly rose again. The process was slow and hard to catch, as it was always happening in the parts of town where you weren't looking. The impression was that of a garden where life had been accelerated beyond the limits of nature. As soon as the Nocturnal put her down, Oriana leaned against the railing.

"Is this still Lucerìa?"

"It is, and yet it isn't."

Oriana frowned.

"Is that a Riddle? Will you pluck out my eye if I don't guess the answer correctly?"

The Garaude's face became hard as a statue's.

"No, milady, this is no Riddle. This is Lucerìa as it appears in the Second Night. It is the fiefdom of Serapide. Do you know what she rules in the Night?"

"Storms, I think. And battles. And dreams."

"Yes, and cats, and owls, and the nightmares that go deep to the end of existence, to the Hour of the Wolf, where the Dark Sun shines eternal."

"So?"

"This is not Lucerìa, not really. It is Lucerìa's Dream."

"And who dreams it?"

"The city, of course."

"Silly. Cities don't dream."

"Maybe in other parts of the world they don't usually. Some cities sleep dreamlessly, some don't sleep at all, some have constant nightmares. They say that these days, the city of Paris dreams of bodiless heads rolling in its streets, while London has fancies of steam and machines that can fly like birds. Some unborn cities are still Dreams themselves, hovering like mirages over the places where men will build them. But of all the cities in the world, only Lucerìa's dreams are accessible. For here the Night was born, and it is in this land that the Nocturnals have made their home. You see? In the Second Night, on this night and a few others, the city changes at every instant. Each moment, it contains different streets, different squares, different walls. Some are taken from its past, some from its future, some belong to a possibility that will never be. Take one alley instead of another, and you won't ever be able to return to the Lucerìa you knew. You would spend your whole life in a Dream as solid as bricks, marrying, having children, until one day it would cease, and you would find you had lived a life of delusion, your existence wasted while the real world left you behind."

Oriana shuddered.

"So I'm dreaming, then?"

"No, that's the privilege of traveling with our kind. You'll need to fall asleep only to enter the market, as soon as Serapide seeds it in the Second Night."

"How will I come out of it, then?"

"I'll guide you."

"So you'll be with me."

"I cannot. Only people who are alive can enter the market."

"But you just said—"

"I'll give you a piece of me. It will be as if I were there."

Even if the oddness of the answer upset her, Oriana felt somehow reassured. Despite his eyeless face, for some reason the Garaude didn't scare her.

"There is something I don't understand. This Dreamarquise—"

"He is the cat most talented at dreaming. Once he was a ferocious alley cat, but after he was wounded in a fight, Serapide granted him the Boon of dreaming with such intensity that it took on a second life of its own. Here in the Second Night, the cat's dream-self can go almost anywhere, even into my master's forge. That's how the two met."

"I see. And they were friends until he stole the Hammer thing."

"The Deep Red Hammer."

"That one. Why is it so important for your master?"

"It is one of his best tools. It can work materials few smiths could even dream of—"

"What? What is it?" Oriana cried.

Gobbo screeched madly, pointing with his clawed hand. She looked up. A shooting star—only it was too slow, too fiery, too *blue* to be a meteor—cut the night like a razor, leaving a turquoise scar in the tissue of the dark.

"Milady, hold on to me, we must follow. Quickly."

"We're going to fly, aren't we?"

"There is nothing to be afraid of."

"I'm not afraid. Will you sprout wings?"

"I already have wings. *Grow.*"

That last command was given with a voice of cold stone. Then the eyelashes on the Nocturnal's cloak grew. Before Oriana could draw two breaths, they were the size of her palms and encased in an iridescent membrane that made them look like fins.

"*Fly,*" he said, and much to her astonishment, the iridescent eyelashes began to flutter in waves, the way tropical fish swim, so fast she could feel a wind on her face.

"Hold on!" said the Garaude, and Oriana hugged him tight, like she hugged her dad when he carried her to bed.

Oriana saw Gobbo jumping up and down and screeching on the belfry's terrace, so far below now. She hid her face against the Nocturnal's chest. It was too much: the dead, the dream-cats, the task ahead. But what was really overwhelming was the joy she felt in this moment, a joy so profound she knew she would never be the same again. Beneath them, silent and unmoving, was a city of wooden bridges and Doric porticos, of asphalt motorways and neon signs, of gothic spires and baroque arches, a mix of present, past, and never-will-be, a city alien to her and yet—in some way—a place she felt she belonged to more than any other on earth.

The Garaude began his descent. The Seed had landed within a gated Renaissance garden, and the entire block was illuminated by its bluish glow, its shadows leaning on one side. The girl noticed that they were not alone in approaching its gates. In the alleys below, a dozen men and women were rushing in the same direction. They ran with their arms parallel to their bodies, as if they had been tied and forced to run downhill.

"Those are the dreamers," sounded the Nocturnal's soft voice.

"How did they arrive here before us?"

"Is that a Riddle?" mocked his dark lips. "I don't know, milady. Some dreamers stumble onto the market the instant Serapide throws her Seed. How it is so, none can say."

They glided down toward the iron gates of the Renaissance garden. These were common in northern towns—mazes of moss-covered fountains, lime trees, and horse chestnuts—but certainly not in any Luceria she knew. And yet it felt familiar, in the way places are sometimes in dreams. The gate was in a small piazza bordered by ivy-covered palazzos. From above, Oriana glimpsed the market tents, growing like burgeoning bluebells all down the tree-lined lanes. As soon as the dreamers came in view of the market gate, they stumbled, their steps slowing to an unsteady pace. Oriana felt herself yawn just from looking at them. It was as if her weight had suddenly tripled, and she staggered under the load.

"Milady, listen to me. You are able to see the Secret Market of the Dead because of the Tokai my master made you drink. However, you're not one of the dead, nor are you sleeping. This is an immense advantage in the market. For the dead are tricky and will try to manipulate you into buying something from them. But this you must never, ever do. Do you understand?"

"Of course," she said, yawning again.

"As I mentioned, you'll have to be asleep to get in, but it is also of the essence that you wake up as soon as possible."

"A-and how would I do that?"

"Just remember to look at your hands."

"At my hands?"

"Aye. But you must go now. See? The gates are closing."

She turned. Not only were the gates closing, but also the palazzos all around them had begun to scatter, moving farther away from the garden.

"Quickly now," said her guide.

"But . . . you haven't told me what I must do after I'm inside! How will I find the Dreamarquise? How will I even recognize the Hammer?!"

"Just go, I'll tell you later. Stretch out your hands."

She obeyed, her palms up.

The Garaude bent over. With a black-gloved hand he touched his mouth and removed it from his face. Oriana looked wide-eyed as the Nocturnal pushed his mouth into her right palm. It stuck there, like a wound with teeth. With the same gesture he took off one of his ears, the left one, and fused it with her left hand.

"Speak to me," said the mouth, "and I will guide you."

A moment later the square around them widened like a gaping mouth and the Garaude was swept far away.

Oriana gasped.

"Don't leave me!" she screamed at the distant cloaked figure.

"I am here," said a nearby voice.

She looked down at her palm. A shudder.

"Now, milady, enter the market or our quest is over. Now!"

With her last ounce of courage, Oriana rushed in, sliding through the iron bars. They were already so narrow that her left arm got stuck. Savagely she pulled, wrenching until the iron gave way and she fell backward, into the darkness behind her.

EIGHT

She was walking, this much she knew.

Yet it was as if her mind was out of joint, for she didn't know herself, nor did she know her surroundings. She was outdoors, in a place crowded by large white tents and dimly lit by hanging oil lamps swaying in the wind. A throng of faceless people walked alongside her, yet their steps had a purpose hers didn't. There was something important she had forgotten. What was it? It was so difficult to concentrate, her thoughts scattered like a column of smoke blown by the wind. She looked up. Under a white tent, sitting on a stool, was an old woman wrapped in white shawls. In her wrinkled hands was a wooden box containing hundreds, maybe thousands, of crooked iron nails. From time to time someone from the passing crowd picked up a nail.

She smiled to herself. Of course. She was at a market.

The crowd was no different from one you would expect at any other fair: farmer boys, craftsmen in their green waistcoats, some gentlemen in white wigs. And yet there was an uneasiness in the air. The people around her were silent. In fact, she noticed that the whole market was quiet. No bleating of sheep, no barking, no women's shouts, no firecrackers, no sounds at all. Odd. Oriana couldn't remember if voices and loud noises were common in a market or not. In her mind both things were true. A market was both a place of incredible clamor and one of utmost silence.

The market stalls were set up everywhere. Not only in the

garden lanes, but also on the terraces, inside the shell-shaped fountains, and on top of the gargantuan statues. There were white tents winding through the lanes like candid snakes over brittle stone elephants, inside deep grottos, within huge chestnut trees. At first, the vendors seemed ordinary enough, but the lamps never illuminated their faces. She could see their clothes quite well: the fishermen's white hats, the prostitutes' red shawls, the farmers' yellowish cloaks, even a bishop's garments. But their faces were always in shadow.

Everything for sale was secondhand. There were hats, rings, scarves, lamps, scissors, wheels, chairs, golden teeth, wooden handles, tin cups, belts, and stoves on display. Yet, curiously, each stall sold only one object. Oriana noticed a short, shabby, shadow-faced farmer selling dozens of the same dented cup. They were identical in every way, with the exact same dent. She could feel it to the touch.

The moment Oriana touched the cup, two things happened. First, the market suddenly became less quiet. She now heard whispers and faraway songs. The second was that her entire being was pervaded with a deep-seated desire for the cup. It was as if her whole body was shaking with an unquenchable thirst and only the cup could sate it.

The vendor called to her in the softest murmur.

"Name it. Name the one thing. Name it."

What was she supposed to name? What was it that she had forgotten?

"Why is it so difficult to remember?" she muttered.

Another soft voice answered her.

"Because you are not asking the right questions."

Oriana knew that voice.

"Sorry, I've changed my mind," she said.

She walked away, more enthralled with the buyers than the wares for sale. There were two kinds of shoppers—the indecisive buyer who went from stall to stall, searching in the heaps of objects, but never buying anything; and the cautious one, who probed, looked sideways, went on, circled back, and doubted, before finally taking an object. The transactions were fast; each time, the vendor laid an open hand on the buyer's forehead, sending them reeling backward.

"What do they take from them?" Oriana whispered.

"The vendor asks you to name a thing, something that matters to you a great deal. A brother. A trade you love. A home. If you accept their trade, whatever you name will become like a dream to you. A living ghost."

Oriana shuddered.

"A-and in exchange the dreamers get what, old junk?"

"You didn't think so, when you held that cup in your hands."

"Right. But now I can see that it's mostly junk."

"It's not the objects for sale. It's the Moira that is in them."

"A destiny? I'd rather leave empty-handed."

"Would you, now?"

"Yes!"

"Prove it."

And she looked down at her hands.

There was a strange wound in the middle of the right palm. It didn't hurt. Its lips were thick, soft, as if . . .

The mouth opened and spoke.

"Welcome back, milady," it said.

NINE

The market's whispers became a roar, tall waves crashing in her mind.

The place was alive with sound now. There was no noise from any animals, as there were none, but the hawking of vendors was so ghastly it made her skin crawl. The voices were singing, beautifully if isolated, but all together dissonant. Now she understood why some of the dreamers seemed drunk. They were being hammered by the songs of the dead but didn't understand what they were hearing. She did, but only because she had woken up.

"Why do they call out like this?" she asked.

"It's their only hope. To sell what they are—and dissolve."

"Riddles again, Master Garaude?"

The mouth on her hand tightened to a line.

"The objects are their Moira, how it manifested in their lives. The stronger their Moira, the more they must sell. That's why they need several customers to buy in."

"I still don't understand. How is this junk their Moira?"

"Look at the stalls and tell me what you see."

Oriana looked around and frowned.

"I see a warrior selling a rusty old sword."

"What else?"

"A fisherman with dozens of the same old wig. A child selling a silver shoe. A lady in emerald selling an ivory comb. I don't understand! Some sell hundreds, some just the one."

"Listen to them. Closely."

Oriana stepped toward the narrow stall of the emerald lady. She wore a striking dress of the deepest sea-green, almost glowing in the lantern light. Oriana couldn't make out her face in shadows, but she imagined that she saw a frown of terrible arrogance. Her stall sold just one ivory comb. It was one of the few items for sale at the market that didn't look like junk. Even so there were no dreamers crowded around her booth. Perhaps because the emerald lady was not shouting but singing ever so softly.

> Comb your heart, comb and burn
> Burn green, burn deep, burn bright
> May Envy be the others' demise

The song was sweet, mesmerizing, but Oriana tasted horror, as if its lyrics spoke of murder.

"Why does she have so few customers?" she whispered.

"She doesn't need them. Our lady has sold all but one of her combs, and now she is waiting. See how earnest she is? She is about to be set free."

"Free?"

"These are the dead whose tales are the weakest. Their stories weren't strong enough to transform them into Night Saints. That is what they sell, and what the dreamers buy: a destiny. Look at the Dame. The moment a dreamer buys her last comb, they will become proverbial in her place, and she will dissolve."

"But who are they? The sellers, I mean."

"They are those whose passion made them what they were, until their behavior became like a mask that people recognized straightaway."

"How come I've never heard of them, then?"

"Oh, but you have. *A shoe of silver makes iron soft.* And there is your silver shoe. *An old woman's mirror is always* empty. And there you have your mirrors. *A dead man's sword is his best friend . . .*"

"Those are just the stupid proverbs Cetta says all the time!"

"Proverbs are stories. Long ago they were about real people, Diurnals like you. Someone, at a Vigil's fire, recounted the life of a man or a woman they all knew: the old crone who always looked in the mirror, hoping to see the young woman she once was; the old soldier who died in bed with his sword; the cobbler who made a foot fashioned of silver to shape his shoes, but then was robbed and died in despair. And though their names were lost over time, their stories were not. So these people, long dead, live on in the Night, a flicker of a story, not told enough to become a Nocturnal, just pervasive enough to exist."

"Oh, but this is silly! You're saying that *Comb your hair every day and you'll go the Dame's way* refers to an actual—" She stopped and looked wide-eyed at the shadow in emerald green. "Oh my god, it's her, the Dame."

"Do you know what her proverb means?"

"Don't worry too much about how you look, or you'll waste your life away."

"See? You don't have to know the details of her life story to get the gist. She spent what little she had on looking beautiful, combing her hair by the window every day, hoping some Duke would pass by and marry her."

"But he didn't."

"He did. But he was a violent man and strangled her."

"Oh. And why would a dreamer buy a Moira like that?"

"Ah, milady! I forget that you are a child. Having a Moira means to have a destiny. Not everyone has one. Many, most even, don't. They live lives unrecorded, unremembered, unaccounted for. That's why people dream. And cats, and hills, and rivers. So that they can relieve themselves of the burden of form and become something larger than themselves. And here, right here, they can buy a new Moira, at a price—their loves, ambitions, whatever they held dearest in the Day, traded in for a destiny that will echo throughout the centuries to come."

Much to her surprise, Oriana felt her eyes burning.

"Why?" she cried, outraged. "Why would they do something so horrible? Sell everything that is so dear to them for what? A story!"

"Milady, you are too young to understand. Is there nothing you really Desire? Something you can't picture your life without?"

"My brothers. My father. My mother."

"Ah, but this you already have. I mean something you wish to accomplish. Something you wish to *gain*."

Oriana fell silent. She had never really thought about it, not in those terms at least.

"I guess one day I'd like to help my father in the smithy," she said at last.

"What if you can't? What if that call is denied to you? What if the thing you really want is not allowed to you?"

Oriana frowned.

"Is this what Nocturnals are good for? Scaring little girls?"

"No, milady. I just wish you to understand that sometimes a destiny denied is twice a destiny."

"Well—" she began, then stopped.

In front of the emerald lady's stall there now stood a woman. She was similar to the hundreds of dreamers Oriana had already seen, with her half-closed eyes and drunken gait, but set apart by the dozens of ivory combs attached to her shawl, making her look like some strangely decorated tree. She was also her mother, Donna Lena.

At first, Oriana assumed that she must be mistaken. The woman in front of her was younger than her mother. She was also more beautiful, her skin radiant, almost glowing. And her expression was one that Oriana had never before seen her mother wear—a badly sedated hunger. But those hawklike features were definitely hers, there was no mistaking them. Silently, the Dame offered Donna Lena her last comb.

Dreamers and vendors turned their heads. The lady in green was about to be liberated. Someone else would become proverbial in her place. Oriana felt the urge to snatch the ivory comb and run, but a memory echoed in her ears. *Beware the Emerald Dame.* And Oriana knew—as one knows things in dreams—that she couldn't fight what was about to happen. Whatever you gave at the market was freely given. She watched helplessly as Donna Lena stretched out her white arm and snatched the comb. The Emerald Dame placed an open hand on her forehead and pushed. Donna Lena reeled back.

"Mamma," Oriana whispered, "what have you done?"

She hadn't expected an answer, but Donna Lena opened her eyes and stared straight at her. Then, with the utmost quiet, she said, "I did what had to be done to get your father that commission for the door handles. We'll be rich and happy."

Oriana bit her lips savagely.

She didn't know what her mother's words meant exactly, but she guessed it was something nasty, something that in the waking world Donna Lena would never admit.

"Why? Weren't we happy already? Weren't we rich?"

"You won't have to do what I did. You won't have to work all day and all night, like I did. And you won't even have to have children if you don't want them. You'll be a lady. Respected, loved. Feared, even."

"Mamma, why are you saying this? I don't want to be feared!"

Paying no attention to Oriana's words, her mother caressed her left cheek. Oriana shuddered. Donna Lena's hands were warm, real.

"Mother, what did you give the Emerald Dame?"

The woman stared vacantly at her.

"I don't remember. Well, sometimes I do. But it doesn't hurt so much anymore. Less so every day."

"What did you give her?" Oriana asked in a broken voice.

Donna Lena smiled her sweetest smile.

"Why, you of course. All three of you."

A breath later, she disappeared. And not just her; the Emerald Dame and her stall were gone too. For a time, Oriana Siliceo stared at the ground. She told herself that this was just a dream. But she also knew that somewhere in the Day a wheel had been set in motion. Her father's door handle commission made him a rich man, and it was all because of her mother's dealings at the market. She couldn't stay a moment longer.

"What's the fastest way out of here?"

"You wish to leave now, milady?"

"Immediately."

"But the Dreamarquise is still at large, and we must—"

"There is no *we*! I don't care about your master's treasure or about that stupid cat! And I'm not going to continue with your quest. Your market already damaged my family, and I won't stay here a second longer. I need to go home."

"That's very unfortunate, because if this is your choice, then you won't ever leave."

"What!"

"You made a deal with my master. Either you deliver your end of the bargain, or he will *own* your fate. I had instructions to lead you home only after you completed your part. If you don't, I can't bring you back."

Oriana bit her knuckles until they hurt. She felt that every moment she spent here was more damage done to her family back home. But there was nothing she could do.

"Are you his dog, then," she said at last, "that you'll obey all his orders?"

"I am much worse than his dog, for he owns me already."

"I am not a thing to be owned."

"That is of no significance. He is the greatest maker of the Black Court. A living thing to him is no more alive than a stone. Less so, even, for he can do wonders with just a pebble."

Oriana shivered, and then retorted, "Right. Like the stone he told me he would turn me into before smashing me to pieces to mold into something new."

"That was not an idle threat. My master is not the boasting Baron of Twilight, nor the mad Marquise of Fullmoon. He weighs his words long before letting them out of his mouth. If he said that he would turn you into stone, this he will most certainly do."

"I'll run away then. I'll sail to Africa, where the sun always shines!"

"He is Lord of the Under-earth, his fiefdom bleeds into the Day as well. And his Moira is now linked to yours. Wherever you go, he'll be there, until you die. And after."

Oriana repressed a shudder and hugged herself.

"There is another reason why you should care about the Dreamarquise of cats," the mouth continued. "For it was by following him in a dream that your mother found the market and the Emerald Dame."

Oriana blinked.

"B-but why would my mother have followed him?"

"Have you not guessed yet?"

Oriana opened her mouth wide, her face flushed.

"Oh vile, vile traitor!" she cried out at last. "Let me wring my hands around his fat neck tomorrow. I'll make him beg for mercy!"

"Tomorrow morning is a world away, milady. And I doubt my master will have the patience for that. Anyway, it would be of no use to find the cat awake. After all, he is the Dreamarquise only when he dreams."

"Well, then. I'll kill him here, after I get the Hammer back!"

"Kill him, milady? Here he is just a Dream."

"All the better!"

"I am not sure whether you would find it easier to kill a Dream or a Reality. I guess it depends on the kind of person you are."

"Let's find out," she said.

TEN

She began searching through the stall-crowded garden, inside the moss-padded caves, along the beech tree lanes where the dreamers wandered somnambulantly. Yet she never saw a single cat, nor any other beast.

"Your master was wrong. There are no animals here."

"That's because you assume that those you are seeing are people."

"Well, what are they then?" she frowned.

"Dreamers. And if a city can dream, so can its rivers, and hills, and trees, and animals, even cats. Cats, in fact, dream most of all."

"But everyone here looks human!"

"To you maybe, because a market is a human affair, after all. So that's what you expect to see. But have you looked hard enough?"

She eyed the sleepwalkers more closely. Earlier she had concentrated on the ways they interacted with the dead instead of considering them individually. When she did, she noticed something odd. Not all the dreamers were in the same state of stupor. Some looked and acted as if they were almost awake, walking steadily, mumbling to themselves, and even opening their eyes for an instant. Finally, Oriana spotted her first nonhuman dreamer—a middle-aged woman wearing a half-decayed wedding dress. Her face was plaster white, her hair matted with mud and leaves. But as she blinked up, Oriana saw that she had windows for eyes. Small, yet perfectly defined: four glass panels separated by a cross of wooden frames painted green. The woman shut her eyes and tottered away.

"Who—what was she?"

"Some buildings are semi-sentient, milady. They dream of their inauguration as men dream of their infancy. They age, too, like human beings. And some, just very few, desire a conflagration of destiny, a new beginning, or maybe an end, that will be long remembered."

Once she got the hang of it, Oriana saw not-human dreamers everywhere. They were always given away by a small mannerism, a tiny detail of their attire, or something else out of place. That young blond man in a cassock, floating from stall to stall as if pulled by some secret undercurrent, his hair was not really blond. In fact, it was not hair at all. Oriana realized it when he stood under the direct blaze of a stall's lantern: each single strand of hair was a drop of water, dripping so slowly from his scalp that it traced an illusion of length. As for its color, it simply reflected the golden halo of the lanterns.

"A river," Oriana murmured in awe. "That man is a river."

There were many others. Scrawny women with long, fidgeting fingers walking in sleepwalking clusters, roaming from stall to stall, suddenly halted, all at once, so still it looked like they had put down roots. Indeed they had, for a moment. There were the men whose heavy, muddy cloaks made them look like walking boulders. The cheeks of a half-drenched girl with pale, greenish skin, suddenly bloated like a balloon, then deflated with a very quiet croak. And an old woman, bent by age, wore a faded cape that whirled into a mass of black feathers in the blink of an eye. Oriana stared at the crow-cloak, entranced.

"My master was right; you do have a talent for recognition. The Duke's sister—better not to say her name here—calls these the garments that make the dreamers appear human dream-tokens."

In the stall to her right, a little girl in a white cuff licked her own hand thrice. It was a gesture any little girl might have made, but something in the quickness of it, in the way she indulged in it, made Oriana stiffen.

"I think I saw a dream-cat," she whispered.

At once, the other girl turned to her, eyes wide open.

"What is happening? What is the dream-cat doing?" The Garaude's voice made them both jump.

"I think she saw me. And heard you! Rats, she's getting away."

"Chase her, milady, fast!"

Oriana ran. But the market was crowded with hundreds of dreamers, and it wasn't easy to push them aside as they were all bigger than her. The girl-cat seemed preternaturally agile, diving under the skirts of the black-clad matrons and dodging the bulkier dreamers with ease. Oriana chased her through the swirls of the labyrinthine garden, into small rococo grottos filled with lanterns, alongside putrid artificial ponds, over intertwined bridges and narrow cypress lanes. The girl-cat turned her head to look back from time to time, then sprinted even faster. Oriana caught only a glimpse of her—a brown dress, sandals, a white cuff—before she took off, and began to wonder if she was just a scared little girl of Oriana's own age, after all. Finally, they bolted onto a tufa terrace filled with weeping angels. The girl headed toward one of the marble statues and simply blinked out. Oriana halted so abruptly that she almost crashed into it.

"What is it?" asked the Garaude. "Did you get her?"

"No," panted Oriana, "she disappeared."

"Disappeared? How?"

"I don't know! Look, there is something wrong here. I've seen dog-dreamers, horse-dreamers, bird-dreamers, but only one cat. If she even was one."

"She clearly was. My master's sister loves felines. That's

why she granted them a collective Boon: when one of her own Dreams, such as the market, appears, they can become aware that they are dreaming. This ability makes cats fierce opponents in the Second Night, should you face one."

"But that's the point. I can't, because there aren't any! Wasn't the Dreamarquise supposed to do his stunt at the market? That's what your master said! So where is he? And where are all the other cats?"

"You are right, milady, it is odd. Perhaps the cats knew the Duke would send someone to retrieve his Hammer."

"You think they're hiding from me?"

"Maybe. Milady, please describe what you see."

"It's a terraced garden like all the rest . . . only it's full of statues and trees and there are fewer stalls. It's, I don't know, different somehow."

"How?"

"Well, there are fewer dreamers, and I can't really say why, but it looks ghoulish. It looks a bit like the garden outside the walls of the cemetery in Lucerìa. The statues and trees look the same."

"Ah, the scoundrel! It's a nested dream."

"A what?"

"Our Dreamarquise knew the Duke would send someone for him, so he created a nested dream. A dream within a dream, if you like. One you cannot reach without first making it through another. He took the Dream of Lucerìa's cemetery and pasted it in here."

"Sorry, I am lost. Are we still in the market or not?"

"We are, but *they* are not! Search well, milady, you should be able to find something different from the rest, something the dream-cats can recognize easily and use as a passageway."

Oriana looked around.

The angels were indeed beautiful, even more odd in this

dreamscape than in the real Lucerìa. Their marble bodies were covered in phosphorescent moss, in glowing lichens, red spongia that hung like beards from their maiden faces. Their faces! They were each covered by the angels' hands, all except one. That angel must be the way through.

She drew a long breath and stepped toward it.

At once, the cries of the vendors faded away.

Oriana turned around and saw that the stalls had disappeared too. She was still within a vast, terraced garden just outside a tall wall encircling a small hill which she knew to be the cemetery. Even from where she was standing, she could see the lumini lit for the dead, like a cloud of glowing eyes staring at her across the six terraces. A stronger light shone on its summit, as bright as the half-moon, a bluish beacon of sorts.

Someone hissed at the base of the wall. Oriana looked down in time to see the girl-cat crouched and baring her fangs. The poor thing was so scared that Oriana could barely understand what she was saying.

"I didn't do anything!" she hissed. "Grandpa says I mustn't even look at the stalls, but I didn't take anything!"

From experience with her brother, Oriana knew the girl-cat was scared enough to attack her if provoked. So she backed away, and in the tone of voice she used with Oriano when he was upset said, "Don't worry, I won't tell your grandpa. You have my word."

"Do I still have to go, then?" asked the girl-cat. She seemed to calm down, and scratched under her white cuff.

"Go?" frowned Oriana.

"To the Parliament. Grandpa said it's educational, but I think that's the grown-up word for boring. The market was *much* more interesting."

"Oh yes, you must go. That's why your grandpa sent me here to fetch you. But he said you can take that off, if you want," she answered, pointing at the white cuff.

"Really? Can I? The Dreamarquise said I was never to take it off."

"That was at the market. But now you are safe."

Oriana's answer satisfied her. As soon as she took off the cuff, her face grew fur and whiskers, and her body a long tail. She was still half-human, but the animal part was taking over fast, until at the base of the wall sat a cat, or rather, a striped kitten with a cuff in her paws. Oriana scooped the cuff away from her. The cat hissed in anger.

"Go back now!" said Oriana. "Get away from here or your grandpa will have you bitten like you deserve!"

The kitten hissed again and vanished.

"W-where did she go?" Oriana asked, crouching on the ground.

"You told her to go back, and she did. To the waking world."

"She didn't die or anything?"

"I thought you wanted to kill dreams by the hundreds."

"Can you just answer me plainly, Master Garaude? Just this once."

"No, milady, she just woke up."

"Good," she sighed. "Let's see if this works as I think it does."

Oriana fastened the cuff around her wrist and felt the strangest impression that dozens of cat tails were brushing her legs.

"I don't feel any different. But, phew, I stink."

"That's her smell, and it will help you appear more like her, to a cat at least. But that's not all that's different about you."

She patted down her body. "No? I guess I—"

She shuddered as her hand grazed the tip of her tail, thin enough to poke through a ripped seam on her skirt. Oriana stroked it with absent-minded fascination.

"Where do these dream-tokens come from? Can dreamers make them at will?"

"The Dreamarquise can. I heard a story in the Under-earth. They say there was a Dreamarquise of cats in Germany, by the name of Hinze, who dreamed of boots."

"Boots?" she asked, blinking.

"Yes, his master's boots. They say that he transformed them into dream-tokens so powerful that he was able to look like a man not only in his master's dreams, but also in the dreams of his king. He pretended to be a hunter and brought him the splendid beasts he slayed, on behalf of his master. So impressed was the king at the hunter's offerings, that when he finally met Hinze's master in the flesh, he gifted him a county and his own daughter's hand in marriage."

"And this happened for real, in Germany?"

"Or France. Or Sicily. Possibly."

"But how can that be? Something either is or is not."

"In the Day, perhaps. In the Night, so many possibilities are born and unborn, that one can't really say what is real, and what is not."

"This is all very interesting, but I still don't know which way to go."

"Is there a door somewhere? A gate or a passageway?"

"No, just a wall."

"Follow the wall, then. And be careful."

She began circling the tufa wall, looking for a door or an arch of some kind. But the wall was smooth and had no openings.

"This is stupid! Why would the Dreamarquise nest a dream within a dream if no one can get inside it?"

"To keep *you* out. And it has worked, apparently."

She begrudgingly kept her silence until, after a time, her quiet steps returned to the same angel she had stepped out from. She had walked an entire circle around the cemetery and found no way in.

"Damn," she whispered. "What now?"

You're quite late.

Oriana spun around like a feather caught in the wind. For the words came not from her palm, but from the top of the wall. A gray tiger cat looked down at her with bemused eyes. It didn't look anthropomorphic at all, just like a very big cat. He did feel somehow familiar to her, though Oriana certainly didn't know of any cat that could talk in the Day.

So? Coming or not? The Election has just started.

The cat's mouth had not moved. It was not exactly words she heard, more like his *intent*, just like with the market's vendors.

"You mean up there? How? There's no ladder."

Pitiful. This is why I'd never guise myself as a human.

Such was his tone of reprimand, his tail flapping in scorn, that Oriana felt her own wilt in shame. Was she cat-blushing?

Jump, you idiot!

As instructed, Oriana crouched down and jumped. Her feet and hands brushed the wall very slightly before she landed atop it softly. She blinked in amazement. Not only had she reached the top of the wall in a blink, but she was also perfectly balanced on it.

The tiger cat purred in approval.

Now, come quickly. The Dreamarquise gets tremendously irked if he's interrupted during his Boast.

Swiftly, the tiger cat jumped down to the other side of the wall.

Oriana scuttled behind him. And jumped.

ELEVEN

Oriana took in her new surroundings. They'd crossed into the dream-version of the old graveyard of Lucerìa. Built on the slope of a hill, it was shaped like an amphitheater with seven graduated terraces. Oriana and the tiger cat stood at the crest of the bottom one, from where they could see the highest terrace and the stone balustrade encircling it. Broken Doric columns were scattered all around among thick hawthorn bushes, ivy-covered weeping angels, and tall cypresses. And seated on the traceried balustrades, the moss-covered tombstones, and marble statue heads, each with its attentive eyes pointed in the same direction, were hundreds of cats of all shapes and forms.

The farther they sat from center stage, the more they looked like the cats Oriana was accustomed to seeing. However, even these were bigger and fiercer than the cats in the Day, for this was how they'd dreamed themselves. The closer they were to the bottom of the arena, the more they looked human. Each wore one of the Dreamarquise's distinctive dream-tokens—an earring, a scarf, a hat, a scabbard, a pair of boots. Indeed, at first glance, the closest rows to the stage seemed crowded with men and women. They sat on tombstones, gentlemen smoking their cigars and ladies cooling themselves with their fans. Still, they could be given away by a gesture, a lick on the palm or a yawning of sharp fangs. All of them had long, flailing tails.

Oriana walked into the midst of that tail-forest as quietly

as she could, for she felt like she was entering enemy territory. There was a strange tension in the last rows, a palpable and growing unrest in the form of harsh, pervasive purring. Oriana passed by two huge Siamese, when one of them glanced at her and said to his mate,

Here comes another. I say this human fashion has gone too far.

The she-cat yawned in the way of annoyed cats.

Why yes. I dare say we are not the only ones to think it so.

The tomcat yawned, too, showing his long, white fangs.

Let's wait and see, then.

Let's.

Oriana passed them quickly, a faint shiver on her back.

"What were they talking about? Where the hell are we?" she whispered in her hand, putting the other over her right ear so that no one else could overhear.

"I should have guessed. We are at the Cats' Parliament," answered the Nocturnal. "Once every seven years the cats of Lucerìa elect their Dreamarquise. It appears this year they've chosen to do so during this market. That must be why my master sent you here. I didn't know. My master keeps his own counsel."

"So Marfisio was elected here, seven years ago."

"In another Parliament, yes. Tonight, either he'll be confirmed, or they'll elect another cat to be Dreamarquise."

"I see. And the Dreamarquise commands all the cats in the world?"

"Of course not; only in Lucerìa. And he doesn't command them, he decides the style of their dreaming in this city. This, in turn, affects how they live. See tonight how many cats are guised as he is? He's been busy giving out dream-tokens during his rule."

All the crowd stared ahead in anticipation. Sitting under a massive Lebanon tree were three dream-cats in human form.

As Oriana sat down, she studied them more closely. One was a Persian cat, or rather, a middle-aged man who couldn't have been anything else but a Persian, his flattened features giving him away. Dressed like a Navy Admiral, with a tricorne hat and a generous blue mantle, he was in the middle of reciting a fervent speech. Seated behind him there were two other dreamcats. One was a woman, or rather, an elegant she-cat with green eyes and long dark hair, jewelry made of shimmering beads and coins at her neck, a colorful skirt made of intricate fabric. She looked indeed more like a wandering adventuress than a lady. And the other, Oriana recognized straightaway. He looked like a man in his thirties, with a drooping mustache and an arrogant nose. He was beautifully dressed, a flamboyant Spanish soldier in a large Venetian hat that boasted three enormous red feathers.

And yet in spite of his attire, Oriana felt like she was meeting a man she'd known since he was a child. It was the way he sat and the way he looked at the Admiral, as if smiling at a secret joke. But truth be told, even without noting his familiar mannerisms, Oriana would have recognized Marfisio at once. For the Dreamarquise of Luceria had only one blazing green eye. The other was covered by a black leather patch.

The Admiral finished his speech and swept his hat on the ground to collect a cat applause, that is, the silent slash of tails. Much to her irritation, Oriana discovered she was doing the same. Then the Persian sat down, and the Dreamarquise stood. He spoke out loud like a man, not using his intent.

"So," he began, "I was talking the other day with the Khan, when he asked me, 'Growler, what have your last seven years been like?'"

"Who the hell is Growler?" Oriana whispered.

"That's him; it's his name," the Garaude answered.

"No, his name is Marfisio."

"Cats usually have three names. The one humans give them,

if they get the chance, though they don't like to be reminded of these while in the company of other felines. Then there is the name other cats use. His being Growler. And last, there is the name they have for themselves. When you see a cat looking in the middle distance, smiling softly, they are contemplating their true name. And none less than a God can take that away."

"So I said to him," the Dreamarquise continued, "nothing special, your Imperial Majesty. In the First year after I was appointed Dreamarquise, I stopped the Thule invasion by farting so fiercely that all the Thulians' beards flew off their faces and into the air for miles until they landed on their wives, and that's why Thulian women have beards. In the Second year, I jumped onto the moon and killed all the rats living there. That's why the moon is so full of holes—those are the rodent lairs I exposed. And in the Third year, I marched with half a million tigers and conquered the great island of Dundeya, close to Ceylon. I had a fancy to drink only good tea, so the cat of the British King, himself a Dreamarquise, agreed to grant me a yearly supply of black chai if I returned Dundeya to his human, and so I did, at least for as long as my galleons are replenished. In the Fourth year I felt like a smoke, so I took a swim over to Hy-Brasil. There I sang so beautifully that all the parrots of that continent fell in love with me. With their help I extirpated half of Hy-Brasil's tobacco plantations, and gave smoke to all my friends, as well as to the King of England, who is now a friend too. In the Fifth year I got bored with smoking and drinking tea and decided to go hunting. I hunted elephants in Sudan, gray wolves in Germany, whales in Thule. I hunted bears and leucrotas and giant apes and chimaeras. I killed more than one hundred thousand wild boars and used their meat to feed all the poor in Naples and Reggio. In the Sixth year I got tired of it all and went deep underground, and there I befriended the Emistuchivio with the tales of my adventures and an offering of my tobacco and excellent tea. We became such good friends that he showed me his wonders, many of which must remain hidden and never, ever fall into the wrong hands. Of course, I waited for him to fall asleep and stole one."

Silence. Oriana could see the cats' eyes gleaming all around. But the Dreamarquise remained perfectly silent, as if he had forgotten all about his Boast. Until the big tiger cat who led Oriana inside jumped up on a half column and purred with his sharp intent.

Show it to us.

The Dreamarquise grinned.

"I know," he said, "that many of you think my rulership has been too . . . human. That I gave out too many dream-tokens so that you could take humanlike dream-forms. Well, to those I can only say: in my Seventh year as Dreamarquise, I decided to crack Serapide's Seed of Dream. Thus, her Dream will spill out into Lucerìa and become reality. For one Night you will not be the feeble cats of Day, but the dream-cats you are now: powerful, fierce, invincible. An army, you will enter the houses of the humans who mistreated you, who drowned your kittens, who starved you, and you will hunt them in the streets. For pleasure, to toy with them as you please. And it will not be a Dream, it will be real. It already happened in the dream-city of Ulthar, eleven thousand years before this day. Are you with me?"

The gray tiger cat growled again, his tail flailing behind him.

And how would you do that? How can you crack the Seed? he challenged.

The Dreamarquise tweaked his mustache, a mischievous glint in his one eye.

"With this," he answered. A swift movement revealed that in his free hand there was now a hammer. Oriana put a hand to her mouth. It was the most beautiful hammer she had ever seen. Long and lean, its traceried body made the slightest curve before forming a horse's head, all in perfect details. Such was the craftsmanship that it could have been a mere ornament, yet it gave an impression of power, of harnessed strength and subtle might.

"The Deep Red Hammer!"

The sound of Oriana's outburst echoed through hundreds of flailing tails.

"Indeed." The Dreamarquise smirked. "One of the Duke's best tools. It can bend and break the most fragile of substances and the most unfathomable. Even Serapide's Dreams."

And her Seed? Where is the Seed? the tiger cat demanded.

"Can't you see its blue light shining on the top of this hill? Here is where it landed when Serapide cast it. I built my nested dream around it, so that neither she nor the Duke's agents can find us before we finish our business. Now I will go right to the top, wield my Hammer, and bring it crashing down on the Seed. Then you will be able to enter Lucerìa as you are now and take your vengeance from all the citizens of the Day."

Oriana had never heard such a large and impassioned throng of cats meowing and growling and purring all at the same time. It was inhuman and unearthly.

"Watch the Hammer carefully," whispered the Garaude, "before he hides it again!"

But his advice had come too late. The Hammer disappeared. Was it in the hat he'd replaced atop his head? No, it wouldn't be able to fit. Neither could it be in his waistcoat. Under the Lebanon tree, the she-cat raised Growler's left arm.

"Parliament of cats! Is there anyone who knows of a reason why Growler must not be reelected as Dreamarquise?" the she-cat inquired.

The cats were as still as the tombstones on which they sat. Not a purr to be heard.

"Is there any of you here who thinks he or she has a better claim than he to earn this title? Speak now or be silent evermore."

Again the deepest silence followed.

"Good. It is with my deepest pleasure, then, that I declare Growler of Lucerìa—"

"Wait! I do! I have something important to say!"

TWELVE

Oriana's cry turned four hundred and seventy-two heads and tails toward her. They stood in unison, humanguised and not, looking at her with eyes of solid gold. Oriana walked among them with feigned calm, her heart racing.

"Milady, what are you doing?" asked the Garaude.

"I just want to have a closer look. Now, be quiet."

As she got closer, Oriana found herself in the midst of the cat-whispering.

It's Purrer.

Purrer who?

The granddaughter of Harp-tooth.

How dare she insult the Dreamarquise.

Instinctively Oriana touched her cuff as she strode toward the she-cat and the Persian. As for the Dreamarquise, he was looking at her with iron-hot intensity. Oriana swallowed. Would he recognize her as easily as she had recognized him? But Marfisio—Growler—just glanced at her cuff. That token and her cat smell was enough to identify her as Purrer.

"What is it, child? This is a serious matter," the she-cat adventuress warned. "If you don't speak now, you could be tried for Misconduct by the Parliament."

Oriana bit her lips. She could feel all those eyes scratching her skin.

"Speak, then!" said the Admiral, flashing his sharp teeth.

She looked around. Her mind was numb. Not only could

she not invent a story to save her life, she was also unable to utter a single word.

"Well," said Growler, "this proves an old point of mine, that only cats of age should be allowed at Parliament. It's quite clear now that this child—"

"Oh most terrible, most horrible of liars!" Oriana cried out.

Growler froze, his eye narrowing to a feline slit.

"What did you call me?" he said quietly.

"I called you a liar *and* traitor! You are betraying our trust with groundless stories. You haven't seen the Duke's forge, nor are you his friend, nor do you know his secrets. But most importantly, that which you've shown us is *not* the Deep Red Hammer!"

At that, the feline crowd hissed as if scorched by boiling water. The Admiral drew his saber.

"Treason! The little one dares to speak of Treason!"

"Beware, child," said the she-cat, "these are heavy allegations."

"Heavy are his lies," replied Oriana, chin up. "My truths are feathers."

"Then give us proof now or I swear by our saber-toothed ancestors that I'll rip your guts open!" said the Dreamarquise.

"I'll prove it, to all of you."

Oriana smiled to hide her swelling terror and realized that the Parliament was actually waiting to hear her out.

"Well, he says he knows of the Duke's secrets."

"I do! He told them to me as a sign of true friendship after we shared my Hy-Brasilian tobacco and my Ceylon's tea."

"Good, then. So what is the seventy-times-folded-mansion?"

Growler squinted his eye.

"You're making that up!"

"I see. So you don't know."

"There's no such thing!"

"The seventy-times-folded-mansion is a metal castle that can be folded like a handkerchief and put into a pocket."

"Preposterous. This child is just playing games!"

"Am I?" she asked.

Without adding another word, she put her hand in her pocket and retrieved the handkerchief. She began to unfold the mansion, and with every turn it grew, and grew, until it became half as tall as the Lebanon tree. It had spires, and doors, and turrets, and one little Moorish window, right at the top.

As the cats started to reel back, wild-eyed, the she-cat cried, "Enough!"

Oriana stopped. All the cats looked at the mansion with deep longing, for such is the power of the treasures of the Under-earth.

"How do you possess such a thing," croaked Growler.

"I bought it with my services to the Duke."

"What services?"

"He asked me to steal for him the Thin Chain from the seven Wyrms who guard it under the Mountain of Secret Fire. And this I did."

"And what is this Thin Chain?"

"A chain so thin it looks like a silk scarf, and yet so strong it can hold back one thousand horses at full gallop. Do you wish to see that too?"

The Dreamarquise stepped back. Oriana folded up the mansion until it was small again and put it back into her pocket.

"So you see," she exclaimed, "Growler doesn't know the treasures of the Duke. His Hammer is a fake."

"It is not! Can't you see? She must be a spy from the Duke!"

My granddaughter is no spy, Harp-tooth growled, his fur standing up.

Yet the other dream-cats eyed her with suspicion. Oriana cleared her throat and addressed the audience.

"He is good at tricks, I must admit. A flash of his hands

and you all thought you saw the Hammer, but in fact you didn't."

"It was the Hammer!" protested the Dreamarquise.

Harp-tooth jumped up in front of the crowd, eyes ablaze, and commanded, *Then show it to us once more.*

"Yes, show it to us again."

Show it!

Hat in hand, the Dreamarquise saluted them, making a mocking sweep to the ground. And again, in his hand, the Hammer appeared. Oriana could feel its beauty in full force. For the seventy-times-folded-mansion was an artifact, while the Hammer was a tool. It wasn't just beautiful, it was capable of creating beauty.

"What do you think now? Is it real or not?"

The cats reeled back, even Harp-tooth. Oriana was watching, too, not the Hammer, but Growler. Was the Hammer disguised as one of his golden buttons? Or maybe his white ruffle? Both times, the Dreamarquise had swept his hat to the ground. Oriana considered it carefully. There were only two red feathers adorning its top. Suddenly, Growler raised the Hammer over his bare head.

"Is that enough or do you want me to break the moon? I could shatter the earth and wake its fires. Shall I?"

All the dream-cats crouched down, human and beastly alike.

"No, Growler, forgive us," said the Admiral.

"Good, then," said the Dreamarquise, then gestured to Oriana. "Now, seize her!"

Before Oriana could take a breath, the she-cat and the Admiral grabbed her. She tried to wriggle away but their hold was a clawed vise.

"Now, Parliament of cats, how do you judge her?"

The answer was unanimous.

Guilty! Guilty of High Treason!

"And how will her Treason be punished?"

By hanging! Hang her! Hang her on the Lebanon tree!

"This is the Parliament's final sentence. Pray, bring a rope."

Someone in the crowd produced a rope.

It was woven with human hair, ugly as the deed it was going to be used for. Oriana had no doubt that what was happening to her was a dream, for it was. And she was going to die in it. Growler put his hat back on. At once, the Hammer disappeared. It might as well have been on the moon with Growler so out of reach. And so, before the two cats tightened the noose around her neck, before the Dreamarquise gave the signal and the Admiral pulled the rope tight, Oriana shouted:

"Marfisio, stay!"

The Dreamarquise crouched down. It lasted less than an instant, but all the cats saw. Immediately they started waving their tails. First the kittens, then the older cats, human-guised and fully animal, all the Parliament, laughed at Growler. He stood in front of Oriana, growling in fury.

Who are you? How do you know me?

"So she does know you," the she-cat confirmed.

The Dreamarquise turned around.

"This is of no consequence," he said.

"Wrong. For our Parliament cannot bear to be ruled by someone who is on such humble terms with humans. Maybe Harp-tooth's kin was right, after all."

"But I have the Hammer!"

"You could as well own the moon and the stars. What are they to us?"

"Would you pass on our vengeance, then? Would you wait until we become like the cats of Ypres? Hunted down every winter for sport?"

"Those are old customs, and the humans we know don't

practice them. Let the Dreamarquise of Ypres take revenge, if he wants."

"But humans offend us! They kick us and starve us and torture us!"

"Yes, they do—but only if we let them. You did. I didn't. My human is Roma, and she knows the value of freedom. For this I respect her, and she me. We are equals."

This exchange had not escaped the Parliament, which had fallen silent again. By now most of its members were cats once more, having discarded their dream-tokens. Foulards, boots, earrings, fans, they were all cast down as the creatures reverted to their original feline shapes. Again, Harp-tooth stepped forward.

Growler, Dreamarquise of Lucerìa, we depose you of your title.

Growler staggered back. All the Parliament's eyes were upon him. In a single motion, Oriana removed the noose from around her neck and snatched the Dreamarquise's hat.

"Thief!"

She was fast, but Growler was faster.

With one hand he grabbed her, shaking her so hard she yelped. And yet it was Growler in the end who screamed, crouching in pain. The mouth on her palm had bitten him. Still in shock, Oriana stepped back, only to discover that the rest of the cats had closed in on her, a swarm of widening eyes, sniffing her and smelling her real scent.

A human. A human among us. A human at the Parliament.

Oriana looked down. Her white cuff lay on the ground. It must have come off during Growler's shaking. The Admiral, the Roma, the other cats, were all staring at her in horror. As for the Dreamarquise, he too had lost his dream-token. Without his hat, his one-eyed face was becoming wilder, fiercer, his mouth fanged. From it came a low, deep growling.

You!

"Run, milady," screamed the Nocturnal.

Oriana ran.

Never in her life, neither before nor after, did Oriana Siliceo sprint as she did with the whole Cats' Parliament at her heels. Her only salvation was that her cat-form was fading gradually. She still had some feline agility left when she raced through the cemetery and up toward its summit where the Seed lay. She hurdled forward, finding footholds on gravestones, railings, and marble steps, moving as fast and as nimbly as she could. Luckily, she had the advantage of surprise, for never before had a human being infiltrated the Parliament of cats, and her sacrilege held the shock of first times.

For a while she climbed alone, listening carefully and alert as she leapt from one terrace to the next. She had already reached the fourth, when her worst fears took the shape and sound of a rumbling noise. It was a soft roar, the kind you would expect from a flood, feeble at first, then growing in strength. Her feline nimbleness was fading fast, leaving her sweating and panting like the human child she was. The moon was just full enough to illuminate the cemetery with its snowy candor. She reached a marble buttress surmounted by a cypress and she looked up to find another glow. It wasn't the moon, though almost as bright. It shone from the very top of the graveyard, behind the crooked gates of a Moorish mausoleum shrouded in ivy, a bluish flicker. The Seed! It was her only way back home, to her brother and father, to Donna Lena . . .

The noise rising behind her made her turn again. A flowing mass climbed up from the terrace below, a river of fur and golden eyes. As it drew nearer, it branched out, spreading over the marble balustrades, dodging the cypresses, the bushes, the tombstones, and the weeping statues, quickly surrounding her. Fear rooted her to the ground. There was no use in running. They were too fast, and far too many. She would never hug her brother again.

"The Hammer, milady! Use the Hammer!"

In a daze she looked at her hand. Then, she plucked the longest feather from the Dreamarquise's hat. It instantly transformed into the elegant shape of the Deep Red Hammer. In her palm she could feel its power, the force of breaking. She looked up and saw that the stone buttress overhead supported almost the whole terrace. She stared down at the approaching army of cats.

"Garaude, what happens if they die here, in the Dream?" Oriana asked.

"They will wake up immediately, like Purrer did," he answered. "Why are you smiling?"

"Because it's not so easy for you to kill dreams, after all."

"Oh, shut up."

Using the cypress's roots as handholds, she climbed until she was on top of the terrace. Then she took a deep breath and at the top of her lungs shouted, "Hey you, mouse-chasers! You fish-stealers, you tame tigers! Come here and get me!"

The rivers of cats paused for a moment, then converged on her like the fingers of a hand. Oriana felt her heart drum furiously, and yet she waited until the soft roar of paws was deafening, the forest of tails almost engulfing her. She kept waiting until the first of them, the freshly deposed Dreamarquise, jumped on top of a tombstone and stared her down with his only eye. His hat, his boots, his cloak, his human guise were gone.

Give it back! Give it to me and I will save you, I will bring you home safely, I swear! I'll do anything you want!

"Because of you," she said, "my mother traded with the dead. Undo it, and I'll give you your precious Hammer back. Can you?"

Whatever you say, just give me the Hammer and I'll fix it.

"How?"

I don't know! I will figure out something!

"Sorry, not convincing enough."

Oriana swung the Hammer against the top of the buttress.

A breath later, sixty tons of earth and stone erupted as if from a cracked dike. Oriana screamed as—using her last drop of cat agility—she jumped onto the low branches of the cypress. The tree tilted like the mast of a sinking ship but didn't fall into the landslide below. The cats were less fortunate. Growler and the first ten rows of his peers were vaporized. The ones immediately behind scattered as fast as they could to avoid the stone avalanche. The rest took cover behind tombstones and iron fences.

When the earth's roar finally ceased, Oriana found herself dangling from a cypress branch. She was bruised and bleeding from the many cuts on her arms. But she was safe, and, most importantly, victorious. The old cemetery looked as if it had been raked by a Titan's claw; a path of destruction laid open tombs and mausoleums. In the stillness, a few surviving cats bellowed in pain. Oriana picked up the Hammer from the ground and started to climb up.

A few hundred steps later, covered in sweat and mud, and caked blood, she arrived at the mausoleum. It stood on the top of the mound, a marbled dome atop a frescoed wall and an arabesque iron gate. Oriana could see the Seed illuminating the frescos as she approached them. They depicted a battle between Christians and Muslims. The pictures held a peculiar appeal, lifelike in a way Oriana had never seen before. Each of the soldiers' faces was rendered in vivid detail, no matter how tiny, as if the painter had been personally acquainted with every one of them.

"Oh," she said, "this is truly beautiful."

"Thank you, milady."

The little girl looked down at her right hand.

"You made this?"

"The man I was did, yes, centuries ago."

"Then, Master Garaude, you were a true artist."

"You do me too much honor. But now, please go to the Seed, for the Second Night is at an end, and we must return home."

The Seed looked like a medlar fruit, only it shone with pure, icy light.

Oriana bent forward and touched it.

THIRTEEN

Stepping out of Serapide's Dream was like walking through a waterfall, only in reverse. Oriana felt filthy and bruised and tired beyond imagination. She stood in a long, rectangular piazza, next to the portico of the custom house. Her home was just two streets away. Above her the moon had set, the starless sky almost violet. Before long it would be Dawn, another region of the Night. Oriana staggered toward the arch. There, in the deepest shadow, was a blazing dot of fire, glowing on and off like a pulsing red-coal eye.

Three shadows waited for her. Two knelt and the third one—though short—was standing. Gobbo growled as Oriana approached the arch. The Garaude looked up once with his eyeless face, then lowered it. As for the Duke of Under-earth, his grin bit a thin white pipe. He extended his hairy hand and Oriana gave him the Hammer. She had not expected a word of gratitude, but she had expected some words, and was baffled by his silence. The Emistuchivio inspected his Hammer quietly as Oriana watched.

Suddenly, he looked up.

"You wielded it," he said.

Oriana was too exhausted to be scared.

"And now you'll tell me that I shouldn't have, and because I did, to save my life, I'll owe you for three hundred years, and you're going to turn me into a stone or a goblin to serve you. Well, do as you please, I've done my part. As for your precious mansion, you can have it back. Here, I don't want it anymore."

She took the handkerchief from her pocket and handed it to him.

The Nocturnal didn't move.

"You do me a great injustice, Oriana Siliceo. We Night-Ones may be considered treacherous, and indeed we are, but we always pay our debts. I more than others. The mansion is yours; you've earned its value in full."

"Still, I don't want it. What would I do with it? I'm not a princess, I'm the daughter of a smith. This is no treasure for me."

"I will hold on to it for you, then, if you wish. But the mansion is still yours. You've also returned with my tool and landed quite a blow to my sister. In fact, it is now I who owe you, Oriana Siliceo."

"I don't want anything from you."

"That is wise, though there are popes and emperors who would burn to be in your place. But as I was saying, you wielded my Hammer."

"What of it?"

"Would you like to learn how to use it?"

Oriana blinked, stared at the Garaude, then back at the Duke.

"Is this another trick? Or a Riddle?"

"No, it's just a question. Would you like to learn its secrets?"

"What for? To break mountains and split rivers?"

"That is not what the Deep Red Hammer does. Oh, it can break apart mountains, all right, but I didn't make it for that purpose. This is a tool to work with the subtlest of substances. It can shape air and fire, but also Hope, Dream, and Despair, as if they were solid alloys. With it you could make a ring of water, a helmet of Fear, or a sword of Longing."

"That's impossible."

"In the Day perhaps, not in the Night. I could teach you."

Oriana saw—as if it were right in front of her—the red glow of a forge. Next to it she could picture the hunched silhouette of the Duke striking the anvil with a hammer, and by his side a woman with black hair. She wielded a pincer, helping her master to hold the metal in place on the anvil as her eyes reflected the forge's fire. With a jolt Oriana recognized herself. The vision faded. Finally, she cleared her throat.

"I can't. I'm my father's firstborn, I am to become his apprentice along with my twin when we come of age. I'm sorry."

"Don't be. You've shown me your loyalty to your family, a virtue I value more than diamonds. Still, my offer remains valid for some time. Give me the mansion."

Oriana handed it to the Duke, who stowed it in a pocket of his leather apron. He did the same with the Hammer, until it disappeared entirely.

"This I'll keep safe for you, along with the Hammer. When the time of your apprenticeship comes, I'll ask you again."

"I won't change my mind; I'm sorry."

The Nocturnal smiled, his pipe glowing.

"I am not. You've served me well, Oriana Siliceo. You may go now, my Garaude will take you home."

The Major One stepped back into the darkness, Gobbo hopping right behind him. Their steps echoed down the arcade before fading. Then the Garaude stood up, took her by the hand, and escorted her out.

It was the moment right before Dawn, when the sky is still dark but there is a forewarning of sunlight; the time when bakers light their ovens and roosters call. And yet Luceria was quiet and still as if it had been frozen, more like a recorded image than a real town.

"We must hurry, or my father will see us," she said, but the Nocturnal shook his head.

"No? Why not?"

The Garaude stopped and tilted his head to one side.

"What's wrong?" Oriana asked. "Why don't you . . . Oh, sorry."

She raised her open palm to him. The Garaude bent over. With his fingers he took his mouth and placed it back on his face. His full lips curled into a smile.

"Milady, we are still walking the paths of the Night. As long as we are on them it will always be Twilight. Time is different here."

They walked in silence until they reached the fountain next to Oriana's house. She could see the drawn blinds of the main room. Behind them Oriano and her family were asleep. A wave of tiredness washed over her.

"I can't go in like this. My mother will kill me," Oriana worried, suddenly aware of her muddy cloak, the caked blood on her arms, her disheveled hair. Invoking her mother called up an image, the Emerald Dame giving away her last comb. Oriana stared blankly ahead. "I failed, didn't I? I didn't make Growler undo her bargain."

"I don't think anyone could have done that. Once a bargain is struck in the Night, it is binding until death. And sometimes, beyond."

She shuddered. The Night was not her friend, after all.

"Will she become like that Dame? Proverbial, I mean."

"I'm afraid I can't read the future like the children of Uriene. But there is something I can do for you. Look here."

The Nocturnal took an eye from his cloak and handed it to Oriana.

She looked into it and, to her surprise, found that it reflected her as if it were a mirror. But the image she saw was a different version of herself: her clothes were dry, her arms unharmed, her hair combed. She looked beautiful.

"What is this?"

"An image I collected of you."

Oriana felt her cheeks burn.

"Well, I certainly don't look like this."

"You do now."

She touched her arms.

The cuts had disappeared, as had the mud from her clothes. Even her fatigue had evaporated. The Nocturnal put the eye back on his mantle; it blinked twice.

"We must say goodbye, milady."

"I told you not to call me that. I'm not a lady."

"You are to me, Oriana Siliceo."

Oriana grasped her arms at the elbows.

"Do you have a name? It seems unfair that you know mine and I don't know yours. Or was I not meant to ask?"

"Of course you can ask. It's just that, well, no one has asked me in a while."

"What is it, then?"

"My name is, or rather was, Scandar."

"It's beautiful, and it suits you. Well, I must go now, Scandar."

She turned toward her house, but her legs would not let her move forward.

Something rooted her to the ground, but this time, it was not fear, or fatigue, or enchantment. She slapped her forehead and faced Scandar.

"Aren't you forgetting something? It wasn't just your mouth you gave me, was it?"

She raised her left palm where Scandar's ear rested like a fleshy butterfly.

"Here."

But the Nocturnal shook his head.

"I didn't forget it."

"No?"

"No. It is my present to you."

"Oh?"

"So that any time you want, you can speak to me at night. I will listen to you, any time you want me to."

Oriana stared at him warily.

"And you won't eavesdrop? For your master, I mean."

Scandar's face darkened.

"This is my initiative, not his. I am a slave, but even a slave has some freedom. Still, if you don't want it, I will take it back."

Oriana stared at her open hand for a while.

"No. I trust you, Scandar of the Garaudi."

The Nocturnal's cloak became alive with blazing eyes, a starlit night all his own. Then he took her left hand and kissed her palm with burning lips. Immediately his fleshy ear sunk inside her layers of skin, completely hidden.

"I'll be there, if and when you want me," he said.

His stone-cold hands held her for a moment longer, then let go. Oriana met his cloak's gaze once more. Then she turned and ran straight through her front door, across the main floor, and upstairs to her bedroom. Oriano was still sleeping in their bed, curled up and blissfully unaware. Oriana took off her cloak and shoes and put them on the chair. And yet she still felt incapable of lying down. Instead, she quietly walked over to the small window that looked down at the street. He was still there, cloaked in stars, looking up at her.

She watched him for a long time, as the sky brightened into a purple slate. Then, little by little, the Nocturnal began to fade—first his face and hands, then his shadow, and lastly his cloak, its eyes closing one by one, like stars going out until the gray street was empty.

PART II
THE CHALLENGE OF PEERS

FOURTEEN

"Facts, not opinions! Things, not words! Notions, not fancy! For this is the Age of Reason and we are its newborn children! Let us then sacrifice the vainglory of abstract speculation to the altar of common knowledge! For all men and women are worthy of being educated and thus delivered from that pernicious illness of intelligence that is superstition! This is our current endeavor: Everything that responds not to reason must be eradicated! Give us physics, then, not poetry; give us jurisprudence, not novels; give us economy, not art: for they are a better bread than—what, what, what is it now?"

"I really wouldn't insist on that eradicating superstition part too much," said Oriana. "I'm sure there will be priests at the salon too."

"Of course, of course. But even they, these days, at least the ones who would be invited to Alfonsina's salon, even they—"

"I really wouldn't say it."

"All right, no superstition. Blast it, I lost the thread!"

"They are a better bread . . ."

"Thank you. Hmm . . . for they are a better bread for our ailing minds! Indeed, we should be more obliged to the philosopher who teaches us how to eradicate weeds from a meadow than to some pompous dissertation on the composition of the soul. For if it's true that souls are merely a collection of sensory impressions, then we should cultivate these impressions with facts, things, and notions, and not with the most dreadful fancy!"

This speech, along with its brief interruption, was given in the semicircular niche of a tall mahogany library to an audience of one, a young girl of almost fourteen. As for the man giving it, he—Fernando Pignatelli, Count of Villabianca—was quite a sight to behold. During his performance, the white silk shirt containing his belly sailed up and down the book-crammed room, while its owner perspired to an alarming extent. His pale, wigless, dark blond head, puffed from exertion, resembled that of a cherub who, having been blown all out of proportion, had taken on the consistency of a lush mozzarella. And yet his round olive eyes, jittery with excitement as he leapt around the room, still held such childlike gaiety that, were it not for his frumpy mustache, he could have easily been taken for a young boy who had unexpectedly ballooned into adulthood. And indeed, Count Villabianca was almost thirty-four, the only surviving heir of a noble family fallen into ruin. All that was left of the estate was the palazzo in which he now stood, and its library, a coach, and ten acres of farmland. The typhoid fever of 1734 had taken his parents, siblings, aunts and uncles, and many other relatives, leaving only a distant cousin, Alfonsina Ravallo Vernarecci. Hers was the high society salon, the best in Lucerìa, that Count Villabianca had been trying to infiltrate for a decade.

"So, what do you think?" he asked, drying his sweat with a tarnished handkerchief.

"I thought it was fairly good."

"Really? You're not trying to flatter me?"

"Do I ever?"

"Right. Have you guessed where I drew inspiration?"

"Hmm . . . I think it was a mixture of Genovesi, Filangieri, d'Holbach, and Verri, with a dash of Voltaire."

"You noticed that! The superstition part was his."

"A nice touch, but we're still not in Paris."

"Alas, we are not," he conceded. "What? What is it now?"

"Well, to be honest, it is not a conversation at all. I may not be a sophisticate, but in the novels I've read—the ones you gave me—people usually talk about one topic at a time. And wait for a response. Yours was a *lecture*."

"I know, I know. But how else am I going to prepare?"

"You don't have to prepare. You just go there and talk to people. That's what I'd do, were I a gentleman. Or a lady."

"But you are not!" he said. "I mean, Oriana, Gesù, that's not what I meant to say. You're the most apt pupil I've ever had, but you've never had to mingle with *them*. They aren't really human, you know."

"You look and sound quite human to me."

"But I'm not one of them! I've never even seen any of them, except at mass. I've spoken to my cousin only twice in my life and she is a dreadful lady indeed. And then there are the Mezzacasa . . ."

Oriana's chin lifted.

"The ones who kidnapped the Baron of Twilight."

"Oh, would you please stop saying things like that! Sometimes I despair of your education. You can't carry on like a country girl! Night Saints are an unhealthy peasant superstition that must be era-di-ca-ted. How can we call ourselves children of the new age if we go on believing in Wiccae and Wyrms and . . ."

Before her tutor could utter the conclusion to his reprimand, his voice was drowned out by an outraged yowl. Reno, Villabianca's decrepit hunting dog, who had been snoring quietly, was howling in protest. Oriana leaned over to give him a mighty ear scratch.

"What's wrong with him?" The count frowned.

"Maybe he has different opinions on the matter of Nocturnals."

"Funny. You know, Father once said that at Twilight, all the dead hounds of Lucerìa hunt with the Baron for the treacherous souls of traitors—"

"Who's the superstitious one now? Anyway, let's not get distracted. I don't see why you care so much about that salon. They haven't even invited you."

"They might."

"But you don't even like them, you said it yourself."

Villabianca sat down, flustered.

"You can't understand. You're too young."

"Well, you are my tutor. Pray, teach me, sir."

"Don't mock me, Oriana. I'm not in the mood."

"Nor am I. I've been sitting here for the better part of two hours helping you practice all the High Society Good Topics, and I haven't seen any hint of my early birthday gift—no, I haven't forgotten about that. And now you won't even tell me why you want so badly to attend this salon of yours!"

"You know, you really shouldn't talk to your tutor like that," he admonished, then softened. "Oh, Oriana, don't you see? Look at me. I'm fat. And old."

"You are quite fat, yes," she said with an affectionate smile, "and nearly as old as my father."

"And what's worse, penniless. Do you know what that means for someone like me? It means my family name, my estate, will die with me. It means I am nothing. What have I done with my life? If only I could finish my father's map, but I can't even do that. If only—"

"You want to go to your cousin's salon to find yourself a wife."

If a mozzarella the size of a human head could blush into the shades of Twilight, that is exactly what the count's cheeks would have looked like then. He coughed a couple of times, his face cyanotic.

"That's a huge oversimplification," he protested.

"We want facts, sir, not opinions!"

"To hell with facts! What's your opinion? Tell me! What do you think? Am I hopeless? Should I even try? Speak!"

The count stood. Huge as he was, he was tiny in comparison to the enormity of his own distress.

"I think," she said deliberately, yet delicately, "that were I a lady of this town, and I had the pleasure of speaking with a gentleman of your kind, with your intelligence and knowledge of philosophy, not to mention your understanding of Newtonian physics, I would be madder than the Marquise of Fullmoon not to be flattered by any proposal to become your wife."

The count's lips quivered once, then his tremulous cheeks softened.

"Oh, Oriana, what would I do without you? How would I be able to stand this wretched life if I hadn't met you?"

"Ah!" she laughed. "Now, if Mamma Emma heard you say that—"

The words had barely escaped her lips when, from the other side of the room, came a creak, then a thump, then another. In a single rapid motion, Villabianca seized his wig and put it back on, a little askew, while Oriana noiselessly dragged her chair to the desk, sat down, picked up her quill, and raised it as if to write. Even Reno put his head down. A few moments later the door opened, and Mamma Emma entered. She was a robust woman of fifty-seven who carried all her weight in her dropsy legs, dragging them along like a convict would his chains. Carrying a tray with both hands, she surveyed the library in one swoop, her gaze finally landing on her godson. Villabianca straightened his wig and inspected Oriana's writing above her shoulders.

"Have you finished writing your essay, miss?"

"Yes, sir, I think I have."

"Good, we can have our chocolate and biscuits, then."

Oriana turned and smiled to Mamma Emma.

"Thank you, Mamma Emma, I was really hungry."

Mamma Emma had once been the count's wet nurse, though

she was more than a servant and not much less than a mother. She put down the tray with the steaming chocolate.

"Has the beast been fed?" she asked, meaning, of course, poor Reno, whose nervous tail revealed that he had heard her.

"No, Mamma Emma."

"Leave it to me. You know, Reno is the last of his pack. The son of the son of Villabianca's last legendary pack of hounds. Your father had ten of them, the best breeds from Naples. Ah, he was a true gentleman, your father, he surely was. I certainly don't see *you* hunting with ten hounds in Foggia's woods for wild pig."

"Probably not, Mamma Emma. Unless they were hunting me."

Oriana's face contracted to stifle a smile. The count's eyes flickered.

Mamma Emma frowned and said, "Now, signorina, don't you mind Don Fernando's jests. He might not look as valiant as his Spanish ancestors, but his blood is the very same as the D'Avalos's, seven hundred years of uninterrupted loyalty to the King of Spain, not like that Mezzacasa half-breed! Don Fernando is a Villabianca, and so will be his children."

"I'm sure of it," said Oriana. The old nurse was about to reply but instead looked up at the ceiling as if her eyes could drill through the wall.

"Did you hear that? It's that leak in the attic, maledetto!"

"Leak?" asked the count.

"You might sleep as a baby, but *I* hear everything that happens in this blasted house, oh yes, I do. The great summer rains filled the attic cistern with rain, let me tell you, and it leaks down, leaving me sleepless all night. S*omeone* will have to do something about it, if he wants more chocolate."

Mamma Emma stared at her protégé. The count's cheeks inflated in protest, then caved.

"All right, I'll have some more," he said.

"That's my dear boy." She beamed. "I'll fetch it straightaway."

She proceeded out of the room followed by three sets of eyes: the count's, the girl's, and the hound's. Oriana started laughing as soon as she heard her limp reach the bottom step.

"What was all that about continuing the lineage of my ancestors?" Villabianca complained.

"That was the best part," Oriana laughed. "I thought I would die! I reckon she has found you someone, Fernando, or else thinks she has."

"Good lord, you might be right. Must be some old crone like that widow she suggested could be the mother of my children, at sixty-three."

"Here she comes again. I can hear her downstairs. Listen, I've helped you as best I could with your Good Topics and a deal is a deal: Where is my reward?"

The count's cherub lips pouted.

"So vile of you to turn our visits into a business transaction."

"You could always give me them all at once, I wouldn't mind."

"And then have you vanish for weeks? Never!"

"I won't vanish for weeks, and you know it. Where else would I go? But Fernando, please, she's coming back upstairs, and I need to go."

"All right, all right, I guess it's only fair. Here."

The count paced toward the smallest cabinet in his library and slid open a wooden panel. Oriana wet her lips. Behind the panel she saw a plethora of model houses, bridges, towers, porticos, even—all made from cork and wood—the remains of a seventeenth-century presepio, a scale model of a nativity scene.

"I'll take the tower. I've never had a tower before."

With the rapacious swoop of a bird of prey, she seized the cork tower and slid it into her waist pocket. And just in time, for the door opened again.

Oriana collected her gown and with a curtsy to the count said, "I'll do my homework, sir. Thank you very much for today's lesson."

And with that she departed, fast as she could, brushing a hasty kiss against Mamma Emma's left cheek before bustling down the steep flight of stairs.

"What's wrong with that Siliceo girl?" cried the nurse. "She's running like a pack of Nocturnals is chasing her to her death!"

Her words still clung to the air when Reno sprang up from his spot and let out a loud yowl of canine protestation, as if, had he possessed the gift of speech, the old dog would have recounted such a tale as to turn Mamma Emma's hair white.

FIFTEEN

With the quick double step of her mood and age, Oriana Siliceo skipped through the muddy courtyard of palazzo Nicastri, her dark hair wild in a way her mother never would have allowed outside the house. The late August storms had soaked the ground and made the weather uncharacteristically mild for the season. It almost felt like spring, and the palazzo's baroque portico was blooming in white oleanders.

"Morning, Zi' Nicola!" called Oriana as she approached the portico.

"Mornin', signorina," replied the old carver, working with his chisel at a large mirror frame embellished with laurel leaves. He sat on a stool in front of his workshop, his blond son sawing a large log just behind him.

"It's coming out beautifully, I think," she said.

"Very kind of you to say so, signorina," he said, then, in a lower voice so that his son couldn't hear, continued, "I have something for you."

The carver limped inside his workshop and returned with a small parcel.

"This is for your mother. Cevese, wild cherries from my brother's orchard."

"You are so kind, thank you, on her behalf too."

Zi' Nicola smiled, and then quickly winked at her. Oriana beamed, then turned and ran up the great staircase.

When Oriana was nine years old, the Siliceo family moved to the second floor above the piano nobile where the count lived. On the ground floor of the estate was the apartment of Donna Marisa, the gatekeeper, and in the courtyard Zi' Nicola's wood-carving workshop. The Siliceo family occupied seven frescoed rooms and a huge, tiled kitchen. Oriana had her own room, with a real bed, and a real cupboard filled with real clothes. Her tall, large windows—full of light in the day—looked over at the courtyard below, and she sat and read her beloved illuminists there without anyone disturbing her. She should have been happy, really, and yet only felt truly contented during her lessons with Villabianca or when her hands were busy.

Oriana pushed her green chair against her bedroom door before allowing herself to look at the contents of the parcel. She had to be very careful to make sure that Donna Lena didn't find out about her secret pastime. Inside were cherries, darker than currants and sweeter, too, but underneath them was a smaller paper envelope containing a bundle of tiny nails, almost as thin as needles. Oriana retrieved the arabesque paper screen she used to dress behind while Cetta was making her bed. Swiftly, she arranged it in front of the secretaire her mother bought her, sprung open its secret panel, carefully took out her Sanctum, placing it on the desk. Then, Oriana fished from her pocket the model tower Villabianca had given her and carefully separated its cork walls. She inspected its spread-out pieces carefully.

"What will I make you into? Will you be the baby steps of my staircase? Will you frame a window, or become a beam? Let's see."

Using her tools, an old chisel and a knife, she cut the raw part of the cork into a smaller strip, which she bent until it formed a circle. She fixed the shape in place with one of the needlelike nails. She repeated this twice, creating a sort of barrel. She had decided that the tower would work nicely as a slack tub used to temper iron. She chewed one of the cherries and, using her fingers, started to paint her barrel with the juice's dark hue.

At eight years old Oriana had been content to create stories to amuse her brother. But as she grew up, her fancy had morphed into a deep hunger to make, to create, to craft with her own hands. This need of hers was a guarded secret she could never entrust to anyone, especially not her mother. Donna Lena would deem her pursuits useless, of course, and remind her of all that had been given to her, including her lessons with the count, for the purpose of turning her into a lady. She knew this with the same certainty that she remembered the Emerald Dame.

Sometimes it felt as if the market had never happened, that it was a half-forgotten dream, one she could only glimpse when asleep. Reading Voltaire's essay "On Superstition" and then musing about the Night Saints was jarring. What if she *had* been brainwashed by the superstition of her class and social milieu? In moments of doubt, Oriana opened her left hand and whispered into it. In the Day, she couldn't remember what words she had uttered, yet she knew they were said, cold pebbles stored in the icy well of her mind.

After she returned from the market, Oriana struggled to accept what she'd learned about her mother—to buy herself a new Moira, Donna Lena had traded in the Reality of her children. Had Donna Lena become a totally different person, with long, needlelike fingernails dripping poison and forever enveloped in an emerald haze, Oriana could have hated her without guilt. But the market's influence was subtle. At times Donna Lena acted like the person Oriana knew and loved. She still tried to teach her famous opera arias and cooked parmigiana di melanzane like she used to. However, when her mother absentmindedly called her "titilla," Oriana's soul ached. For even in her most affectionate gesture, she sensed a vacuity, a coldness, as if the figure in front of her was not flesh and blood but a hunger with a face.

Oh, the new Donna Lena could be careless to the point of cruelty—sending Tato to military school at the young age of six and scolding her twin brother by calling him undeserving of the food, clothes, and home she'd given him. But mostly it was the way she sometimes behaved as though they weren't there at all that marked the Dame's influence. One day, when Riano—as his street friends now called him—came home with a gash on his thigh after fighting with his urchin pals, there was so much blood they thought he needed a surgeon. Donna Lena, however, was busy refurbishing the drawing room's walls with Genoese fabrics. She quickly scanned Riano's wound, instructed Oriana to press a piece of cloth on it, then serenely finished instructing the workers. It was only after her son was about to faint that Donna Lena retrieved a needle and thread from her apron and stitched Riano's leg herself, all the while dispensing orders to Cetta.

As soon as they moved into palazzo Nicastri, Donna Lena had built a small altar in the kitchen using an old image of the Madonna. But the lantern that burned by its side day and night was made of dark green glass. Every time Oriana passed by it, she couldn't repress a shudder. It felt like the Emerald Dame's influence over the Siliceo household poured forth in green ripples from that lantern, soaking Donna Lena's actions in verdant vibrations. This was painfully evident to Oriana every time her mother ordered her and her brother about. Somehow, the Siliceo siblings were never enough: not well-mannered enough, not well-spoken enough, and, in particular, not well-dressed enough. But while Oriano could get away with a scorching remark, Donna Lena's demands on her daughter were on another level entirely.

In time Oriana had come to loathe her toilette sessions, the long stretches during which she had to sit completely still while her mother arranged her hair and clothes with her cold, hard hands. Oriana couldn't even leave the house without her mother doing and redoing her hair, until she was deemed perfect.

It was one of the many reasons why she had lost touch with her childhood companions. After her return from the Secret Market, she had tried to invite them to her family's new house. But her change in status, she discovered, made her even more isolated. When she did go out, the boys of the contrada were mockingly deferential, addressing her as "signorina." And yet Oriana felt in the boys' mockery a new boldness, an omen of manhood fast approaching.

The girls were even worse. Less clownish than the boys, they talked about little else but amore. Not love like Oriana had read about in her books, but a matter-of-fact business born from a single glance, a single touch, a single word. Such were the perils of her age, it seemed. The girls chattered in the patios while plucking chickens, whispering about secret meetings under a balcony, in the darkness of a courtyard, or—they said, shielding their laughter—in the fields. Oriana didn't take long to understand what to meet in the fields meant. She also realized her old friends were not as seasoned as they wanted to appear. Oriana suspected that all their brazen talk of lovemaking was intended to shock her ladylike sensibilities. When they found her impassable, they pursued the subject to its limits, sometimes blazing red at their own tales.

"Have you heard about Antonina? Her moroso, Gianni, was caught by her father under her balcony."

"No!"

"Aye, Gianni said they would elope before the harvest."
"No, you have it wrong; they broke up!"
"You don't say!"
"Gianni is with Teresina now. They met in the fields last summer. And that's not the worst of it: she is with child!"
"Madonna mia, how old is she?"
"Fourteen next month."

Angia was among them, gossiping with reddening cheeks. How her old friend had changed! The thin candle had become a voluptuous torch, taller and brighter than the rest. Once in a while, however, she would eye Oriana with a shade of apprehension, the memory of the Duke's power lingering between them. Oriana could have talked about what happened openly now, if she wanted to, as the Tokai had worn off. But since she had returned from the market, she had come to realize that the Night held a subtler power over her as well.

The truth was, Oriana was afraid to speak of the Nocturnals to anyone, lest she attract more of their attention. Not that she needed to. Something of the Night had smeared her with its colors. Their effect might have been unseen by Diurnals, but it was not unfelt. And so people shunned her, even boys and girls her age, acknowledging her with a bow that became less and less mocking as time went on. The years passed, and when Oriana turned thirteen—the age her grandmother was betrothed—Donna Lena became her jailor, and Cetta, her warden. From that moment on she was never allowed out of the house alone. She became the living doll her mother saw her as, and palazzo Nicastri was her dollhouse.

Once, she confided in Riano, and it was one of the most painful conversations she had ever had. Her brother was eating an apple by the salon window, his brand-new redingote flashing in the sun, looking proudly at his glass reflection while she sat disconsolate, self-consciously touching her newly ribboned hairstyle.

"I think you should consider yourself lucky," he said.

"And why would that be?"

"Because you girls can take it, we simply can't. All those laces, those ribbons, it would just drive us insane. Lucky you are a girl."

Oriana stared at him with such speechless alacrity that her twin gulped down his bite.

"Oh. You think I'm insulting you, but it's quite the opposite. Don't you see, sorella mia? I can't stay put. That's why the boys love me, because I'm always up for some fun. But you, my dear sister, you're something else. You read, you know things I couldn't understand in a million years. I'm as shallow as I am well liked."

"Now, don't be so hard on yourself."

"I'm not. I know myself. And you know what? So does Mother. She knows what metal I am made of. More copper than iron, I'm afraid. I think Father suspects it too. I'll never be a good apprentice for him. That's why they sent Tato to the military academy, so that he won't become like me. I know it's hard for you, sorella. I'm only saying that, in a very different way, it's hard for me too. But you know what? Even if I am scared, I know I'm not alone. We're in it together, the two of us, aren't we? And when the apprenticeship comes, you'll stand by me. Won't you, Sister? Won't you?"

Oriana hugged her brother so fiercely she felt his collarbone. The thought of it still brought an acrid taste to her mouth. They had grown so apart in recent years. It wasn't that she loved him any less, or that he did her. It was because he could never really understand how unequally they were treated. Oriana had not been allowed out of the house for months after going to the spring market. Her twin brother could skip mass, steal apples from their neighbors, shove a washerwoman into the public washbasins, nick the bishop's rooster with a stone, and not even get a beating for it. In fact, the lazzari, the town's street urchins, loved him for his antics. Even their father could not suppress a smile when he heard about his son's misdeeds. He had a way with people—his "shine," he called it—that allowed him to get away with almost anything.

Oriana wondered what would happen on the day their apprenticeship began. Their fifteenth birthday was in late August, a year and a week away. She knew that her father would have to work hard to make Donna Lena accept her path. In truth, Oriana could see her point: her dress-up doll, the brilliant pupil of a count, working with coal and fire; people would gossip, as they always did. In the end though, it was Mastro Peppo's decision and his alone. After all, wasn't Angia working in her father's butcher's shop? And likewise Germana, the engraver's daughter in via Luccoli. All the fancy laces and hairdos in the world could not change the fact that Oriana was the daughter of a smith.

Still daydreaming, Oriana felt a puff of air behind her, then her twin brother's hand grasping her hard by the shoulder.

"Ori! Are you hurt?"

Oriana bolted from her chair with such vehemence that her brother stumbled back onto the paper screen, knocking it to the floor. His sister looked at him with the trembling outrage of a woman who had been surprised in the nude. For the small construction that lay on her desk was her soul stripped bare, and her baffled brother was looking straight at it.

"Close the bloody door. Now!" she hissed.

Riano scampered to close the door. His sister put the miniature slack tub in the Sanctum and cleaned her hands on a cloth.

"I-I'm sorry, I saw all that red on your fingers, I thought you were hurt. But what in the name of the Dark Sun is that?"

Oriana closed her eyes and sighed.

"What were you thinking, sneaking up behind me like that."

"Sis, I'm sorry. I didn't—"

She turned, eyes ablaze.

"Mother mustn't know. Promise me."

"Of course. But what is it?"

She bit her lips until she felt her lower teeth hurt.

"It's . . . my work. My Sanctum."

"It's beautiful."

She felt her cheeks scorch.

"You think so?"

"Why would I lie to you? It's bizarre, but it's . . . I've never seen anything quite like it. All those stairs and those . . . what are they?"

"Bellows. To blow air into the fire."

"Oh my god, it's a smithy! But how can you know what it looks like? You've never even set foot inside. Father never let us!"

"Diderot's *Encyclopaedia* has many good drawings of one."

"It looks too big, and there are too many . . . what are those?"

"Statues, obviously."

"I see that, but statues of what?"

"Garaudi, mostly. Some Wiccae. A Wyrm. A very small one."

Riano burst out laughing.

"It's like the tales you told me in bed when we were little!"

"You think this is a joke. That I made it to amuse you."

Riano's face sobered up.

"No, I'm sorry. I have a talent for saying the wrong thing at the wrong time; I'm not very apt with words, I'm afraid. What I meant is that I love it. I think Father would like it too."

"You think?"

"Of course. Did you make it to show him?"

"No. At least, I don't think so."

"Why did you make it, then?"

Oriana remained silent. She didn't know. Why would one

make such a thing? A tool is a tool, a gate is a gate, a door is a door. But why take the trouble to make an object that was more than its function? And why had she added Nocturnals? She hadn't sought out their stories, not since the Teller aunts had stopped visiting. One time, she'd asked Villabianca if there were any books about the Night Saints. Of course there were none. Their stories could not be so easily trapped. Their tales changed every time they were told, always different. But what about pictures? What about engravings? What about statues, etchings, bas-reliefs? Could they live on in them? Maybe. Even though she had never consciously thought about it, Oriana found herself wondering if the objects she created were in fact their effigies. She turned to her twin.

"Listen, this is our secret now; it's between the two of us."

"Of course. Do you trust me so little?"

"I do trust you, but as you said, words slip from you at times."

"You have no confidence in my—"

A soft knock at the door prompted Oriana to hide the secretaire behind the paper screen, and not a moment too soon. Cetta peered in.

"Dinner's ready," she said. *"The sea doesn't wait for the salmon."*

"We are coming, Ce', don't fret," said Riano.

"You should. Mastro Peppo is here."

"Father? I thought he was still in Caserta!" said Oriana.

"He's here, with guests."

"You must be mistaken, Cetta," mused Riano. "We never have guests. Maybe it's some convict trying to hide in our pantry, some gentleman bandit like in the novels Ori reads."

"Now, young master, don't get all fresh with me! If I say there are guests, there are guests! How dare you make fun of me!"

Once again Oriana noticed how Cetta's scolding words always sounded more severe than the shape of her face. It was hardly a secret that Riano had become her favorite, probably because he was now the same age as her eldest son when he died. Gone were the days of her impartiality; what little affection Cetta had left to give was bestowed on him.

"Calm down, Cetta, I believe you. Just tell us who they are."

"Well, if you must know, there's two of them. One I know, the other I don't, but I can guess he is quite highly connected."

"A stranger? Oh, Cetta, this *is* news!" he exclaimed, almost hugging her.

"Well," the old maid repeated, a bit flushed, "I'll tell you what's more: the master wants to speak to you. Yes, to both of you. Well? *Sunrise waits not for the idler.*"

On the white dinner table, two rose-shaped lamps blazed with a peculiar twilight tint, casting the plates in copper halo. Ceramic, not wood, plates alongside silver cutlery, for this was no ordinary family get-together. Since he had been given a commission at the royal palace in Caserta, Mastro Peppo was almost always away on business and very seldom at home. And during this visit, he had brought two people with him: his old apprentice, the same Bruno who had accompanied them to the spring market in Foggia, and another gentleman from Caserta.

While they ate, Oriana glanced around the table. Her father's presence always made her heart ache. Since the beginning of his good fortune, Mastro Peppo had aged quite a bit. There were now white patches on his bald head, like moss on a statue. But most striking of all was how the master craftsman now draped himself in a thin shroud of sadness, quite at odds with the state of his flourishing business, as if the mere act of his presence required effort. Bruno, on the other hand, was the same old Bruno, jolly as always, and yet plumper, broader, and huskier—in short, more man than boy. As for the out-of-towner, he wore a fashionable wig over a fashionable face, with two bushy eyebrows raised in what seemed to be perennial surprise.

The stranger was introduced as Signor Bernardo Merello, personal secretary of Vanvitelli, the famous architect who was in charge of the new royal palace in Caserta. His presence frosted the Siliceos' every gesture. For while Signor Merello was a civil servant, he was nonetheless an agent of the king. Finally, the gentleman broke the silence by complimenting Donna Lena on the pasta and the Lacrima Christi wine. Oriana's mother replied by asking how the royal residence was coming along, and if His Excellency was happy with the new rose-shaped gates he had ordered. Signor Merello's eyebrows leapt again. He reported that Vanvitelli liked the gates very much. In fact, he liked them to such an extent that he had requested Mastro Peppo reside as master smith in Caserta. The king himself would grant him the position and an annual income of five hundred gold ducats.

"Oh, but this is wonderful news!" Donna Lena said, temporarily losing her ladylike composure. "We must toast! Cetta, bring more Lacrima."

Oriana looked at her father. Finally, Mastro Peppo put his wineglass down.

"I've been offered good coin to sell my smithy here in Lucerìa. But I don't want to sell it. The Siliceos have been smiths in this town for over two hundred years, maybe longer. We aren't gentry, but our trade is very old. I will take the position in Caserta, but on the condition that I may keep the family business open here in town."

This speech, the longest she had heard her father utter in years, took on a surreal quality. Giuseppe Siliceo was master of the smithy. Whose permission was he asking? Oriana looked at her mother. Donna Lena smiled like her lips had been curved-up blades.

"So we won't be moving to Caserta," she said.

"I will. You won't. You'll stay here, the three of you."

Donna Lena glanced up. For the briefest instant, Oriana could have sworn she saw an emerald flicker in her eyes. Her mother smiled thinly.

"What of the smithy, then? Who will be its new master?"

"I will," answered Bruno with his mouth full.

"You," Donna Lena said, "will."

"He is of age, and he has passed the final test of his apprenticeship to become a master smith," said Mastro Peppo.

"So the smithy will not belong to the Siliceos, after all."

"It will. This is the deal I have made with Bruno. On the day he becomes master smith, he will take on a new first apprentice," he said, looking at Riano, who almost choked.

"B-but, Father, I'm not yet of age!"

"You will be a year from now. We have asked the Guild for a dispensation for this year, and they have agreed. A week from today, on the day of your birthday, we will hold the ceremony for Bruno's new mastership. On that same day he will stipulate a contract with you to make you his legal heir. Then, when you are of age, you will become master of my smithy. And thus, it will all stay in the family. Is that understood?"

Donna Lena nodded briefly.

"And Oriana?" Riano interjected.

"What do you mean?" he asked.

"The two of us, Oriana and me, we should enter the smithy together. We are both firstborns, we are twins. Won't she be with me on that day?"

There was such an edge of panic in Riano's voice that Mastro Peppo glanced at his guest with some irritation. But when the smith looked at his daughter, his eyes softened again.

"Will you see this through with your brother, Oriana? Will you do that for me?"

She felt her chest caving in, though she couldn't be sure whether in joy or sorrow. For there was an edge of prophecy to her present bliss, a foretaste of pain yet to come.

"Yes, Father, I will."

"Cetta, pour wine for my son and daughter. To this agreement."

"*Seal it with wine, and the deal is done!*"

"Concetta!" spat Donna Lena.

"Sorry, signora, I'll fetch the wine, signora."

Cetta turned around and exited the room in such a speedy sprint that Riano burst out laughing, followed by Bruno. But no sooner had their guffaw died down than they heard a duet of voices from outside.

"What is that?" demanded Mastro Peppo, scowling.

The door creaked opened and the only manservant of the house, a freckled redhead who answered to the name of Gianni, peered in.

"I am sorry, master, but the count has insisted that I—"

"And so you have, my good, diligent fellow. Now you may step back," Villabianca interrupted, stepping inside. As soon as he entered, guests and hosts alike stood up in one fluid motion. The count looked at them in dismay. "Dear me, you have guests."

"My lord, this is Signor Merello from Caserta. You know Bruno. Count Fernando Villabianca, our landlord."

"Honored to meet you, my lord," said Merello, bowing.

"The honor is mine, but I really must apologize. Donna Lena, Mastro Peppo, my coming was ill-timed. Please accept my apologies and pray continue with your dinner."

"What is it, Vossia. Pray, tell us," insisted Donna Lena, a flicker of amusement in her green-gray eyes. "It must be important."

"Oh, Donna Lena, it is! Quite so! My old nurse, Mamma Emma, just received this card from a servant in the livery of the Vernarecci."

Villabianca looked at Oriana. She twisted her napkin.

"Is it an invitation to Vernarecci's salon, sir?"

"It is, it is!" answered the poor count, so completely beside himself that he would have run to hug his pupil had the table between them not prevented it.

"I'm really happy for you, sir. I'm sure you'll cut a fine figure and prove all your talents."

"Me?" laughed Villabianca. "The invitation is not for me! It is for you, Oriana. You have been invited this very Friday, at six o' clock, to palazzo Uva along with the finest ladies and gentlemen this town has to offer!"

SIXTEEN

The count's carriage rumbled through the empty streets of Lucerìa. The sky was a forge, the clouds melting in streaks of orange and gold. It was the first time that Oriana was outside after sunset since the market. She looked up, searching for a patch of darkness to detach itself from a chimney and blaze to life with shining eyes. She bit her lips. Had Scandar forgotten her? And his master, had the Duke of Under-earth erased her from his book of debts?

She looked down the empty streets. There was always an edge of danger in Lucerìa at night. After dawn no one would talk to strangers—they could never know for certain if a kind face was a face at all. Even at sunset, one would walk to their destination at a brisk pace. There were many tales of travelers distracted by a song, a scent, or a stranger, who were never seen again in the light of Day. For this reason some buildings at crossroads housed a candle-lit niche with an image of the Madonna. Only, these Madonnas wore black-blue cloaks made of human nails—their nacreous sheen glinting at the candles—and crimson stars for eyes: Our Lady of the Night, Queen of Dawn, Saint-Spouse to the Grim King. If a traveler got lost in the different regions of the Night, he could always go to her image and take hold of one of its red ribbons. Made by the finest seamstress, the ribbons connected each Queen on the block—a web of veins branching from building to building—and guaranteed a safe passage to the end of Dawn.

They had just driven past one of those niches when the coach turned the corner and the noble palazzos of Lucerìa came into full view. Encrusted in ivy, their marble structures were somber in the shadows, all dark save for the tall windows flickering in candlelight. The proximity of her destination redirected Oriana's anxieties.

She could not fathom how or why she had arranged it but was certain that her mother had a hand in the invitation. She glanced at her reflection. Her hair was coifed à la fountain, and she wore a crinoline hoop skirt, with a puffy green padding to widen her slim hips. She felt stiff, constrained by her bodice and the count's bulk at her side. And yet in the end, she didn't think it would be that bad. She wasn't attending a ball, after all. She was going to a salon, a place for philosophical discussion. A bump in the road jolted her back to the present. She looked at the sullen count who—quite uncommonly—had scarcely spoken a word.

"Are you upset that they invited me?" she asked.

"Upset! *Upset!* My dear child, how could I be upset? You've made me prouder than I have ever been in my entire life."

"And why would that be, my lord?"

"Because, my insolent bird, they have heard about the extent of your education. Which, I must confess, I had no little part in. And yet I have a recommendation for you, one you should listen to very carefully. That habit of yours, of mentioning the Night . . . not here, Oriana, not now. To these people, nothing reeks more of peasant spirit than those plebeian yarns."

"Well, I *am* the daughter of a smith!"

"Not anymore. From the moment you step into that parlor, you'll be born afresh. Almost. But if you speak like a farmer, they'll stop listening to you. Is that what you want?"

"No," she conceded, sulking.

"Good, then. Look, we've arrived."

Two servants in red livery and white gloves opened the carriage door holding a flaming candelabrum over their heads. Another servant, the maestro di casa, escorted them across a dark courtyard and up to a wide, shallow staircase. After two flights of stairs, Villabianca was taking in long, shallow gasps of air. Oriana waited for him to catch his breath and reapply a bit of powder. The count caught his reflection in one of the mirrors and grimaced.

"I look like a whale who swallowed a hydropsic elephant."

"It'll be all right, really."

"It will be most horrible, but I'm grateful to be here. I owe it all to you. Allons-y!"

Following the servants through parlor after smoking room after sitting room after parlor, they arrived at a large, double oak door that the butler swung open, announcing their arrival to the hosts. At first, Oriana was blinded. Seven oil lamps hung in front of seven mirrors, their light reflected in an endless mise en abyme of the same room, its infinite replicas lost in a silver haze. But when her eyes adjusted, she found herself in a large, yellow-curtained drawing room filled with stuccos and mirrors. The bright, golden space was entirely filled with a wig-wearing crowd of people, all of whom were very much intent on sizing her up.

At that moment, Oriana experienced the most bizarre of impressions. It was as if she were in two places at the same time. One was palazzo Uva, the other inside the mirrors. The two places stood one in front of the other, separated only by a thin layer of silver. And what she saw within the mirrors could just not be. The reflections of the wig-wearing gentlemen staring back at her did not appear to be human. They were men-cats, of the same kind Oriana had seen at the Parliament, with fur and tails and thin white fangs. And as they stared at her with wild, lush, hungry eyes, Oriana felt her lungs turn into leaden clouds ripe with dread. This time, there was no escape; they would catch her and reveal her as the impostor she truly was. And they would feast on her flesh with vindictive joy.

"Are you all right, my dear? You look pale as a lily."

The count's words broke the dark enchantment of her heart. She was back at the salon. There was no beastly mirror world, no catlike faces scrutinizing her with inhuman appetites. But her intuition stayed all the same, for she was an infiltrate in their ranks and—she sensed—not at all welcome. As they walked in the drawing room, she heard snippets of their conversations. Maria Carolina, the queen, had just delivered her firstborn, and some gossiped that she had gone back to her lover on the same day. And Tannucci, the prime minister, his notice was due. Now that she had given an heir to the crown, Maria Carolina could sit in the minor council and depose the old stink with a vote. Oriana could not help but blush, both amused and unnerved by the vulgarity of their remarks. Their tales seemed not all that different from the ones Tellers recounted at the Vigils, except with kings and queens instead of Nocturnals.

They traveled to the back of the room, where on an embroidered chair sat a portly old woman wearing a tête de mouton hairstyle, all curls and pink ribbons, and a pair of glasses she raised to peer at her guests. She could be none other than their host, Alfonsina Ravallo Vernarecci. She looked like a shortsighted turtle wearing a flamingo on her head.

Beside her a stout, pot-bellied gentleman in his forties, dressed in a fashionable waistcoat and speckless wig, summarized the merits of their guests. Suddenly, the baroness beamed in their direction, raising a hand to be kissed.

"My dear cousin, you and your pupil are most welcome."

"M-my lady, I am flattered."

"Indeed you are. But what about this little birdie? Can she talk? I am sure you've taught her as much."

"I'm very glad to meet you, madame." Oriana blushed and curtseyed.

"Oh, but we are glad to meet *you*, my love. Tales of your achievements have traveled far, exaggerated as they must be."

"They are quite certainly so, madame."

"Most certainly so, but still. My husband here, Count Gaetano Lombardi, my second husband, in fact—I hope that doesn't shock you, my dear, but at my age I am far beyond social pretenses—my husband is a man of his time, oh, I love him so very much for that, and he is very keen on the new French ideas of education."

"They are not totally new," corrected Lombardi with a fashionable air of intelligence, "but their consequences will be far-reaching. I've heard that you've read the *Encyclopaedia*, mademoiselle."

"Tous les suppléments que je pouvais trouver."

"Oh, how lovely, Cousin. You've taught her French!"

"She knew French before we met, madame."

"Did she? Most impressive."

"Don Giacomino, the archpriest, taught her."

"A priest!" sneered Lombardi. "Ah, but the church's hold on education is at an end! Tannucci's dismissal of the Jesuits is just the start, mark my words. We shall offer a new education to a new generation. We will eradicate superstition one mind at the time, and—"

"Do you find my husband funny, my dear cousin?"

"No, no, not at all!"

"Then why are you sniggering? You look like a cat who's just swallowed a fish. And in your case, it must have been a pretty big one."

Villabianca's white cream cheeks became tremulous.

"It's j-just that I hold very similar views, madam."

"Oh? Pray, tell us about them."

Villabianca shot Oriana a panicky stare. A small crowd of wigs had formed all around them. Oriana nodded slowly and the count cleared his throat.

"Fats, not onions!" he bellowed. "Things, not words! Potions, not fancy! For this is the Age of Treason and we are . . . w-we are . . ."

Villabianca flushed, stammered, stalled, and came to an abrupt halt.

What followed was such a heinous roar of laughter that Oriana thought they might be buried under it. Her tutor looked at her in naked despair. Quivering like a blade just drawn, she turned to the garrulous crowd and said:

"What my tutor *meant* to say is that in this age we shouldn't care so much for empty speculation but for factual knowledge. I would rather read Newton than Metastasio."

The sniggering receded to a murmur.

"Have you read Newton, Signorina Siliceo?" asked an elderly gentleman with a tight waistcoat and a white powdered face.

"I-I've read Algarotti's *Newton for Dames*."

"For Dames," sneered a plump gentleman with prominent eyes.

"Well at least she's read that! What do *you* know of Newton?" another cried.

The plump gentleman blushed.

"Do you agree with the Omnipotence of Education?"

"Do you mean Helvétius's view? Most certainly so. But I do think that he is wrong on one point: We are not equal in intelligence," Oriana answered.

Lombardi smiled, triumph in his eyes, and exclaimed, "That nails it! Yes! Women and men have the same capacity for learning, just not the same *kind* of learning. For your feminine sensibilities lean more toward poetry and—"

"I am sorry, sir, but that's not what I meant," Oriana interrupted. "I can't say I care much for poetry or for music or other things suited to 'feminine sensibilities,' as you put it."

"Oh goodness," lamented the baroness, "they haven't taught you how to play the violin or sing? How barbarous! I am very disappointed in you, Cousin, for depriving such a sweet child the balms of music."

"But I am not deprived, ma'am," retorted Oriana. "What I meant was that we *all* have different kinds of intelligence. Not just men and women, every one of us."

"But then how must we educate? If intelligence is different from one man to another, how can we find a common ground to impart knowledge?"

"We do have a common ground, sir. We all want to be happy, and to flee from pain, as Pietro Verri wrote. That is already enough, but there is more. I think we all have a fundamental need, one that is at the core of learning."

"And what would that be?"

"What Vico has said. We can only know what we create ourselves. And so we crave to create. To give life to thought and emotion. To shape meaning and . . . sorry, excuse me, sir, to give meaning to shape and form. The *way* we give birth to these creations differs, as per our disposition. For some it could be words, for some, yes, it is music, for others it is friendship—for I believe friends to be a creation of the heart—for some it is the family business or the family itself, but we *need* to create. Because if we leave this world without having created anything, then we haven't repaid our debt to the Creator. We were made. And so we have to make."

The silence surrounded her like a thick fog that shrouded the light.

"You are right, Oriana," said Lombardi. "Indeed, we are all creators. And that's where women and men differ, for your true creative vocation lies in your children."

"No, sir," she said.

"No?" Lombardi frowned.

"I don't know if I'll ever have children. I don't think all women should. Not all of them have a talent for family. Some of their talents lie elsewhere. Maybe they were destined to create other things."

"Signorina Siliceo," said Lombardi, "if you are so passionate about the need to create, and if having children is not your calling, what is, then?"

Oriana blushed and unconsciously stepped back. They were all looking at her, every gentleman in the room.

"I—I don't know, sir."

"My pupil is tired, maybe we should—"

"Not so fast, Villabianca," said the plump man with bulging eyes, "it's all right to hear all that philosophical twit-twat about creation and the different intellects. But when we get to the bottom of it, what is it that a woman can create, besides children? Can you sing, signorina?"

"No, sir."

"Do you embroider?"

She shook her head.

"Do you write verse, music? Can you draw, or dance?"

Silence. The haze around her was getting thicker and thicker.

"So!" said the plump man. "For me this is the end of the matter. She can't create a thing; she only wishes to."

Oriana pressed her lips before speaking up.

"I think I would make quite a good smith, sir."

A murmur of outrage rose all around her, hissing and sizzling and rippling like waves over a human pond.

"A smith? A woman!"

"That's preposterous. Nonsense."

"Do you work in your father's smithy, Oriana? Does he let you wield the iron tongs, or bend the horses' nails for him?"

"Now, Perrucci," cautioned the baroness, waving a finger,

"don't overdo it. However clever she might sound and look, Oriana is still a child, and you will show her some kindness."

"Oh, but it is precisely *because* she is a child that she must be taught a lesson. Isn't that what education is for? So, miss, tell us, how are you planning to learn the secrets of your trade?"

Oriana looked up defiantly.

"By becoming my father's first apprentice."

The murmuring turned into peals of laughter.

"Is that so?"

"Very much so. In five days' time my brother and I will be commenced in my father's smithy. I will start from there."

"You see, Baroness Vernarecci, I was right. The child must be taught how to distinguish between fancy and reality."

"But it's true, sir! Signor Merello from Caserta was our witness!"

"Oh, you could have the Empress of Austria as your witness, and it still wouldn't change a whit. This is the law, child, not a figment of your imagination."

"But as a firstborn, surely I—"

"It–does–not–matter! The Smiths' Guild stipulates that only the male firstborn will be the legal heir of a smithy. And of this I can assure you, for—as it happens—I am lawyer of the municipality, the one who draws up all the Guild's contracts. No smith in this town, or in this kingdom, would risk the gaol to take you on as his apprentice."

A sudden icy quietness overtook the room. Perrucci's words had changed the mood of the salon. In a haze of pain and confusion, Oriana looked at Villabianca, desperate for a rebuttal or a show of support on his part. But her tutor averted his eyes, not daring to look at her.

What followed afterward Oriana couldn't quite remember. It was like being in a dream of golden-framed mirrors and candelabra, of doors opening in front of them and closing behind. By some means they must have reached the courtyard, for suddenly they were waiting for the coach to bring them home. The baroness was with them, shrouded in a dark blue cloak, speaking to Villabianca in slow whispers, her lips shadowed by the hood. Oriana didn't hear much of it except the very last sentence, which the old lady delivered with overly dramatic intensity.

"You're every bit the fool I remembered," she said to the count, "but your pupil is a true gem. Pity you don't deserve her."

In the warm late-August night, the empty streets of Lucerìa basked in half-moon splendor. Far beyond the town walls, above the crickets' concerto, one could hear the wind rustling through the wood, rippling through the dark majesty of the Night.

Inside the carriage Oriana listened closely. It was as if through her hearing, she could grope the valley beyond, a bodiless hand searching. The Night Saints were out there, this much she knew. Unseen, lips silently mouthing her name behind thickets, above trees, inside abandoned wells, recognizing her for what she was, an outcast of the Day.

They were in Lucerìa too. Oriana tried to discern which part of the Night they were crossing through. It was way past First and Second Night, and there was no full moon in the sky. Had they yet reached the Hour of the Wolf? It certainly felt so, for the domain of the Grim King did not just occur at a given time, it could also be a feeling, that of being at the very bottom of the Night. And for the briefest moment, Oriana thought she felt the presence of the King himself—a sun in reverse, one that didn't give light but sucked it in. Had she the strength, she would have exited the carriage to grab hold of one of the Queen's ribbons to ground her.

Instead, she recalled the mound by the road to Foggia, a prehistoric structure predating the Romans, and, according to the Tellers, the site of the Duke of Under-earth's original smithy. Oriana wondered what would happen if she asked the coachman to drive her there. Would the Emistuchivio remember his promise? And more importantly, would she really ask for his help? That idea, which in the hours of the Day still held some delight, in the Hour of the Wolf froze her blood to ice. For every citizen of Lucerìa knew that to live among the Nocturnals is to belong to the dead. Even in this dark hour, Oriana knew that she wanted to live. Now that her life's dream had been dismissed as nonsense, she wanted it even more. Only at that moment did she understand Scandar's words—a destiny denied is twice a destiny.

Next to her Villabianca cleared his throat.

"Can we go home now? Please, Oriana," Villabianca pleaded. Oriana didn't even look at him. "All right, then, I'll ask the driver to make another round."

For some time now they had been driving in slow circles, their coach a ship without a harbor. It was the count's idea to let her cool off, yet the steam was still very much inside her, burning. How could she have been so stupid? Did she really believe she could be her father's apprentice, after everything she had heard and seen? True, Angia worked for her father in his butcher shop, but only at the counter. Like all the women Oriana knew, she was viewed as inconsequential. It all seemed so obvious now. She hadn't seen the truth because she didn't want to. She had always been a gifted and precocious child and had assumed that rules would be bent for her, broken even. But she was just a doll to be dressed and tutored as Donna Lena pleased.

"You knew," she finally said.

"Oh, praise the Lord! I thought you had lost your sense of speech entirely. I'll tell the driver to bring us home at once."

"You knew that I couldn't be my father's apprentice."

"Well, if you had told me that was what you had in mind—"

"Oh, but I did tell you, didn't I? Several times. I told *you* and no one else, Villabianca. You are the only person in the Day who knew about my desire, until tonight. You knew I was deadly serious about it. You always did."

"I did, yes, but what good would have come of it had I crushed your childhood dream at such an early age? With time—"

"If you speak another word about patience, I swear to you I'll open this door and smash my head on the pavement; may my blood be upon your hands!" she screamed. As soon as the words left her body, she collapsed, face in hands. Her sobs were so bitter that Villabianca embraced her.

"Oh, my dear, it'll be all right. Someday, when you own palazzo Nicastri, together we'll ask Zi' Nicola to take you on as his apprentice. You'll carve wood instead of iron, but you'll still be a creator, just as you said. Tonight, you made me so proud, Oriana. You are my mouth, my words, my soul, and much more than that. You've surpassed me, Oriana. That's what every teacher secretly wishes for, to see such knowledge in his pupil that he could not possibly have achieved himself. This you have done, and done superbly."

For a time Oriana rested her head against Villabianca's chest, her face hidden. Then she looked up, her skin pale.

"Fernando, why would I own your palazzo?"

"I—I didn't say that. You misunderstood me."

She stared on. Had it been someone else, the count could have tried to cover up his blunder, but Oriana knew him too well. He cleared his throat again.

"M-my dear," he said in a choking voice, "it won't happen for some years to come. When the time is right, and you are of age, and you will feel ready, I will be honored to become . . . to take you as my . . ."

Oriana saw, like a picture drawn on a sheet of glass, her mother's smile at dinner.

"She sold me to you."

"Nobody sold you, Oriana! It's just a prenuptial contract, one that won't be signed for some years to come. It's just a proposal."

Oriana could see now how skillfully Donna Lena had played the game.

"And you thought I'd just accept, without even asking me."

"You told me yourself that had you been a lady . . ."

"But I'm not, Fernando," she whispered in a voice so low that the Night had to bend over to hear her. "I'm not a lady. I'm much worse than that, and much better than that. I'm not a lady, but I was your friend. Maybe your only true friend, as you were mine."

They spoke no more.

SEVENTEEN

That night, Oriana took ill and didn't get out of bed for three days. A doctor was called the following afternoon. Don Saverio prescribed her an infusion of thyme and recommended a broth that was delivered by Donna Lena herself in slow spoonfuls that Oriana sipped as if it were basilisk's blood. Donna Lena knew that her wedding scheme had been found out and gloated in that knowledge. Oriana had never hated her mother before, not really, at least not with the vehemence she now possessed. Mastro Peppo came to visit, too, short and brisk as was the custom between fathers and daughters, yet Oriana cherished every minute of it and felt bitterly disappointed when he had to leave to take care of his business.

Then Oriana was alone for hours, looking up at the ceiling of her room, replaying in her mind every word that had been said to her. Nothing relieved her anguish. She couldn't read, she couldn't write, she couldn't play—even her Sanctum lay untouched in her secretaire, for how could she even look at it knowing it was all a lie?

Nights were worse. She couldn't sleep, even as the house lay dead and silent around her. It was so quiet that Oriana swore she could hear the water leak from Villabianca's attic. She wondered if Mamma Emma was hearing it too. For the first time since she was a little girl, Oriana found no consolation in murmuring her fears into her palm. Scandar the Garaude belonged to another world, a world of terrible delight, but not her own. She dreaded becoming even more separated from the world she lived in. Also, to go to the Duke now meant admitting defeat. It meant that the wig-wearing crowd had been right about the options available to her in the Day. And she would rather die a thousand deaths than concede to them that victory.

On the second day of her illness her brother finally came to visit. Their birthday was a few days away, and he'd been busy getting ready for his commencement. Oriana remembered how, many years back, he had boasted about the spring fair without even noticing the pain in her eyes. Now it was the same. Or rather, worse.

"You'll be there, won't you?" he said. "You'll be well soon, and when I sign the contract, you'll be by my side? It's *our* birthday, after all."

She nodded, and then replied, "Riano, can I ask you something? When you said to Father that we'd enter the smithy together, what did you mean?"

"Why, that both of us could attend my commencement! I didn't want you to feel left out," he explained. Oriana stared vacantly at her brother. "What is it, Ori? Should I call Mother?"

"No thanks, I'm fine. I just want to be a bit by myself."

"Sure, you must not tire. You'll see, you'll be better soon."

On the day before her birthday, as she was sitting by the drawing room's large window, she saw a black cat stalking some unseen prey on the rooftop's ridge. She wondered if it had been one of those cats at the Parliament, years ago. Her thoughts drifted to the Dreamarquise. Even though the Garaude assured her that Growler's death in the Night just meant that he woke up in the Day, Oriana had not seen her house cat ever since. She felt a pang of guilt. To this day she did not know what happened to him. Was he still in Lucerìa? Did he hate her for having deposed him of his title? Most importantly, could he forgive her? She hoped so. She missed being able to talk to someone about the Night in ways she never could with any other creature of the Day.

"Oh, Dreamarquise," she murmured. "Where are you? We've been enemies, the two of us, but I miss you. Who can I talk to now that you are gone?"

"You can try me," answered Villabianca, stepping into the room.

Oriana stood up, her blanket landing softly on the floor.

"How dare you come in here! Out!"

"I am sorry, but I must—"

"You *must*? After what you did? Who let you in? It was my mother, wasn't it? To secure her investment, obviously. Did she—"

"Your mother knows nothing of it!" He interjected with such vibrancy of emotion that Oriana staggered and sat back down. "Donna Lena is out with Cetta. That's the only reason I'm here at all. Will you listen to me? Just this once. You owe me as much, I think."

Oriana offered him the slightest nod.

"Good. Can I sit? I haven't slept much in the last two days. What I wanted to tell you is this. Your mother proposed that I become your husband the day I received your invitation to the salon from my cousin. I was shown a contract, yes, and I have to admit that—in the emotional wasteland that is my life—I thought the prospect of you becoming my wife was something desirable for both sides. I was a fool, I can see that very clearly now. For it's true, you were my friend. I took so much pride in your intelligence that I came to forget that you are still a child. Please forgive me, for on my part I cannot find any reason to forgive myself. It's my fault and my fault alone, and if I've lost your friendship, it's the least I deserve."

Villabianca had no sooner spoken these words than he

buried his face in his hands. He wept bitterly, like a small child. For a while Oriana remained perfectly still. Then she stood up, walked over to him, took his right hand, and kissed it.

"You are a fool, but not a wicked fool. This I've always known, but in my anger I forgot. You are still my friend, and you always will be."

Villabianca looked at her from the pale devastation of his face.

"Thank you, oh, *thank you*. Look, this is the contract your mother gave me. I will tear it to pieces and give it back to her tonight."

Oriana studied the paper the count produced.

"No," she said.

"No?"

"Keep it. As long as my mother thinks the agreement is still valid, she won't try to find me any other suitors."

"And you trust me, knowing what use I could make of it?"

"As I said, you are my friend."

Villabianca tried to speak but no sound came out. Instead, he took her hand in his. And so they stayed for a while. Then Oriana stirred, frowning.

"Can I ask you a favor, Fernando?" she asked.

"You could ask me for my kidneys, and I'd give them to you."

"Do you still hold the post of archivist of the municipality?"

"I haven't renounced it yet, I am afraid. My finances—"

"So you have access to the Guild's contracts."

"Sure, all the copies are kept in the archive. Why?"

"Because I would very much like to have a look at the contract my father drew up with Bruno, as well as my brother's indenture."

"Oh, but only a member of the Guild can—" Oriana looked up. He lowered his eyes. "Of course. I'll bring them to you tomorrow."

"Tomorrow is too late. I need to see them today. And I'll need your help with them."

"My help?"

"Legal help. And one more thing: Will you come with me to my brother's commencement? I don't want to go alone."

"Alone? All your family will be there."

"As I said, I don't want to go alone."

EIGHTEEN

On the day of Riano's commencement—that is, on their birthday—the whole contrada of San Lorenzo was in festa. A thick group of bystanders had gathered outside the smithy's open door. Mostly women, many boys, and all the Siliceos' old neighbors peered inside, chatting and whispering to one another, waiting for the ceremony to begin. They'd gathered anticipating almond-shaped mostaccioli, as well as wine and songs and stories, as was custom.

On the first day of their service, all new apprentices signed an indenture agreement establishing their wages and the respective duties of masters and pupils. This was done as in the rest of Europe, although in Lucerìa a distinction was observed between apprentice and "first apprentice." For while an apprentice could be virtually anyone, the *first apprentice* could only be the smithy master's firstborn. By signing his indenture, he became the legal heir of the smithy. This commencement served a dual purpose. Bruno would become master of the smithy, if only ad interim, while Riano would sign the contract that bound him for life. There was no going around it: Either he would serve with honor and become master himself, or the contract would be broken, the family line severed, and the smithy Bruno's.

The Siliceos arrived by coach, an entrance that was already considered too theatrical by the local craftsmen's wives. Indeed, when Donna Siliceo stepped out of the carriage with her children at her side, a murmur of discontent rose among the crowd of women. Since her social ascent, none of the old neighbors had seen much of her. This behavior was considered bad manners in the contrada, and worse still was the prim, ladylike manner with which Donna Lena greeted them on the street. Angia's mother, surrounded by her seven red-haired daughters, shook her head. Not one word of recognition from Donna Lena, not even a real smile, only a sneer-like grin that paired well with her extravagant hairstyle, a lush cascade of dark green ribbons. And so when the gossips saw her parading in emerald pride on commencement day, something in their imagination stirred. It was just a seed, but a seed that had a shape. And when, a fortnight later, Angia's mother scolded one of her daughters, the words came unbidden: "Don't grin like the green lady." This she said, not yet knowing what she meant, its future proverbial meaning still taking shape through Donna Lena's deeds.

Walking beside her were her two children. Riano was dressed like an apprentice in a simple wool shirt and pair of work trousers, while Oriana's face was pale under the elaborate coif of her hair. Together they entered the smithy.

First to greet them was the vibrant odor of coal and burnt chestnut wood. Then the roughness of the stone walls and the sandy gravel floor underfoot. Finally, they saw the large rectangular room lit by two tall windows.

Right in its middle was the forge itself, shadowed by a soot-blackened cowl, dormant like a sleeping Wyrm. To one side was a gigantic bellows, and on the other a slack tub full of brine. Coal boxes and iron bars filled the spaces in between. On every wall wooden racks displayed tongs, chisels, hardies, fullers, hammers, and sledgehammers, a forest of tools like the branches of a tree. In the back of the room six people stood around the anvil. Mastro Peppo and Bruno, dressed in their best attire but without wigs, whispered to each other in conspiratorial tones. Behind them stood three other smiths, all members of the Guild. Finally, on a wooden plank by a window, sat a plump gentleman with bulging eyes, wearing a waistcoat and a silvery wig. The man raised his head at their entrance.

"The first apprentice is here," said Peruzzi. "We may begin."

Riano squeezed his sister's hand. Her face was stiff, her eyes vacant. Peruzzi began to read Bruno's obligations, the dues he must pay to the Guild, the amount he owed his former master, and so on. Every time Bruno said, "I swear," Mastro Peppo slammed the head of a huge sledgehammer on the ground. It was the mother of all hammers, one they called the Beast. Taller than the smith himself, its head alone was said to weigh as much as a grown man. When Peruzzi finished reading, he handed a quill to the new master. Bruno bent over the table and signed his contract with an X. Then Mastro Peppo passed him the Beast. His old apprentice took it with a mischievous grin. For a moment he paused to look at those gathered, the Siliceos and the crowd behind them, and then with sharp cry, he struck the anvil. The hammer's din echoed in the smithy like a bell tolling, a good omen. When at last Mastro Peppo hugged his old pupil, a great cheer rose from the crowd outside.

"Quiet! Quiet out there or we will continue with closed doors! We may proceed. Please, may first apprentice Riano Siliceo step forward."

For a moment Riano was her little brother again. He gave his sister one sharp look of terror, then stepped forward. This time, there was no quieting the street urchins who chanted his name boldly. Riano could not refrain from smirking.

"Riano Siliceo," read Peruzzi, "do you accept your role as Bruno Bucci's first apprentice, serving him as your master for seven years?"

"I do."

Oriana looked behind her. Someone was pushing through the wall of people, an old wig on a white cherub's face. Peruzzi gave the count a fiery stare but went on reading.

"Do you also swear to serve him to the best of your abilities, being at all times punctual and never damaging the forge's property?"

"I swear."

Oriana looked at Villabianca. His face was even paler than usual when he nodded at her. For the first time since she'd returned from the salon, she smiled.

"Do you moreover agree that your pay will be six carlini a month, and that you will not ask for anything else in return for your work for the entire duration of your apprenticeship?"

"I agree," said the boy.

And thus they went on, clause after clause while the crowd's impatience grew. For they had seen the wine bottles, the almond-shaped biscuits, and the salted chestnuts, and were certain this would be a commencement to remember. In this they were not mistaken.

And so after the lawyer finally finished reading and the young Siliceo signed the contract, after Bruno shook his hand and Mastro Peppo squeezed his shoulder and Donna Lena beamed at him, after Peruzzi turned to the crowd to say that if any knew of a reason why this young man could not become first apprentice they ought to speak then or forever hold their peace, a voice was raised, and someone did step forward to say that Riano could not be first apprentice for the very simple reason that there were two of them.

The forge was so quiet you could hear the buzzing of flies.

Had Oriana taken off her clothes and stood naked in front of the contrada, had she fallen to the ground and screamed her eyes out, had she cut her throat and bled to death, she wouldn't have had half the effect on this audience. Her mother, brother, and father, Peruzzi, Bruno, the Guild's smiths, and the black-clad women were all staring at her in such utter disbelief that, for an instant, she pitied them. Trembling ever so slightly, more from the intensity of her emotions than fear, she addressed Peruzzi with a curtsey.

"Miss," he said at last, "with all due respect, you are out of your mind."

"No, I am not, sir. The contract says that in the case of a dispute between two firstborns—twins, that is—over who is to inherit the smithy, one may challenge the other to a contest of three trials. Whichever twin completes the trials better or faster than the other would inherit the smithy. It's written there, so I assume it's the law."

"But this is preposterous! Child, you don't know what you're talking about. No woman can legally be a smith's apprentice!"

"No, but in the case of a dispute, a woman can be *first* apprentice. That is, she can claim the smithy as part of her dowry."

"This isn't a legal court, and you haven't the right to—"

"I have every right, sir. I am my father's firstborn, just as much as my brother."

As she said this she pointed to Riano, who was staring at her with such violent distress that she had to look away. At that moment, her mother grabbed her by the wrist.

"My daughter has not been feeling well lately. Pray, forgive her for her nonsense, she will part at once."

"Mother, this is not nonsense, and I will not part!"

"You will do as a I say. Come. *Now*."

"Eleonora." The word was spoken softly, yet it froze both Donna Lena and her daughter in place. Mastro Peppo looked in the eyes of his two women. Oriana stared at the ground. He was the one she had dreaded to hurt the most. So it came as a surprise when he said, "Let our daughter speak. Let us hear what she has to say."

It was now Oriana's turn to be at a loss. She looked at the

small crowd outside the smithy. Among them she recognized many faces from her childhood, women who had seen her take her first steps, girls and boys with whom she had played in the streets. For a moment she longed to go back to that happy time, before her mother traded away the Reality of her. Then she looked at the pale count and his smile gave her courage.

"Everything I said is written in the contract. All of it. If you don't believe me, please read it over, you'll see that I'm right. It's an old custom, but it's still valid. It's called the 'challenge of peers.'"

"But how in the name of the Santa Vergine can you challenge him," burst out Peruzzi, "if you haven't even been trained!"

"There is a time set for completing each challenge. Usually a month, more if it's needed. The master of the smithy will preside over their progress and see that his two apprentices get the same training."

"Is this true, Master Geremia?" asked one of the Guild members.

The old man scratched the back of his balding head.

"Well, the 'challenge of peers' is indeed an old tradition of ours. Very rarely used to establish inheritance, as it only applies to twins."

"Has it ever been applied to brother and sister?" asked another.

"Not that I know of."

"So it has no legal consequence!" bellowed Peruzzi.

"Well no, sir. Not unless I bring it to court," Oriana admitted.

"You can't! You're a woman, and not even that, you're a child. You're underage, you can take no legal action of any sort!"

"You are quite right, Peruzzi. But *I* can," a voice sounded from within the crowd.

As Villabianca stepped forward, the crowd gave way to the white sail of his vast stomach. Donna Lena stared at it with fascinated horror.

"And what legal claim do you have to Oriana Siliceo to be able to take her part in court?" Peruzzi asked.

The count looked at Oriana, who gave him the slightest nod.

"She is my best pupil, the most intelligent I've ever had—"

"That's very touching, Count, though I'm afraid—"

"And my prospective wife."

His statement roused a tremor of disbelief in the crowd. Mastro Peppo was staring sharply at his wife, who looked away.

"Indeed," mused the lawyer, "today is a day of legal fictions!"

"It is not a fiction, Peruzzi, I have a prenuptial contract that proves it. Here, read it. I'll also spare you any further inquiry into the validity of this dispute, for I went to court this very morning and summoned the justice of the peace on behalf of my future wife. Her case will be discussed in the coming week. And if, as I have every reason to believe, she is proven right, then she is entitled to call for the challenge of peers, just as she has very sharply illustrated to you."

Peruzzi closely examined the contract Villabianca handed him, reading above his glasses. He sighed and returned it to the count. At last, the lawyer reluctantly addressed the young woman who stood in front of him.

"What if the court abides by your reasons, then? Would you pursue such madness? Think it over, miss, this is quite a serious matter."

"I've thought it over, sir. There is only one instance in which I would not pursue my challenge. That is, if my brother agrees to split the smithy's ownership. We will *both* be Bruno's first apprentices, train with him, and, when the time is right, we shall own the business together."

"Oh, but this is unprecedented! The law—"

"Laws can be changed, sir. New times are coming, times of progress and equality. It would be indeed a good omen for Lucerìa if at least twins can be proved to possess the same rights. I have no desire to overrule his claim. But I will most certainly not give up mine."

This speech drew a wind of cold hostility from the women of the contrada. In fact, while the men seemed quite amused by the girl's boastful speech, the women muttered scathing remarks among themselves. Oriana felt their reproach like a scorching heat. And yet she also saw a handful of young women, Angia among them, who were looking at her with gleaming eyes.

Peruzzi turned to Riano, whose silence was now conspicuous. Every eye in the smithy turned to him as well, waiting for an answer. The boy was shaking so badly it took him some time to speak. At last, he looked up, his expression changing from fear to ire.

"Over my dead body," he said, "that's when I'll give up the smithy to you, Oriana. Over my dead body, and not one day sooner."

NINETEEN

A dare, a public challenge between siblings! The girls by the washing basins chattered incessantly, recounting over and over the day they saw Donna Lena—Lady Grin herself—take the twins into Mastro Peppo's smithy. Oh, Donna Lena looked beautiful at the commencement, wearing a hairstyle like a magnolia in bloom, all lush and green, decorated in ribbons and pearls like the Queen of Dawn herself. While poor Riano, spikey like a hedgehog, looked ready to flee from the forge's chimney and fly away over the rooftops of Lucerìa. But the one who most struck the women's imagination was Oriana herself. At the Thursday market, Lucia the artichoke vendor said that she'd never heard someone of her gender and age speak this way, and so Oriana must've drunk from the Fountain of Truth guarded by a Wind Wyrm. Its waters had granted her the power of prophecy, for all the men listened to her argument, even the Guild's lawyer.

All the women of Lucerìa speculated and gossiped, and not just the peasants and the artisan's wives. Rumor had it that even Baroness Vernarecci herself had sent a servant to listen for news of the court's proceedings. Unsurprisingly, most women over twenty-five, be they noblewomen or peasants, condemned Oriana. For they had been taught that it was highly improper for a young woman to talk back to an assembly of men, and even worse to challenge them. They would have scratched their daughters' faces raw, had they dared to confront their brothers and fathers in such a fashion. Oriana's name was like acid on their lips. How skillfully she had seduced the poor count into doing her bidding, and she was not even fifteen! No wonder her mother had gone so odd. And they were even more contemptuous of Mastro Peppo. Had he been a *real* father, he'd have beaten his daughter black and blue to put some sense into her. Others suggested that the smith had his own reasons for staying quiet—he had not just a lover, but an entire second family waiting for him in Caserta, which was why he was moving there in the first place. But not everyone in Lucerìa felt this way. Though there were many girls Oriana's age who criticized her, at least out loud, more than a few kept a stubborn silence, their eyes brimming with insolence. They were the first to wait outside the tribunals, to inquire about Oriana or the state of her trial. Every day, street urchins loitered outside the palace of justice at noontime, and when a gentleman of the jury finally came out, the boys flocked around his wig.

Six days after Riano's commencement, the jury closed the proceeding with a verdict that caused a minor uproar. Neighbors called out to one another from their balconies, vendors stopped at the gates to sell wares and news, street urchins clustered on the steps of the Duomo, and ladies sent their maids to the market to find out if the rumor was true. For whether it was due to Villabianca's involvement, or simply because there wasn't any other way to circumvent the law without changing it, in the end the court gave Oriana her first victory. A challenge of peers would be set, and its winner would become first apprentice.

While the town buzzed, Oriana was locked up in her room. She had been there since the night of her brother's commencement. Only Cetta was allowed in with her tray of bread and soup. The young woman passed the time reading, mostly letters from Villabianca in which he kept her updated on the court's proceedings, but she also spent no little time on her bed staring at the palms of her hands.

"Oh, Scandar," she sighed. "Why didn't you warn me that growing up was like this? I would've come with you right away."

At times, in the wakefulness before sleep, she thought she could see the outline of an ear growing out of the skin of her palm. But when she opened her eyes fully, it was never there. And yet she couldn't shake the growing feeling that someone was listening to her, waiting for her call. Then, one night, as she lay in her bed reading about the life of Spinoza, holding her breath as she read about his dismissal and excommunication, she heard somebody tap on her door.

"Come in," she assented, thinking it Cetta.

Oriana sat up straight when Mastro Peppo walked in.

They had not talked since that day at the forge. The smith was still dressed in his travel cloak, the mud on its hem fresh. He must have just come back from Caserta. The bed creaked when he sat down. Oriana felt her cheeks blaze.

"Father, I'm so sorry, I swear. You mustn't . . ."

Her voice trickled down to silence. The smith rested for a while, his face flushed, his hands restless in his lap. She looked at them. His fingers were thick like old roots, and yet his wrist was almost disproportionally thin, like it didn't belong to the master craftsman he had become. For the first time Oriana thought of the young man Giuseppe Siliceo had been. Beardless, he would have looked a lot like Riano.

"Papà," she asked, "did you always want to be a smith?"

He looked up at her in mild shock. She thought she had overstepped her boundaries, but then he smiled.

"In fact," he said, "I didn't. I had to when my eldest brother died."

"You didn't? Then, what did you . . . I mean, *who* did you want to be?"

Mastro Peppo ran a hand over his bald head.

"A gardener," he said. "I wanted to grow flowers and medical plants."

Oriana wanted to ask more but didn't dare.

"Why, Oriana?" he asked finally. "Why didn't you ask me?"

"About you wanting to be a smith? Father, I—I—"

"Why didn't you tell me you wanted to work in the smithy?" he pressed. Oriana stared at him. He didn't look angry, just curious. She had expected fury, not this. He met her gaze. "Your great-grandmother, do you remember her?"

Oriana shook her head. He smiled thinly and wet his lips.

"You would've liked her."

"I would have?"

"She was a smith," he continued. "With a great flair for bonding alloys. You know those small, traced locks we still have in our cellar? They were her creation, from conception to execution. That's how talented she was. A natural."

"She was a smith?" Oriana asked, her eyes opened wide. She thought her father would add something, but he didn't. She cleared her throat. "Was she in the Guild's records?"

"No. Of course not," he replied matter-of-factly. His tone made her shrink back, but then Mastro Peppo smiled. "But she was an excellent smith. Grandpa took most of the credit, but she didn't care. She just loved her craft."

"The people, did they know?" she wondered. He nodded. Oriana sucked in a deep breath, understanding what her father was trying to tell her. "I am sorry, Pa, I couldn't have guessed . . ."

"You couldn't have. But I should've seen it sooner."

They stayed in silence for some time, the darkness of the room ripe with emotion.

"Oriana, this challenge, it will change Riano, but I think for the best. As for your mother, she'll oppose you fiercely."

"I know."

"Tomorrow I'm leaving for Caserta, and this time, I will not be back for a month."

"Father, no, please! If you leave me, they'll—"

"I must, Oriana. Signor Merello has been patient, but if I don't go back to Caserta now, I'll lose my position."

"Of course. It's a lot of coin."

"The coin is welcome, but it's not that. It's my work. And it's important that I do my work well. Do you understand this?"

"Yes, I think I do."

"Then you know why I must go. In any case I spoke to Bruno tonight. He'll give you a fair chance, both of you. I don't care who wins. But I do care that you have your chance."

"So this position in Caserta, it's what you desired most."

"Not the position, but what I can do with it. Look."

The smith retrieved something from his pocket. It was a rose, a steel rose made of eleven crowns of petals.

"Papà, it's beautiful!" Oriana exclaimed, thinking of the paper rose her father had given her mother during their courtship. It had been lost during their move to palazzo Nicastri.

"I thought so too. I wanted to give it to your mother but . . ." He trailed off. Then, turning slowly to his daughter, he asked, "Are you ever afraid of her, your mother?"

"W-what do you mean?"

"I think you know what I mean."

"I . . . really don't know what to say."

"She's changed, hasn't she? Yes, I think you know what I am talking about."

She stared at him, unable to utter a word. The honesty of their conversation was so intense that she was surprised not to taste the blue spirit in her mouth. Nocturnals had been part of her inner life for so long that discussing them with another felt like recounting her dreams as if they'd happened in the light of Day.

"Father?"

"Do you really understand why it is that I must go?"

Oriana stood up.

"Papà, can I show you something?"

Before he could answer, Oriana took the candle, set it on a stool, walked to her desk, and opened its first drawer. She touched a spring, and the desk came undone. The smith stood up and looked at the model hidden inside. Oriana raised the candle over her head.

"What is it?" asked her father, moving toward it.

"It's my Sanctum. My heart and soul."

But there was no need to explain, for it could be nothing else. It was a scale model of a smithy, one that only Piranesi could have dreamt. Constructed from painted cork, squares of cloth and linen, buttons and latches, wooden splinters and nails, there lay an ideal smithy as seen in Diderot's *Encyclopaedia*. Or at least that had been its starting point, for instead of one hearth, it had six. Oriana's Sanctum was divided into three different floors, with six cork staircases connecting them via six different landings. Each hearth had two bellows, one for each side, so perfectly made that they looked as if they actually worked. On the little wooden racks, no longer than a finger, were fullers and chisels, tongs and hardies, hammers and pokes, all the tools of a smith, in miniature, made precisely to scale. And scattered throughout were cork statues painted violet, peeking out from the walls and the chimneys, the Night-Ones: Mazapegul, Wiccae, Nuriae, Wyrms, Basilisks, and Garaudi, an entire forest of Nocturnals.

Mastro Peppo took it all in. Oriana's candlelight reflected

not only his wonder, but also the proudest flame that had ever burned in a smith's heart. Then his expression changed.

"You've met them, haven't you? There's no denying it. It's all over you. It has happened to you both, my wife and my daughter. I know it, but I cannot do a damn thing about it."

TWENTY

The night before the first day of the challenge, Oriana Siliceo slept little. It was to be expected, yet she couldn't forgive herself for wasting her energy. She needed all the strength she could muster, as today Bruno Bucci would set the twins' first task and start their training.

There would be three trials, each a routine task easily performed by a master smith. The two would receive three weeks of training before completing every task. At the end of their training period, under the supervision of three Guild members, they were to perform the task in the allotted time. The Guild members would decide whose work was best. The one who scored the most across all three trials would be named first apprentice. And if for any reason a winner couldn't be established, the apprentices themselves could request an additional task, until a clear win was achieved.

That morning, Oriana had chosen her clothes very carefully. A wool petticoat over which she wore a nightshirt, secured by the strings of a checked linen apron. On her head she'd chosen a ruffled linen cap to protect her hair from sparks. Cetta was helping Oriana with the cap when Donna Lena slipped quietly into the room.

"I must take care of your hair," she declared.

Oriana shivered. She had barely spoken to her mother since the commencement.

"Mother, please, I won't need it," she protested.

Donna Lena smiled and asked Cetta to leave them, striding

up to where Oriana stood in front of the mirror. Oriana dried her wet palms on her wool gown. But when she looked up at her mother through the mirror, her heart simply stopped.

Donna Lena's hair filled the room. Every inch of the ceiling, every square foot of the floor, the surface of the bed and the window's deep embrasure, the empty space of the open door, was overtaken by spidery tendrils of her dark hair. It twisted and quivered like a forest of thorns as it pressed against the boundaries of Oriana's room. It was like Donna Lena possessed a Night of her own, a private darkness that had spilled into the Day and demanded to fill any hollowed space. Such was the enormity of her hair that she could have stripped the room of its wallpaper with a simple nod of her head. As her mother's grin drew near, Oriana could smell the market on her, a reek of dead things, and in her own mouth, the blue taste of Tokai.

"Do you know," Donna Lena said, "why I didn't become a capera, like my mother? It's a tale I've never told a living soul. When I was about your age, a baroness came to the house where I lived with my mother, in the quarter just outside the ancient walls of Naples. The lady heard that my mother was the best hairdresser in town and had come to see for herself if her fame was well deserved. She loosened her hair and asked my mother to do her best, saying that if she were really as good as they said, she would get a string of pearls in return. And if she weren't, the lady's servants would cut her hair to the skull. So my mother set to work. She used her best combs, her best ribbons, and her best threads. She even used paper flowers she had made herself and a silver brooch. I worked as her assistant and helped throughout the process. The session lasted two hours, during which not a word was spoken. When she finally handed the baroness a mirror, the lady gasped. It was a beauty, Oriana, a true work of art. If da Vinci or Raphael had set to work on a woman's hair, they couldn't have done better. The gentlewoman looked thoroughly impressed. But when she asked one of her servants what he thought of it, he replied that it looked vulgar and overly done. The baroness explained to my astonished mother that this servant was a coiffeur himself. In fact, he was considered one of the best in the country. You see, his judgment could not be wrong. My mother shook her head, insisting that the baroness had not thought so herself. But the baroness smiled. I'll always remember what she said. 'I think your work is most splendid. But that counts for nothing, for in this world all the standards are set by men. This is the lesson I so bitterly learned, and the one I came to teach you. You are too good for your own good.' She directed her servants to shave my mother's head shortly thereafter. And in the end my mother didn't learn her lesson and died poor, a master of an art that none consider art. But I did. I learned my lesson."

"Mother?"

During her mother's tale, Oriana had averted her gaze from the monstrous reflection in the silvery screen. But now she turned again to look at Donna Lena. It was just her mother. There was no swaying black hair or grinning Dame, just the woman she had been years ago. Her face was pale, her eyes tight with something akin to pain, or regret. Suddenly, she seemed so small, so lonely. Oriana had to fight the urge to hug her, to bury her face in her shoulder like she did when she was little. Her mother sighed, placing a hand over her eyes.

"Sorry, titilla. I'm a little off; you mustn't mind me."

"Why did you tell me this story, Mamma?"

"Why, indeed," she repeated, lowering her hand.

"It won't stop me from doing what I have to do."

"I know it won't. You're stubborn, and I admire you for that."

"You do?"

"It's a quality we both possess. You are my daughter, after all. But returning to the topic of your hair, can't you see? It has too much volume. Unless we do something, it will pop out of the cap and catch fire at the first spark."

Oriana looked in the mirror. Her hair did look a bit constrained. Her mother removed the cap and started brushing through it with her fingers, caressing it softly. Oriana let out a sigh. Donna Lena stopped.

"Oh, I see. It is a nice day, staying indoors must be torture. Let's go out, then. I'll do your hair in the courtyard."

"You will?"

"Why not. Come, get your shawl."

They dressed and ventured down to the courtyard. The September day was blessed with blue sky and warmed by a steady sun. Donna Marisa, the gatekeeper, passed by with a bucket full of ashes, acknowledging them with a curtsey. Oriana sat on a straw chair, listening to Zi' Nicola's gentle rapping from the workshop, while her mother began straightening her curls one by one with an ivory brush. Brushstroke after brushstroke, the girl relaxed, her mind focusing on the task ahead. She hadn't seen Riano in days. They hadn't spoken since the day of his commencement, and Oriana was ashamed of their estrangement. Maybe she should have said something to him. If only—

Tzick. Something like a black feather fell onto the ground. A lock. A lock of her hair. Oriana tried to pull away, but her scalp was held tightly by icy fingers.

"Mother? What are you doing?"

"I'm teaching you a lesson. Be quiet now."

Oriana screamed and scratched and bit, just as Growler would have. But the Emerald Dame was back, and Oriana was helpless against her; Donna Lena's hands held her in place with impossible strength, fueled by her Moira. Oriana had no choice but to endure, holding back her tears, hoping it would end soon, that it wouldn't be as shameful as she feared.

Time coagulated around her. She could feel the blades of the scissors coming together, cutting a new lock with every snip. Others gathered in the courtyard to watch the spectacle. Zi' Nicola, from his workshop, shook his head. Donna Marisa whispered to her husband under the arch. Even Mamma Emma looked on from the balcony. Oriana felt her shame burn, setting fire to her cheeks and stinging her eyes.

Then the scissors stopped.

On the ground, all around, lay her dark hair, as if she were a tree and autumn had come for her. Blindly, Oriana groped her head. She could feel her naked skull, the remaining tufts and empty holes a horror to the touch. She removed her linen cap from her pocket, but when she tried to put it back on, her mother snatched it from her.

"No. Your hair is safe now as it is."

"Y-you want me to go out in the streets like this?"

"Why not? Since you're planning to live your whole life as an outcast, you'd better get used to it, don't you think? Oh, you can marry that humbug, but it won't make much of a difference. You'll still be the girl-boy who wanted to be a smith."

"I'm not ashamed of who I want to be!"

"That's what I'm here to teach you," her mother replied. Slowly, Oriana stood up, swaying. But as she headed toward the stairs, her mother called out, "Wait. Your lesson is not over yet."

At the top of the marble staircase, Oriana saw her brother. In his arms Riano carried a large object wrapped in a white sheet. Cetta was with him, bearing a jar of oil and a disconsolate face. Oriana was too stunned to react when her twin set his bundle down. The boy began unwrapping it. As soon as she saw the cork stairs and wooden towers, Oriana released a sharp cry. Her fists trembled with rage.

"You promised! You promised not to tell her!"

"And you promised to be by my side," said Riano, staring fiercely at her.

"Cetta, the oil," commanded Donna Lena.

The widow reared her head back as if in protest. But Donna Lena's green eyes held her like a vice.

"Yes, ma'am," she said finally.

The old maid poured the oil over the Sanctum while the girl watched in horror, frozen in place. But when her brother brought out the flint, something finally broke in her. She ran to him and tried to snatch it from his hands.

"No! Stop it! It's my work! My work!"

"It's peasants' nonsense," said Donna Lena quietly, "and I won't have it here under my roof, not while I am signora of the house."

Oriana turned to her, teeth bared.

"Oh, this is nonsense? Answer me this, then. Who twisted the seventy-two door handles at the Mezzacasa six years ago?"

Oriana caught Zi' Nicola's wide-eyed stare and Mamma Emma crossing herself up on her balcony. Donna Lena must have noticed it, too, for she turned her back to them.

"I don't know what you're talking about," she said flatly.

"Yes you do! It was you at the Market of the Dead who—"

Oriana screamed. A trickle of blood traveled down her lips. Riano, Cetta, and Zi' Nicola each stared at Donna Lena, aghast. She seemed quite in shock herself. But only for an instant, then she righted her expression and wiped the bloodied scissors on her apron.

"It's just a cut. You'll be fine. Cetta, clean her up," she instructed coldly. And to her daughter: "You will not speak madness under my roof again. Riano, the fire."

Eyes downcast, Oriana's twin sparked his flint.

At once, the Sanctum went up in flames. The first to burn were the flags, then the bellows, then the tools. The walls, the staircases, the cork landings, and the six white forges dissolved next. And at last, the Nocturnals, each of the Gaunts, the Mazapegul, and the rest of the Garaudi, blackened one by one like roses forged in Hell.

TWENTY-ONE

On the day of the challenge, Riano looked very different from the happy-go-lucky boy everyone knew. His jaw set, he seemed more like a boy-soldier drafted for war. As for his sister, she arrived at the workshop with a hand covering her shaven head. A boy sniggered when she passed, cracking a joke about a "pruned bush." Laughter followed her like a trawl of shame.

But it wasn't the men's humor that most perturbed her. It was the women staring at her, mostly stern faced, as if Oriana had personally offended them. And yet a younger crowd had gathered too—craftmen's daughters, her age or just a bit older, gazing with hungry eyes. With a jolt Oriana saw Angia among them, her red head blazing in the sea of dark hair. Their reciprocal surprise lasted an instant. Oriana beamed. At once, all the girls let out a primal scream, shattering the scornful silence and rising over the rooftops of Lucerìa like a promise desperate to be kept.

As soon as they entered, Bruno gave them their first challenge. They would have to fuller an iron bar, first making an impression on the bar with the chisel, and then hammering it to smoothness. It was one of the preliminary steps in building a rack, something considered easy by expert smiths. But to be able to do it, the two siblings had to learn different skills in a short time.

The first task seemed the easiest, yet it took them the longest to learn—lighting the forge's fire and bringing it to the right temperature. To do it correctly, they had to put a handful of wood shavings into the furnace and light them. When the blaze caught, they were to pump the bellows, creating a short blast. Once the kindling started burning, they needed to dump a half-bushel of charcoal around the blaze, all while continuing to pump air into it. As soon as the charcoal burned steadily, they had to add more, breaking up the larger lumps with a poke and packing it tightly to create a sort of deep tunnel for the iron bar to rest in.

For days, they built and rebuilt the forge's fire. Both siblings had blisters on their hands by the second day, not because of the heat, but from the continuous effort of pumping air using the bellows. To them the fire looked always the same, and yet it wasn't. With a grin Mastro Bruno would show them how, with the slightest of changes to the placement of the charcoal or the pumping of the bellows, the fire would either blast too fiercely, reaching a welding temperature instead of a forging one, or too meekly, unable to heat the iron. Developing this skill was the core of their work—breaking up the charcoal, pumping the bellows at the right rhythm, inserting the iron bar into the fire without hurting themselves—but not the whole of it. They also had to learn how to clean the hearth of all impurities that could taint the iron. They had to sweep the floor and clean the windows so that the room stayed full of light.

During the first week, brother and sister didn't even touch a hammer, which was quite frustrating as they had imagined blacksmithing to be the art of delivering mighty strikes that sent sparks soaring into the air. It soon became apparent that to be a smith was to have patience and control over his or her gestures with incredible precision. For Oriana this discovery had a profound impact. She found that the building and rebuilding of the hearth distracted from the losses she had suffered, the flames cleansing the painful memory of her

Sanctum. Her model had been a childhood game, a dream of work yet to come. Now, she experienced the work itself. To her surprise it was a relief. For what she'd been so eager to create had never been hers alone. She wasn't a scholar and she didn't want to be one, poring over books and building models. It wasn't that the books she'd read were useless—she knew they would come in handy later on—but now they had to be put aside for more tangible pursuits, and this she did gladly. It was what she had always admired about a craftsman's work, that it wasn't just the mind that learned, but also the hand and the eye, the eye and the ear.

Their work at the forge wasn't just a training exercise—Bruno had work to do fulfilling client orders. Many of the townsfolk, mostly women, used their purchases as an excuse to glimpse the twins' progress. They visited the smithy to buy a handful of nails, a knife, a small shovel, or a spade, while craning their necks for a peek at the Siliceos.

Watching Bruno work was also part of the twins' apprenticeship, perhaps the most important part. To see him retrieve an iron bar from the hearth, give it three blows with the hammer, then place it again in the forge, then another three blows, without ever yielding to the rhythm of necessity was magical, for the man did everything with incredible ease. If this were a normal apprenticeship, they wouldn't have been allowed to touch a tool for two years. Even for a first apprentice, the real training was that of observation. This the two siblings did quite well.

Oriana was astonished at how much her brother had already been changed by the challenge. The old Riano would have fiddled around, picking up and misplacing tools, playing little pranks. But the Riano beside her at present spoke little, obeyed all orders, and when Bruno scolded him for being cheeky, he took the rebuke without a word. Oriana previously feared that their acrimony had risen to such a pitch that even working together would prove to be a challenge. But she was wrong. Bruno's commands were so sharp that there wasn't time for them to argue. Oriana considered her father's apprentice with a newfound respect. She had always thought him a scoundrel. And it was true that Bruno lobbed dirty jokes at everyone in town, was harsh and often ill-tempered, and roared oaths that would make a fisherman's blood curdle; but as a master smith, there was nothing in him that one could object to.

On the tenth day of their training, with another ten to go before their first trial, Bruno began to teach them how to hammer, or rather how to draw out a red-hot iron bar until it was flat, widening the metal in the process. That day Bruno seemed to be in a bad temper, probably because he had been fighting over some girl in town. At twenty-three he was still a bachelor, a predicament which often got him into trouble, for he was not uncomely and had an eye for married women. So it was with an angry zest that he asked Riano to swing the first blows against the heated iron. His first blow almost proved his last. The bar cracked, shooting a fat spark onto his right hand. The boy bellowed, crouching in pain.

"Ah," laughed Bruno, "you bloody fool! Didn't I tell you to watch the color? It has to be cherry-red, not yellow!"

"Why didn't you stop me, then?"

"Because now you know what happens when the iron isn't hot enough. It breaks, and you must start all over. Not today, though. Go home and ask Cetta to put some arnica on the wound."

"B-but I . . ."

"Are you arguing with me, young Siliceo? Do I have to remind you what it says in the contract you signed? Now, scuttle off."

Riano glanced at his sister, then collected his cloak and left.

"Good. Shall we continue? Let's see if you're as dumb as that dumb brother of yours."

Oriana felt a trembling pride as she put her iron bar in the hearth. She waited until the color was right, then took it out and placed it on the anvil. For a moment as she gripped the hammer, she hesitated. A memory came to her from some distant past, a remembrance of the same gesture that she couldn't quite place. Then Oriana swung the hammer and landed three sharp blows, not too hard, not too soft, before stopping. Bruno grinned.

"Is that it? Tired so soon?" he mocked.

"I can't keep going. The iron's changed color already," she explained.

"Oh, so you do listen. Good. Go on, I'm watching you."

And so Oriana continued, putting the iron back in the forge, waiting for it to turn cherry-red, then returning it to the anvil. Before the town's clock tolled the half hour, Oriana was drenched, drops of sweat rolling into her eyes, making it increasingly harder to swing the hammer precisely. Her body screamed and yet her resiliency was due to more than just endurance. She was not only enduring fatigue, she was enjoying it too.

"Enough. Let me see."

Oriana stood aside as the master inspected the bar on the anvil.

"Here, see? It's completely out of shape. And what's this? It's all bumps and holes. You almost cut through the metal," he critiqued. "And yet for your first time, I guess it's really not so bad, after all."

Bruno offered her a mischievous smile, then walked over to a wooden cabinet and took out a bottle of wine with two cups.

"We must toast to your first forging."

"Thank you, sir, but I do not drink."

"Really? That's not what I remember."

Oriana reddened as if slapped in the face.

"Well, I'll toast alone, then. To your first forging, Oriana Siliceo! Ah, this vino is excellent," he remarked, drinking deeply. "If you don't mind me saying, you're turning into a fine woman, Oriana. Not yet, but soon. A couple of years I'd say. Have you already—"

Oriana said nothing but she felt her cheeks scorch.

"A joke, my dear, just a silly little joke, no harm done. Still, your response surprises me. You haven't yet bled, but you're already engaged to that fat gentleman Villabianca."

"I think I should go home now."

"Don't fret, you need not answer me. I know he's just a friend to you, not really a prospective husband. I may be a coarse fellow, but I can recognize love. Or lust. You show neither."

"How perspicacious on your part, sir."

"Oh, don't get all 'sir' with me! I've known you since you were a child, Oriana. At least, I thought I knew you. You gave me the startle of my life that day, with old Peruzzi. 'I will challenge my brother!' Ha ha, what a riot of a puppet show that was! I've always had a liking for theater. It was grand, a real stage trick."

"Glad you enjoyed it."

"I did. But I enjoyed your performance the most. Such courage, such ambition. To own your father's smithy, to start your own business . . ."

"Nothing more than you've done yourself, Master Bruno."

"Oh, I wouldn't say so. You see, I was never first apprentice. I'm master now, but only until you or Riano come of age. And then, ciao ciao, Signor Bucci."

"I am sorry, I didn't . . ."

"You didn't realize? Or you didn't care? I'll be thirty when one of you comes of age and becomes the next master smith. Do you know what that means for me? I think you do. You're smarter than your brother."

"Bruno, if there's anything I can do—"

"Now that you mention it, signorina, there is a little something you could do for me."

"What is it?"

"Marry me. You'll win the challenge and inherit the smithy, and I'll get to stay on as its master. Plain and simple."

Oriana stared at him unblinkingly.

"You can't be serious," she finally said.

"Serious as a nail. It's a business transaction, nothing more. Oh, don't get me wrong, should you change your mind, I'm quite the lustful type. But somehow, I don't think you will, which is still fine by me. Can't you just imagine how much it would infuriate your mother? Donna Lena would just go *insane* with rage. And I'm sure that wouldn't displease you after she pruned you like a bush. *One hand washes the other*, as the old saying goes."

Oriana stared at the ground. In a game of chess, marrying Bruno Bucci would be checkmate. No one would dare object to her privileges ever again.

"And you think I'd want that? To know that my victory was fake?"

"Now, don't be so—"

"You think I need to cheat to win? That I couldn't possibly succeed on my own merit, without a man's help?"

A spark lit Bruno's brown eyes.

"My offer goes both ways, Oriana. I can help you or I can hinder you. You have no idea how easy it is for a master to break his apprentice. I've seen it happen more times than I can count. But it doesn't have to come to that. You're not stupid. You know where your best interests lie."

"I do. And I know that I've no interest whatsoever in your proposal. I will not become your wife. And I will win, nevertheless."

"Now this is pride speaking, not intelligence."

"That may be so, but I won't change my mind."

"Are you sure? This isn't a proposal I'll repeat again."

"I'm sure."

"Well, maybe you're not as smart as I thought you were. Or maybe you think that fatso of yours will help you, or your father will. But they won't because they can't. You signed a contract, and until the challenge ends, you're mine, Oriana Siliceo, to do with as I please. No one in the whole world can rescue you now, not even the king himself. You're mine to break. And I'll break you so badly that when I'm done with you, you won't even be able to recognize yourself, let alone dream of becoming a smith. Does that scare you, Oriana?"

"No," said Oriana, tears of rage in her eyes, "for someone greater than you can even begin to imagine made that same threat years ago, and yet here I stand."

"We'll see about that. Now go home. We'll start tomorrow, before the roosters sing."

TWENTY-TWO

For ten days, Oriana Siliceo made the same half-mile trip from palazzo Nicastri to her father's smithy and back. For ten days, she walked in the rain, drizzle, fog, and weak October sun. For ten days, from daybreak to sunset, she toiled, carrying charcoal, wood, water, and brine around the smithy and delivering iron tools to customers in town. The kind of work she had seen in the first half of her apprenticeship, she now experienced very little. For in the end, it was just as Bruno had said it would be. Not that he was overt about it. To the contrary, Bruno didn't mistreat her, didn't hit her or even raise his voice; and yet not an hour passed without a scolding, her hands were never empty of work, and everywhere she turned she caught Bruno's eyes.

Every time Oriana laid her hands on a hammer she would be interrupted by some errand, so that when she finally got back to the forge, the iron had cooled, and she had to start all over again. That her brother endured none of this treatment was unbearable. Instead, his old self-assuredness had returned, fueled by Bruno's near constant praise. He smiled more often and considered his work with pride. In contrast, Oriana's confidence began to falter. When she was able to work at the forge, nothing went according to plan. The iron suddenly broke under her hammer, even if she had been careful to heat it to the right temperature, or the fuller gave way under her first blow. Was this Bruno's doing or her own?

Once, while she was tending the hearth with a poker, the fire leapt up for no apparent reason, scorching her hand and singeing her eyebrows. She yelped and covered her face. Riano rushed to her, fear in his eyes, but Bruno stood by the anvil, doubled over in laughter.

"It suits you, miss. Goes with that scruffy hair of yours," he jested.

"She's hurt!" cried Riano.

"She should go home, then. If she can't work that's her problem, not mine. That's what happens when you build a shitty fire."

In the end she had to leave. The blister had already grown to the size of a fat nut, and she couldn't risk it worsening. If she missed the last days of training, she might not be able to complete the task. On her way home the usual crowd of street urchins jeered at her. Riano was a hero to them, for he often included them in his pranks and bought them fried mozzarella cones whenever his pockets were full. So it was not surprising that as soon as they saw her, the young lazzari danced around in circles, singing.

Chestnut Riana
her eyes are rapacious
her mouth is voracious!

Oriana was accustomed to it and almost didn't mind. They were so young, so scrawny, so dirty and innocent, that even when they made fun of her there was no malice in their eyes. She could endure them. Besides, sometimes the farmers' wives and daughters piling up bundles of firewood on the street corners for Serapide's festival would offer her respite in the form of basil or rosemary or fresh eggs and a bread roll when they saw her coming from the smithy. But the other women made her grit her teeth. They shut their doors in her face as she walked down the street. Once someone spat on her shawl as she passed underneath their balcony, and Oriana had to wait until she arrived home to scrub off the filth with trembling hands. And though dear old Germana claimed that she hadn't seen her when she threw a bucket of dirty water in her direction, Oriana saw the mirth in her eyes.

Oriana bumped into Angia after she walked past the lazzari. She was running some errand with three of her older sisters. Seeing the Siliceo girl, they sped up, but Angia stopped.

"My sisters think you're mad, that you'll end up in filth and shame," she said.

"And what do you think?"

"Don't you dare stop, Oriana," she said in one breath, before scuttling away to catch up with her sisters.

They barely exchanged words after that, but every time Oriana passed her in the street, she felt Angia's eyes like the warm squeeze of a friendly hand.

By the time Oriana finally arrived at palazzo Nicastri, she wondered why she didn't just go to the count and reveal Bruno's mistreatment. She could write to her father about it. Hell, she could ask him to take her on as his apprentice in Caserta. But in the end, it was pride, just as Bruno had said. Oriana wanted to prove to herself that she could achieve something on her own. How sweet it would taste to see the gentlemen of Lucerìa denied their victory. And, whether well or ill meaning, every one of her potential allies was a man. What value would her victory have if it were owed to someone else? It had to be her, and her alone. The more unjustly she was treated, the sweeter her triumph would be.

That evening, as she was reading a difficult passage from Vico, she looked up and saw something outside. Twilight lit up the rusty rooftops of the nearby palazzo, etching a dozen silhouettes against the sky. Slowly, she approached the window to get a closer look. Between the low chimneys she witnessed the playful dance of impossible children. Mazapegul. Their faces were spiny like hedgehogs', with red-hot eyes. They swirled in the wind as if made of autumn leaves, for Twilight painted their pale skin in bright yellows, burnt oranges, and caramel reds. Oriana felt tears of joy prick her eyes. They said that Ossifrago, the Baron of Twilight, blessed the most unfortunate of the street urchins—the ones who died at dusk—with a new life in the Night, free of poverty or ailment. She stepped forward and pressed her forehead to the cold glass.

At once, the Mazapegul turned to her. She tightened her grip on the window's handle but didn't open it. Perfectly still, the Nocturnals hovered in midair, their eyes shimmering at the blood sun, staring into her.

Oriana shook from the heart. For six years she had longed to return into the Night. But though her hand quivered in anticipation, she couldn't turn the handle. And when at last she opened the window in one wide swing, the Mazapegul were gone. Twilight had ended, and all around, the rooftops of Lucerìa were tinged in the cobalt hues of the First Night.

TWENTY-THREE

On the day of the first trial, the piazza outside the smithy was packed.

A mob of nearly a hundred, mostly women and street urchins, swayed under a wind of chatter. It was smaller than the crowd that had gathered to hear the court's verdict, but more divided than ever. Shouts were tossed from both sides of the small piazza in favor of one twin or the other. Among the spectators, seated inside his gentleman's coach, was Villabianca, peering out from its window. Suddenly, the whispers heightened to a roar.

Bruno Bucci gave the signal. The first trial had begun.

Using a fuller, the twins were each to hammer three impressions onto an iron bar. The catch was that these impressions had to be evenly spaced, and of the right depth, so that other bars could be welded to them later to create a rack. After one understood the basics of drawing out, fullering was easy enough. The two apprentices lit the fire and pumped the bellows. Riano went first. He took the iron bar from the forge, placed it on the anvil sideways, and, with Bruno holding it in place, struck it thrice in rapid succession with the fuller. Then it was his sister's turn. Helped by one of the older smiths, she followed the same process, although, it could be noticed, with a slight hesitation. They repeated the same action, Oriana taking more time than her brother, until each bar bore three indentations. As the iron cooled, they started to chamfer the edges of the dents. And then it was over.

The mob pushed forward to peer inside as the three Guild members judged the results. They closely examined the depth of the indentations, their smoothness and precision, on Riano's bar and Oriana's. Then Peruzzi was taken aside by the jury to hear their verdict. Finally, he turned to both the apprentices and the crowd.

"By the power of this jury," he cried, "I'm pleased to announce that the winner of this first challenge is Riano Siliceo. The two contestants will meet again in three weeks."

Everyone stared at Oriana in dismay.

"That's because you all are men! And that's what men do, isn't it? Scorn women's work even when it's better than theirs!" a woman shouted.

It was Angia, her hair the color of her words.

Before she could continue, the crowd went berserk. As the air filled with the mocking chant of "Chestnut Riana," the shouting turned to fighting. Peasant girls pulled lazzari by their hair, the boys biting them like feral cats. Older women rushed to break them apart. Peruzzi grabbed Oriana by the shoulders and called out to get the count's attention.

"Villabianca, take her away, now!"

The count entered the smithy and took his disoriented pupil by the arm. They fielded their way through the crowd and had almost reached the coach when Rosetta, the basket-maker's daughter, stopped them.

"They've wronged you, signorina, haven't they? They've cheated you of your victory!"

"No, Rosetta. My brother's work was just better than mine."

She answered with a whisper, but her words, or rather their tone, quieted all the women around them. Villabianca dragged her inside the coach and, at once, the coachman set off.

"Treachery! How could we ever think they would play fairly! That they'd allow a girl to outperform a boy at what men are supposed to do best. Of course not!"

Villabianca's distress was evident in the flutter of his big, sweaty hands. Despite their proximity inside the coach, Oriana leaned away, her hands gripping her knees.

"No, Fernando. I meant what I said. Riano won because his work was better."

The count's head reeled backward.

"It can't be," he said. "You're hiding something from me. If only you trusted me . . ."

"I do trust you, Fernando, and I know you mean well, but there's really nothing more to be said. Yes, maybe the training we've received hasn't been entirely fair all along. But as you said, I knew it was going to be like this from the start."

"Then let's protest! Let's go to the court and—"

"And what good would that do? If I go to them now, do you think they would just grant me victory? The court only supported my challenge because they think I'll lose. To teach a lesson to me and to all the young women of this town. And I let them down, Fernando, I let everyone down."

"You are too harsh on yourself, dear."

"Maybe. But what choice do I have? I thought my passion would be enough to conquer all the obstacles I encountered, but I was wrong. I'm simply not strong enough."

They remained silent, the coach rattling over the cobblestones. It was almost dark, approaching that twilight hour when the sky outlines the silhouette of every rooftop. As she looked out through the coach's window, Oriana thought she saw something. Perhaps another Mazapegul had followed her from the smithy. But it was no Mazapegul. Her heart fluttered like a bird in a cage. A shadow had detached itself from a nearby chimney and was extending now into a vaguely human shape. As the coach turned left the shadow stepped forward and followed them from above, crossing along the rim of the rooftop. Oriana leaned out the window to have a better look. And right there, in stark contrast with the darkening sky, the shadow fluttered, then blazed, sparking like a starlit firmament. A cloak made of shimmering eyes.

Cetta entered Oriana's room and put her dinner tray on the desk, then crouched down by the fireplace to light it. It was the first week of October, and the nights were becoming chilly. When she finished with the fire, she turned to Oriana, still lying in bed.

"Do you need anything, signorina?"

Slowly, Oriana shook her head.

"Cetta," the girl asked, "is there any news from Father?"

"No, I am afraid not," she replied. She was about to leave when she paused by the door and faced her young mistress. "Signorina, if I may speak my mind . . ."

Oriana looked up. The old maid sat down on her bed, hands clasped. Her long, lined face quivered as it did every time she was upset.

"What I wanted to say, signorina, is that you were very brave, that day in the courtyard. And I'm sorry, for the oil and the fire."

"It wasn't you. Mother made you do it."

"Maybe. But I did it, not her. I just wanted to say that I am here for you. Both of you."

"You are kind," Oriana sighed, "and your words are most welcome. But there is nothing you can do. Thank you."

Cetta stood up, her hands clenched. Then she bowed and left. Oriana wondered if she had taken Cetta for granted, or worse, resented her for carrying out her mother's orders. As soon as she heard Cetta's footsteps fade, Oriana looked at her left palm. For years now, she had felt Scandar's presence, most often when she whispered into his invisible ear, but sometimes just before waking up, when she felt the touch of a gloved hand against her cheek. But never before tonight had she actually seen him.

"Scandar, I need to talk to you. Pray, come."

A gust of wind roared in the fireplace.

The girl looked around, but nothing happened.

She had spoken into her hand many times before but had expected a different result since she explicitly asked him to come to her. And so she waited for some miracle, but there was none. With a sigh, she reached under her pillow and took out the book Villabianca had given to her in the coach. Poor Fernando. Even his affection could not help her. Oriana opened the slim tome, a dissertation written by an English philosopher translated into French.

By the candlelight she read haltingly, "'Everything that is suitable to stir in us the ideas of danger, and acts similar to the most dreadful terror, is a source of the Sublime: the strongest emotion the human soul is capable of.'" Oriana read the words, but their meaning escaped her. It wasn't that she couldn't understand, but that she no longer cared.

Plack.

A gecko had fallen onto the page. The translucent lizard looked at her with tiny interrogative eyes. Oriana was about to brush it away, when she stopped, remembering something from a night many years ago.

"Is it you, Master Garaude?" she whispered.

TWENTY-FOUR

The left side of the gecko's body quivered and opened like a pair of lips.

"Aye, milady, it is."

His voice was like a dark, silky wine. Oriana's eyes filled with tears.

"I . . . I almost thought I'd made you up. Why so long?"

The lips in the gecko's side curved into a rueful smile. She had missed that too.

"It was not long for me," he said. "Our species swim in different timestreams. Yet I've never deserted you. Every night you talked to me, I listened."

"Then you know why I called you."

"I don't, I'm afraid. Unless it was to accept."

"Accept?"

"My master's offer. Are you ready to come to his forge and become his apprentice?"

Oriana remained silent for a long while, then said, "This was the reason he sent you today. To see if I had lost."

The gecko didn't reply. Oriana stared on indignantly at him.

"I will not accept his offer. I know it's a generous one, but I'm a creature of the Day."

"I see. Why did you call me, then?"

"They are breaking me, Master Garaude, like an iron bar that is too cool to be forged. Every blow I take I'm cracking inside. Soon my lessons with Bruno will start again. But I don't know if I can take them any longer. Everything I do is wrong, somehow. I—I don't know who I am anymore. I should have won, but I didn't."

"That's not surprising at all, milady. Don't you remember what happened at the market? Your mother bought a Moira. Whatever you do, in the end, will end up exactly as she desired."

"But surely Bruno's proposal wasn't her doing."

"Maybe so, but it doesn't matter."

"I don't understand."

"What was the consequence of Bruno's proposal?"

"I told him that I would never marry him!"

"But you'll lose your challenge because of that answer. And what will happen afterward? What will you do next?"

"I—I don't know."

"Think, milady, what is the only possible outcome?"

"I think I would let Villabianca help me and then—"

She stopped mid-sentence. There was no denying she was very fond of Villabianca. If she lost, if she didn't get to be first apprentice, in time, by degrees, the idea of marrying him would become acceptable. For eventually, without the smithy, it would be her only escape from Donna Lena. Oriana would marry the count, just as her mother wanted, and become Lady Villabianca. A dressed-up doll, all in green.

"That's how it is, then," she said in a hush. "My brother's victory, my friendship with Fernando, even my father's departure, it's all her doing. She'll be rich and respected and feared, just like she said she would."

This time, the gecko said nothing.

Oriana continued, "What about your master's Boon? He said he owed me one, didn't he? Could I ask him to destroy my mother's Moira?"

"That would kill her. Would you still ask that of him?"

"No, of course not. But what could I ask him for?"

"It's hard to say, milady. In the end my master is a living story. He does what stories do: he furthers events. Whatever you ask of him, it will inevitably produce more effects than you could possibly foresee."

"He is the patron of all smiths, isn't he? He could help me in my challenge!"

"That would be considered an apprenticeship, I'm afraid."

"Or he could kill Bruno, or blind him, or make him mad!"

For a time, the gecko didn't speak. Then he replied, "That he could do. But you must be very careful what you ask the Night, for in the end our desires shape us. If madness and death and pain is what you seek, madness, death, and pain you shall get. Remember when you wanted to use the Hammer to destroy the Dreamarquise?"

"And I did!" she said.

"Only in self-defense, and only after making sure it wouldn't hurt the dreamer. And it's not dreams we're talking about now."

"So what should I do? Yield? Is that what you suggest?"

"I am not suggesting anything. It's only that, knowing my master as I do, I would consider spending his Boon as the last possible resort."

"Well, then. Would you help me, Scandar of the Garaudi?"

The gecko quivered on the page.

"I can't, milady. I am my master's slave. I'm sorry."

"Still, you are here with me now. Did he not send you?"

"He sent me to the forge today. But answering your call is my initiative alone. Were he to know, he would annihilate me."

Oriana shuddered. With one hand she smoothened the creases on her bedspread.

"You once told me that a destiny denied is twice a destiny. How is it possible, then, that my mother can thwart me in everything all because she stole a destiny from a dream?"

"Dreams are powerful tools, milady. They are the fire in

which people forge their own souls, day by day. Or rather, Night by Night."

"Could I change this destiny in a dream? Years ago, you told me there are certain nights when Lucerìa dreams of itself, creating a dream-version of all its streets and houses. Of its smithies."

"What are you suggesting, milady?"

"I can't train with Bruno, for that's his domain, and there he can sabotage me as he sees fit. But what if . . . what if I find a dream-smithy, a dream-replica of my father's forge, and I train there by myself? I could take advantage of it every night till the next trial!"

"You could . . . if you find your way into and out of the dream-maze. You'll need a Nocturnal to guide you, someone with power over the Second Night."

"Won't you do it?"

"I cannot, milady, for my master's sister presides over the Second Night."

"You don't think Serapide would help me?"

"After you made a fool of her Dreamarquise and stole back the Hammer? I doubt it."

"What about the Dreamarquise himself? We were friends, once."

"Growler? He is lost in Lucerìa's Dream, milady."

"You said that he would wake up!"

"Under normal circumstances, he would have. But Serapide was so cross with him for losing the Hammer that when Growler did wake up, she trapped him in a nested dream. That's the rumor I heard in the Night at least."

Oriana pressed her lips in frustration and looked outside the gray window.

"I see. So, I have already lost my challenge," she said.

"You forget your talents, milady," the gecko replied encouragingly.

"My talents for what? Failure?"

"Do you know how many people in Foggia would have been able to see the artifacts hanging at the Duke's stall and recognize them for what they were? One in a million, perhaps. Even less could have identified the dream-tokens or the Deep Red Hammer."

"What are you getting at, Garaude?" she asked.

"If there is a Diurnal in Lucerìa who could find Growler within his nested dream, it would be you."

She paused to consider before continuing. "Why was Serapide mad at your master in the first place? No, wait, let me guess. The Emistuchivio stole from her, didn't he?"

"That's not how my master would see it."

"But that's how she sees it, isn't it? Which is why she in turn had his Hammer stolen. What was it, then? That the Duke stole from her, I mean."

"Serapide's relic. Although no one knows what it currently looks like."

"Shouldn't the Duke know?"

"The Duke himself is innocent of the theft. An old apprentice of his, millennia ago, stole Serapide's relic to please his master by transforming it into an object of power. Something to make people dream, possibly, though no one knows for sure."

"And the Duke . . . what did he do with the apprentice?"

"Nobody heard from him ever again."

Oriana gulped a cold lump.

"So the bad apprentice transformed the Countess's relic. Can you at least tell me what it was in the first place?" she asked the gecko. "Scandar? What's wrong?"

The lizard was shivering violently, his body pulsating.

"My master, he is inquiring about me. I'm sorry, I must go. Goodbye, milady."

The lips closed, dissolving into the body of the lizard as quickly as they appeared. The gecko flashed blue cobalt, then slowly faded to its original stone-gray hue. Oriana stared at it expectantly. But the gecko was just a gecko, and after a while, she had to let it go.

In the middle of a pleasant dream in which she was back in Calabria, her three sons waving at her across an orange-blossomed garden, Cetta woke up. Holding a flickering lamp, a dark figure loomed over her.

"Our Lady of Night," the maid shuddered under her blanket, "protect me."

"Cetta," whispered the dark shape, "it's me."

At once, the shadow transfigured into a girl of fourteen with badly cropped hair. Oriana turned to put her lantern on the commode.

"By the Dark Sun, miss," choked the widow, "you'll be the death of me!"

"I am so sorry, Ce', but this cannot wait. You said you wanted to help me."

"Yes, but—"

"What do you know of Serapide's relic? I need to know everything you can tell me about the Countess. I know that one shouldn't talk about Them, especially at Night, but no Teller has come to this house since we moved; Mother will not allow it, so it must be you, I'm afraid. Also, you've already asked for protection from Our Lady, so please, tell me."

"Well, Serapide's relic is her left hand. They say it's preserved in a glass case, but . . . signorina, are you sure this can't wait till morning?"

"It really can't!"

"Then I will tell you about her embalmed hand, as well as the Wind Wyrms, the Grinners, and the Lucucelli who guard it. But, if you really want to know more about the Countess, don't you think you should go to the festival?"

"Sorry, what festival?"

"Oh dear, this challenge of yours deprived you of the little sense you had! Signorina, we are just a few days from Serapide's fire festival. If it's her you want to know about, have you considered maybe attending it?"

TWENTY-FIVE

All of Lucerìa prepared for the great fire festival, Serapide's festa grande.

Their preparations began incubating at the end of August, when farmers started collecting bundles of firewood to light up.

A thousand years ago, the Visigoths reached Lucerìa, ready to invade its streets and douse them in blood. The people didn't have an army and braced themselves for the inevitable. But that night, in the Second Night, everyone in town dreamed of Serapide. In her realm the virgin-warrior showed them how to trick the Visigoth army into believing that Lucerìa was protected by an unsurpassable defense. The next day, they lit bonfires all around the perimeter, shrouding the whole town in smoke. Then, to make it seem like their soldiers carried spears, they dressed in pointed caps that, through the haze of the smoke, resembled pikes. Finally, they mounted on horseback and galloped in circles, their war cries accompanied by the deafening roar of drums. Intimidated by the shadows and the unprecedented tumult, the Visigoths fled in terror, believing they were facing an army of ghosts. A thousand years later, on the same night of that victory, the Lucerini celebrated its anniversary.

The ceremony began with the male firstborns of all the important families retrieving their horses from the stables. The Vernarecci, the Varo, the Mezzacasa, and the D'Avalos heirs shrouded themselves in bedsheets as a reminder of that salvific dream and wore the shiny, pointed caps of their ancestors. As the night claimed the land, the townsfolk lit their bonfires and started their procession to follow the statue of Saint Barbara, the Diurnal effigy of Serapide, protector against lightning and fire. When the procession ended, leaving the golden-crowned statue in front of Chiesa del Carmine, the drums began to play, their din building to a roaring pitch and a volley of gunfire—the blanketed riders' cue to start galloping toward Piazza Duomo. They circled it thrice while everyone converged on the square. On the completion of the riders' third round, every Lucerino who owned a rifle would fire it into the air, signaling the end to that part of the celebration. When the riders descended from their steaming horses, they were embraced by the cheering crowd. Now the feast could begin. For each rione had its banquet, each alleyway its festa, each household its dinner party. They would last until the church of Sant'Agata rang for the Hour of the Wolf, three hours past midnight.

Bewildered by the large pillars of smoke, the roaring toasts, and the sudden bursts of laughter, Oriana wandered wide-eyed through the great festa. The last time she attended the fire festival she was just a child and hadn't made it past the horse race. It had not been easy to sneak out of palazzo Nicastri without Donna Lena noticing, but her mother hated all Nocturnal festivals and went to bed early. Cetta's help and the palazzo's gatekeeper's complicity did the rest. It was the first time since the Secret Market that Oriana had been out for a nighttime stroll. After having been the topic of gossip for weeks, she wanted more than anything to walk unseen. But when she did just that, incognito in the nocturnal commotion, Oriana found she didn't like it. For her fear of failure had no other company but her own misery. And yet Oriana wasn't, in fact, alone.

With a handkerchief held to his nose, and a dog-headed cane in hand, Villabianca seemed even more out of place than his pupil. The count had been surprised when she suggested that they join the peasant revelry, but had not refused. She'd hoped that their going out together would help avoid scrutiny, and Villabianca had dutifully complied. Oriana felt guilty, for he had indulged all of her requests, and yet Serapide's festival posed specific dangers. They said that the Countess herself infused her festa with the subtle permutations of Dreams, making people feel intoxicated as if they were drunk on the Night. After becoming Night-touched, Oriana already saw visions in mirrors and was afraid of what else would happen at the festa. If things went awry, at least she could depend on Villabianca's support.

For a good two hours, they wandered among the open banquets, mingling with the crowd and snatching a tarallo or a cup of wine. But the banquets weren't just an excuse for drinking and merriment. After eating, the Lucerini would talk openly about their dreams, sometimes interpreting them. Oriana listened carefully to get an inkling of which nested dream Growler might be trapped in. After all, Serapide's own story was something of a nested dream too.

"There is an ancient Riddle," Cetta told her the other night, "that goes like this: *Is Serapide the Dreaming or the Dreamed?* Some Tellers say that Serapide was a virgin warrior from the Dauni, a shield-maiden with a preternatural gift for summoning storms, a warrior that didn't die in the battle defending her city but ascended to the heavens in the form of lightning. But there is also another tale, about a little girl who, bitten by tzetse flies, contracted the sleeping sickness. They say that because she spent her entire life dreaming, the Night granted her the power to make her dreams real, and in them the girl was a mighty virgin warrior. Some Tellers say that she dreamed about the Dauni she-warrior because she had heard her story at the Vigils. But others contest that this is not how the Night works at all. They say that, in fact, the original Dauni warrior was first born in the little girl's dreams. And yet without the stories of the Dauni, the girl would never have dreamed of the warrior. So, is Serapide the Dreamed or the Dreaming?"

Oriana moved from table to table, catching snippets of dream-tales. A cluster of matrons were listening to Teresa. The basket-maker was recounting how she had dreamed that her house had transformed into a gigantic ear. She could not find her way out! Next to her a farmer smoking a clay pipe puffed out the tale of how his brother became a swarm of emerald bees. He needed a butterfly net to catch all the buzzing of him. Three chairs away a peddler from Foggia made everyone crack up by telling them how a tiny cactus chased him around, trying to bite his balls. Only by hitting him with his hammer was he able to squash the bastard into a pulp.

Oriana noticed something odd about these dream-tellers. The basket-maker, as she spoke, released a maze-like thread of smoke from her ears. Next to her the farmer's shadow trembled, fracturing into hundreds of buzzing dots. As for the peddler, while he guffawed, he spat up a tiny cactus flower. Oriana looked around. No one had seemed to notice.

"Fernando," Oriana murmured to her left, "did you see that?"

She turned. Villabianca was ten steps behind her, resting his hand against a brick wall, white as wax. When she paced up to him, the count raised his handkerchiefed hand.

"I am mostly all right, my dear. It's just—"

The nobleman turned to the wall and gagged.

His disgorging was followed by a spewing of dark matter. Oriana's eyes widened. Her tutor was throwing up shadows in the shape of hounds. They sprinted across the wall as if the invisible dogs projecting them were being chased away. In a wink, they were gone.

"Oh my," the count said, his kerchief pressed to his lips, "how inexcusable that you had to witness, well, *that*."

"Fernando, per favore," she pleaded, "don't act as if you hurt my delicate woman sensibilities, for I haven't got any."

Her tutor humphed. "Thank the Lord at least I didn't spew anything."

"You . . . didn't?" Oriana shuddered, staring at the wall.

"What is it? Oh dear, are you going to be sick too?"

"No, but . . . Fernando, have you recently been dreaming of dogs?"

Villabianca, who was approaching her with a slight limp, halted. A shade of vexation eclipsed the full moon of his face.

"Mamma Emma told you, didn't she? Oh, she'll hear about this! I told her not to mention it. As if you didn't have enough on your plate."

"What in the name of the Madonna of Montevergine are you blabbering about?"

"Well, she must have told you about Reno. How else would you have guessed what I have been dreaming about?"

"What about Reno?" asked Oriana, but already she could see pain sparking in Villabianca's gray eyes. "Oh, Fernando, I am so, so sorry."

She put a hand on his arm.

"He lived a good life," he said, lifting his chin.

Under the bravado, though, she sensed his agony. For Reno was the last living reminder of the family Villabianca once had. However, the count had still found it in him to come with her, exposing himself to the intoxication of the Night. A wave of affection washed over Oriana. She froze. She could feel her mother's Moira working its way into her. It took all her self-control not to jerk her hand away.

"Why didn't you tell me?" she asked.

"With all that you are going through? It didn't seem fair. And anyway—"

The count halted, turning toward the sound. It was one Oriana knew all too well: Riano's laughter. Leaving Villabianca behind, she followed its trail like a fiery thread; and there he was. A flock of boys shrouded in blankets listened to him intently—Lucerìa's scions of true nobility, judging from the crests on their pointed caps. Was Riano recounting a dream about his recent triumph? No, she decided, a dream about his future victory. Then, a puff of black smoke escaped Riano's lips. It wasn't quite smoke, more like black snowflakes. Drowsily they wafted in the nocturnal breeze.

Oriana snapped her hand up and caught one. A dandelion's seed. Black as sin, it dissolved in her hand as if it really were made of snow. A dandelion made of dark dream-matter—Riano must have dreamt of the Farmacia della Pioggia.

"Sister?"

Her twin was staring at her with an intensity that was two parts anger and one part shame. Stop embarrassing me in front of my noble friends, his eyes warned. She said nothing in return but took Villabianca's arm.

"Gentlemen," she curtseyed to the blanketed boys.

As the duo walked away, Oriana thought about how they must have looked to them. A prospective husband and wife strolling together. Stronger than ever, she felt Donna Lena's Moira like a vice, inescapable unless she could gain access to a dream-forge of her own.

She looked up. The dark dandelion seeds still waltzed in the air. There weren't just a couple, but a whole flood of them. And they moved not directionless, but as if coasting along an invisible current. At once, she let go of Villabianca's arm and ran in pursuit.

Oriana couldn't name any specific reason why these seeds might show her the way to Growler, but this wasn't the Day, this was the Night, where intuition, not reason, reigned supreme. Her face pointing upward, she pursued the seeds until she turned onto a narrow alley.

On its walls grew hundreds of dark dandelion stems, black as charred bone. A secret wind blew their heads in the same direction, toward an old shop whose decades of neglect had not yet completely erased its hand-painted sign.

FARMACIA DELLA PIOGGIA

Oriana's fingers touched the peeling paint of the shop's sign.

It depicted a pestle and a mortar, their lacquered colors cracked by time. As for its windows and front door, they were nailed shut by wooden planks. By the look of it the pharmacy had been closed since before she was born. Oriana had never heard anyone mention that the farmacia was still standing. Also, she must have passed by this alley a thousand times, and yet never noticed it. Night-touched. It didn't happen just to people, but to places too. She could not think of a better location to hide a nested dream.

A scurry of steps marked Villabianca's arrival. He was losing his momentum by degrees, his sweaty mass slowing down to a heaving stop. Oblivious to the broth of dark seeds all around him, the nobleman exhaled in one incredulous sigh.

"My dear," he wheezed, "what in the name of sweet Jesus are you doing?"

"Fernando," she replied, "you can either help me get inside, or you can ask me why I must. But know that whatever answer I give you will leave you dissatisfied. So, do not ask."

Villabianca stood silently in place. Then he flashed her a crooked smile.

"Move aside, dear," he said.

Oriana stood aside as Villabianca grabbed his walking cane and wedged its dog head against the plank, unbolting it in a few strong pulls.

"I am an archivist." He smirked. "Do you know how many

crates of documents we have opened this way? Lots, dear, an awful lot."

Again, affection rose in her like a warm wave. She stifled it with a tightening of her jaw and joined him in loosening the wooden planks. Little by little they freed the main door, a stained glass beauty, opaque with grime. Inside it was pitch black. Oriana's neck stiffened.

"Did you hear that?" she said.

"Hear what?"

But his face was tense, betraying that he had heard it too—a rushing sound like one might hear in the deepest jungles of the Americas. Its rainy reverberation bathed her in disquiet. On the other side of the door was Lucerìa's Dream.

"Stay here," she said. "I'll be quick."

"But it's black as coal inside!"

She reached inside her bodice and retrieved the stub of a candle. In six strides she reached a bonfire at the street corner, crouched down to its embers, and lit the wick. She stood up with a smile.

"Here," she said, cupping the flame. "See you in a jiffy."

Without waiting for his reply, she opened the door and walked in.

The mixed aroma of dust, resins, and spices was intoxicating. At first, the flame in her hand only illuminated a faint shimmer from the apothecary vases. Slowly, she made out the rest of the room. Under vaulted ceilings, between wall-to-wall frescoes, was a hall twelve steps wide. At its end, bracketed by two gilded lamps, gleamed a mahogany counter.

The apothecary vases she'd first spotted glistened in the cabinetry's niches just behind it. The rest of the room was a carnival of bronze statues, scales, mortars, mechanical music boxes, glass-stoppered decanters, and potions. Oriana marveled at violet soaps that smelled of Provençal gardens, at candles whiter than Carrara marble, and incense burners in the shape of sphinxes.

And yet nothing felt like it had at the Secret Market. Maybe Scandar was wrong, and she had simply lost her talent. She looked at her palm, wondering if she should call out to him, when she noticed that the sound of incessant rain had ceased. Even so there was still plenty of rain in the shop. Oriana raised her candle. The frescoed walls all depicted Serapide.

The first showcased an approaching storm in the way of Giorgione's *The Tempest*. Only, hidden by the vapors of the storm, loomed an armor-clad giant of a woman, her eyes crying lightning. The second fresco portrayed a large herbarium perfectly in theme with the pharmacy. But on its corner, under a giant fern, lay a bedridden girl. Pale, she looked asleep, her left hand black. Oriana peered closer. It wasn't gangrene, for the blackness was made up of many dots. Her hand was covered in flies. But the third wall drew Oriana's attention like a magnet. It was painted like a cabinet of curiosities. Inside its niches were seashells, glinting gemstones, papier-mâché tribal masks, taxidermized reptiles, fossils, and a mechanical device shaped like a human head. Then she spotted what she'd come here for—a preserved human hand in a portable showcase. Rather small, it must have belonged to a woman. Or a girl.

"Serapide's hand," Oriana murmured.

She could still hear Cetta's voice telling her that every Major One, like the saints of the Day, had a relic. For the Baron of Twilight, it was his left eye. For the Marquise of Fullmoon, his dentures, a thing of nightmares. Even the Grim King was said to have one—his dark, flaming heart. Holding the candle overhead, Oriana approached the fresco. The hand in the showcase was more bone than flesh, and yet one bone was missing, the upper phalanx of the ring finger. Oriana sucked in a sharp breath. It had to be the door to Lucerìa's

Dream! With quivering fingertips, she touched the empty space where the missing bone should be. Nothing happened. She frowned. Was she doing it wrong? Maybe to enter the Dream she had to walk through the wall itself. It seemed solid enough, but she backed up a few steps and then walked straight into it. She yelped and staggered back, crashing into something on the desk behind her, the candle slipping from her fingers. In the newfound darkness she felt dumber than ever. Cautiously, she crawled on all fours, groping for her candle. Instead, her hand brushed a box that tinkled with her touch. A music box. A dim memory reemerged of Gobbo's hands.

"You all—all right?" asked a voice.

She squeaked and turned toward the doorway.

"Fernando, I told you to wait outside!"

"Well, I heard you screaming."

"I wasn't screaming," she protested, but was interrupted by the far echo of a church bell.

They both turned to the alley. A distant clamor rose like a collective cheer. Although Oriana had never been up this late, the voices could mean only one thing—the church rang in the Hour of the Wolf, three hours past midnight. The festival had ended. Soon the alleys would fill with the revelers on their way home. Oriana turned to the fresco, desperate to uncover what she had missed. Not that it mattered now.

"Oriana?"

"I know," she said, and walked past him into the smoky street.

On her way home they scarcely said a word. Three blocks away from palazzo Nicastri, it began to pour. In a few dozen steps they were soaked. Donna Marisa, the gatekeeper, opened the palazzo's double door and motioned them inside.

"Come on up," said Villabianca as they took off their cloaks, his face dripping. "Mamma Emma will help you change; you can't go home in this state."

Oriana considered his offer. It was true that she didn't want to wake Cetta again. Worse yet, she might rouse her mother too.

"Won't Mamma Emma be asleep?" she asked.

"She is often sleepless because of that water leak. Come."

They trudged up the count's staircase only to discover that the nurse's door was firmly shut, the fire in the kitchen extinguished. Cetta was asleep.

"Must be the rain," apologized Villabianca. "It lulls her to sleep. Go to the library and remove those soggy clothes. I'll bring you dry ones from Cetta's room."

Oriana climbed the last flight of stairs with a lit candelabra, the steps creaking under her muddy shoes. As she entered the library, her candles lit the two-tier mahogany bookcases. Dispirited, the girl stared at the books. What good did it do to have read them? Drowsily, Oriana removed her blouse. Swift slants of rain lashed at the gable's window. She ventured a glance outside, her blouse pressed to her chest. The rooftops of Luceria gleamed under the nacreous eye of a half-moon, unperturbed by rain. There wasn't a cloud in the sky. So how could she hear the storm's claws scratching on the glass?

"Here."

She turned. The candelabra's light made Villabianca's shadow look vast. She could not see his eyes. He placed the folded clothes on the desk.

"I didn't hear you come in," she muttered, then, turning to the window, remarked, "Fernando, look outside. The sky is clear. And yet listen! Thunder. Do you think it's the Countess's doing? And if so, why only here at palazzo Nicastri?"

He said nothing.

"Well?" She frowned. "Cat got your tongue?"

When he still didn't reply, Oriana stepped back.

"Fernando? You are beginning to scare me."

"Finally," he said. His shape moved closer.

"W-what did you say?"

"Are you afraid of me, my dear? Afraid that I will take what is rightfully mine."

Her cheeks blazed. In the semi-darkness she was painfully aware of her naked arms, her chest covered only by the wet blouse pressed against it.

"You n-never spoke to me like this. This is not you."

"Not pompous, harmless Villabianca, the fat fool? Suppose for a moment that it was a ruse, a part I needed you and all the Lucerini, Donna Lena included, to believe."

Oriana felt her face burn like it was made of paper.

"B-but why would you—"

"So that you would give me your trust. And sign our wedding contract. That's why I pretended to care about your challenge, but I am so goddamn tired of pretending. I have been indulging you all night, dear, chasing after you like some loyal dog, and I have not even heard a word of thanks in return. And oh, the face you made, Oriana, when someone saw us together. I wished I had a mirror so I could show you. You looked like a thief caught red-handed, such was your shame."

Oriana felt tiny shards of glass in the walls of her heart.

"But now you are under my roof," he added.

She could not articulate a sound. Her terror was palpable, like a cold, dead hand pressed against her bare chest. In one silky stride he closed the distance between them. But though her ears strained, his steps made no sound.

"This is not you, Fernando," she said.

"You said that already," he hissed as he stepped forward.

"No, I mean it. You are not him!"

The shadow stopped. His teeth gleamed in the candlelight.

"I see it all now. I hear the storm outside, yet I can't see it. The staircase always creaks, but I didn't hear you come in. And no wonder! Because we are not really in the count's library right now. Hell, we are not even in Lucerìa. This is a Dream! And you must be one of Serapide's watchdogs. What are you? An Entinazu? A Grinner? A Lucucello?"

As she pressed forward, the man stepped back.

"You have gone mad," he said.

"On the contrary. Answer me this: Can I see your face?"

The man became a piece of petrified darkness. Oriana laughed.

"Ah, a Lucucello, then! A fierce creature, I have been told, a dream-doppelganger. You were good; you gave me quite the startle. But I asked you the Question, so now you are at my mercy. If I see your face, you will die, and yet you can't refuse. So, ask me."

The shadow rippled like a pool of ink.

"Ask you?"

"For mercy," Oriana replied, unflinching.

The black silhouette murmured something.

"I didn't hear you," she said.

"Please," cried the creature. "Mercy!"

Oriana smiled thinly, swooped the candelabra off the table, and shoved it in the creature's face. It had none, but she saw two eye bulbs and a set of candid teeth suspended in his black vacuum. The Lucucello shrieked, its scream turning its body into a gust of red-hot ashes. Oriana stomped them with her shoe.

"That's for making me doubt Fernando, even for a minute."

She looked at the dispersing ashes and shuddered at the thought of spending an entire dreamlife with a nightmarish husband. How easy it was to become trapped within a Dream. Scandar warned her, years ago.

Finally, Oriana righted herself. She was closer to Growler's prison now that she'd entered a Dream, most likely through the pharmacy.

She stared at the gable's window. What if Mamma Emma had been hearing not a persistent leak but Serapide's Dream storm all this time? Of course. Growler's nested dream had always been there, in her own house, a few steps beyond the wall of sleep.

With a flick of her hand, Oriana unlatched the window.

TWENTY-SIX

Without transition, she was outside.

On the rooftop incessant needles of water pitter-pattered against the red clay tiles. The downpour created a barrier of sound her steps could not penetrate. Under the raging storm Oriana saw the rooftops of Lucerìa as they could never be in the Day—not low, shingled roofs but mountainous towers, tall chimneys, turrets, and far in the distance, between the booming bolts and the zigzag irradiations, a buttress raised like a horizontal spine hiding a half-moon. She was in one of Lucerìa's Dreams, this she knew already. But how she would find her cat and release him, she had no idea.

"Growler," she called, but she could not hear the sound of her own voice.

Squinting her eyes, she advanced tenaciously, the winds galloping past her. She heard a moan between the chimneys, like the note the wind makes when it squeezes through a crack in the window. Oriana jumped to a new roof, slid a few feet, and caught her balance. Another rumble above her head. And again, that moan. She opened her eyes wide and looked up. The storm held captives in its belly. Faces, claws, limbs, and wings danced in and out of her view among the chimneys' silhouettes until, at last, the wind disclosed its exquisite horror.

At first, she thought she was seeing some sort of battlefield banner with inlaid figures. Only, this was no two-dimensional piece of cloth, but a festoon of sleeping bodies intertwined limb by limb, human and animal. She spotted a naked maiden with milk-white skin and red hair, her bent knees braided together with a swan's neck, its pearly wings embracing a small slumbering child like a blanket. A sleeping donkey bit that same child's hair, and the beast itself was ridden by a fat matron with a boa constrictor wrapped around her neck. It went on and on. The limbs and heads were oddly misshapen, as if their pliant, waxlike bodies had been stretched and compressed to fit inside a transparent tube. And though they were all asleep, their mouths were agape, giving off an eerie moan as if they were trying to wake themselves up but couldn't. These were the dreamers who had run afoul of Serapide.

And then, after it seemed it could not get any worse, the festoon of bodies coiled around a crooked chimney and *stared* at her. This was no typhoon, but a creature. Its face was made up of the misshapen arms of the dreamers—two closed fists for its eyes, three dozen fingers for its teeth, a child's palm for its tongue. Its claws, grasping the edges of the chimney, were the hands and talons of the creatures it had trapped.

"A Wind Wyrm," Oriana exhaled.

The creature contracted its fist-eyes.

"You are trespassing," it said, its voice modulating the dreamers' moan.

"I am here," she said, stifling the tremor of her lips, "to bring back the old Dreamarquise of Lucerìa, a cat named Growler."

The Wyrm's head tilted, its finger-teeth twitching.

"He is in my custody," it said.

"I will gladly have him back, if you please."

The creature tilted its arm-jaw.

"My Lady wants him here, and I only oblige her."

It half turned, the sleepers' hands spasming and pointing toward the great tower.

Oriana looked past the Wyrm to the black spire. The intermittent fulminations ignited the black clouds surrounding the tower, punctuating a titanic shape. Immense, half-charred by fire, her profile was still hauntingly beautiful. Long lunar hair to her shoulder, the Countess donned a full armored breastplate, her metal chest shimmering in the flash of purple light. A potter-maker in front of her wheel, Serapide's hands were shaping the black spire like clay. Utterly ignoring her, the Countess went on molding the spire and her Dream with it. The Wyrm's face turned back to her, the dreamers' hands reassembling into a grin.

"My Lady will be glad that her faithful servant devoured an agent of the Thief who stole from her."

"The Thief . . . You mean the Duke? I am not the Duke's agent!"

"That may well be your last lie before joining the others in their eternal symphony."

"S-symphony?"

"My Lady loves the music made by the children of the Night," said the hands-face.

Music! Suddenly, a memory from long ago, of a tent and the Duke inside it, came to her. She pressed her lips. At last, she had something.

"If I was trapped in your belly, your Lady would never be able to recover what was stolen from her."

The Wyrm's finger-teeth opened and closed, eager.

"You claim to know where her relic is?" the voices moaned.

"I don't claim. I know where her stolen finger bone is. Or rather, *what* it is."

She could feel the Wyrm's urgency in the Sleepers' bodies, tossing and turning in a collective throb. The creature wanted to swallow her, badly, but it didn't dare. Yet.

"Tell me, then," it demanded.

"And have you devour me a breath later? I should think not. You will let Growler go, and *then* I will tell you."

The creature hunched over the chimney like it was ready to lunge at her. Oriana imagined the arms of its mouth reaching for her, dragging her inside where she would sleep with the others in an eons-long nightmare.

Something was happening inside the Wyrm. The tangle of dreamers spasmed, restless in the black satin of Night. Hand and claw and wing passed forward a wet bundle of fur. Then the dragon's body retched, its face opening like a fleshy flower, and spewed a brown mop. Oriana lunged forward, trying to catch the wheezing bundle. Instead, a yowling comet descended down on her, sinking his claws into her shoulders. Oriana tried to swat the cat away, then stopped. She simply went limp, staring straight into Growler's one-eyed fury. Finally, the cat's bellowing turned into a low growl.

"I am sorry," she said, and hugged him tight. "I really am."

The cat sank his claws deeper into her shoulders, but she didn't try to break free, his howling taking on a morose quality.

"Tell us," the voices entreated. "Where is our Lady's relic?"

Oriana looked up. The creature's patience was wearing thin. Rearing like a cobra, the Wyrm was about to strike, this time for real. Yet she didn't dare to tell him. For what was stopping the Wyrm from eating her afterward? The bundle in her arms boxed her ears with both claws. Oriana gasped, and did the only thing she possibly could.

She woke up.

In the alley the rain was crushing down like a hammer of sound. Oriana's body was numb from the cold. Behind her a scurry of steps marked Villabianca's arrival. He was losing his momentum by degrees, his sweaty mass slowing down to a heaving stop. The nobleman exhaled in one incredulous sigh.

"My dear," he wheezed, "what in the name of sweet Jesus are you doing?"

Oriana turned to face the farmacia. The rain splashed against the planks that nailed the door shut.

"Oriana? What is this?" Villabianca asked again.

The count was drenched to the bone but still tried to shield her under his cloak. Guilt overflowed from her as she thought about how she had doubted him.

"Sorry," she said, "I wanted to see the Farmacia della Pioggia for myself."

"No," said Villabianca, pointing, "I meant *that*."

She looked down at her chest. Clinging to her drenched bodice, the old cat bellowed like a trumpet from Purgatory.

"Oh," she said. "Well, the poor thing was drowning in a puddle. I couldn't just leave him, could I?"

"Did it . . . he hurt you?"

With her free hand Oriana touched her ear lobe. She could feel the warmth trickling down it. The cat's rage had drawn blood, even outside the dream.

"Well, he was scared. He needs a roof over his head."

"I see." The count frowned. "Are you planning on keeping him, then?"

She looked at him. She couldn't risk Donna Lena recognizing her old cat. After all, he was the one who had brought her to the Secret Market.

"Fernando," she finally said, "I know no foundling feline could ever fill the vacuum Reno left in your heart, but . . . could I ask you one more favor?"

TWENTY-SEVEN

In palazzo Nicastri night was a river.
It flowed down in quiet rivulets from Villabianca's staircase, streamed through the porticos, and pooled in the main yard. A dark, feline silhouette floated in that inky quiet. Soundlessly, it climbed down the steps from the count's quarters, sailed through the courtyard, then swam upstream to the Siliceos on the second floor. In front of their double door, the silhouette sat. Only its tail, a flexuous metronome, gave away its impatience.

As if in response to some unheard cue, the cat scurried to a small window overlooking the landing. He jumped inside the kitchen and ignored the shawled figure snoring by the fireplace, continuing down the hallway. The cat passed a succession of rooms before stopping in front of a hand-painted door.

He slid through its open slit and went straight for the bed. As soon as his paws landed on the quilt, Oriana shuddered awake and raised her head.

"Growler?" she mumbled. "Is that you?"

The cat stopped, its tail flailing silently. Rubbing her face, Oriana sat up. Growler flapped his tail disdainfully against her nose and jumped off the bed.

"Wait!"

Oriana threw off her covers and gave chase.

Outside, the corridor's only light was the green lamp in front of the Madonna. The cat skipped past it, Oriana scuttling barefoot right behind him.

"Please," she hissed at the sprinting shadow, "wait!"

She had followed Growler right into the drawing room. Between the card game table and the patterned Genoese fabrics was a cat the size of a bear. Taller than palazzo Nicastri's gate, he sat in perfect stillness, his tail quiet at last, his one eye shimmering in moonshine. Oriana exhaled a mixture of fear and relief.

"This is a dream, isn't it? You came to me in your sleep. So, speak up!"

At once, Oriana was down on the carpet, Growler's huge paws holding her in place, his muzzle pressed against her face, reeking of chicken livers.

Did you really think it would be enough, to ask forgiveness once.

"No," she said, choked by his weight, "but how many times do I have to ask for it? I did when I freed you and in Fernando's library and now—"

You handed me to Lady Serapide for six years of torture!

"Because you wanted to split her Dream and let it spill into the Day! Do you really think she would have just let you? And had you succeeded, don't you reckon Serapide would have punished you with a lot worse than six years in her purgatory?"

Still, it was you who—

"You let my mother follow you to the Secret Market of the Dead! She sold her bloody soul because of you!"

The cat's head backed away.

That was unintended.

"Even so, without you, I wouldn't be in this predicament. My mother would still be my mother, and I would not have to find a dream-forge to stop her. Now, take your claws off me!"

Slowly, the cat retreated. Sitting under the moonlight, head tilted, he looked at her expectantly. Standing up, Oriana smoothed her nightgown.

"Now that we've established that we both mucked each other up, are we good?"

The cat licked his left paw.

"There is something I have to ask of you," she finally said.

The cat stopped and stared down at her.

Of course. How naïve of me to think you just saved me because it was the right thing to do. No, you needed a favor from the Dreamarquise.

"Listen," she said, frowning, "if there was anyone, anyone at all I could ask for help, I would, but there isn't. And they are killing me. Just today Bruno . . . you remember Bruno, well, he is the head of my father's forge now and he threatened me in such a way—"

You are just making useless human noise. Why should I care?

"Because we were friends once. Yes, you and I were friends. Before I even knew who you were and what your dreaming had done to my mother."

The giant cat stared at her for a long while. Emboldened, she stepped forward.

"I need someone to bring me to a dream-forge, a dream-version of ours, so that I can resume my training without Bruno harassing me."

His eye gleaming, the bear-cat resumed licking his fur.

Even assuming that I help you, and I haven't conceded just yet, how do you think we will get past Serapide? As soon as I enter her Dream, she will unleash her Wyrm.

"She won't, because you will tell her where her stolen relic is."

The cat stopped licking, tilted his head.

You know where her finger bone is?

"I do. Serapide's finger bone has been transformed into the tiny dancer of a carillon, a music box I saw in the Duke's realm years ago. From what he's told me, the Emistuchivio himself is innocent of its theft."

I wouldn't be so sure; he is quite a treacherous one.

"Anyhow, you will enter Serapide's good graces once again. You see?"

It still won't be a stroll in the park. Lucerìa's Dream is a deadly maze. One wrong step and we could end up lost forever. Also, you will have to wait until the Day of the Dead.

"That's in three weeks." Oriana frowned. "It's way too far away. I won't have enough time to train for the next challenge."

Moreover, there are nearly infinite dream-replicas of Mastro Peppo's smithy. Most of them, I'm afraid, might be lethal.

"Why lethal?"

Because a building doesn't dream like a human, and cares little for human comfort. We'll find smithies full of blood instead of air, or built upside down, or with doors made of liquid fire. And though there might just be one or two smithies that are habitable, and maybe even one that is similar enough to yours, the problem will be finding it.

The girl stared blankly at the carpet's red-and-blue pattern.

"What if," she said at last, "I bring something with us from the real forge. Cetta says that in some folk rituals, people find someone missing by using a lock of that person's hair. I'd guess that you can do the same with a place."

The cat looked sideways at her, his one eye gleaming in the moonlight.

Interesting. To use an object of the Day to act as a dream-compass. That might work. But it would have to be the right kind of something, or it could lead straight to our death.

"Leave me to it. It seems I'm rather good at appraising items for their hidden value."

Growler resumed grooming his fur once again.

Even with a compass, we will be traversing Lucerìa's

Dream at the most unstable of times. Serapide's foulest creature will be on the prowl.

"Ah! You've said 'we' twice now. So, we're doing it! But wait, didn't you say it was impossible to enter Lucerìa's Dream if not on certain nights?"

I never said it was impossible. I said you would have to wait until the Day of the Dead.

"While you don't?"

I am a cat. I go wherever it pleases me, whenever I like. As for you, the town's dreaming and wakeful states are not black and white. Lucerìa begins to dream little by little. Even now, outside this dream-room, you could find parts of Lucerìa's Dream double. Its roads would be brittle like ice in spring and just as dangerous. Only a skilled dream-cat like me could tread on it and, even then, with some risk.

Oriana reached for his massive whiskers. The bear-cat stopped licking and opened his eye wide. When the girl started stroking his fur he didn't move. Instead, a soft humming sound reverberated throughout the room.

"Growler," she asked, "would it please you to be my dream-guide?"

TWENTY-EIGHT

For the next challenge of the trial, the Siliceo siblings had to build a forked fire poker for use in the home. It was simple enough, since they could use an iron bar without having to change its mass. But first they had to learn two new techniques, bending and cutting, using the pickup tong and the rodded chisel, both needed to split a flat iron surface in two. Just as during the first challenge, Riano got to practice on the anvil with these tools while his sister toiled around the workshop. Oriana wasn't even allowed to touch a chisel, but she watched attentively.

It was almost the end of their morning shift. Oriana sat by the tool table, pretending to sweep wooden shavings to the floor while secretly inspecting the forge to find her target. Stealing an object from the smithy under Bruno's malevolent scrutiny was worse than difficult, it was bloody dangerous. Even if her idea of using it as a compass in the Night worked, there was always the chance that, if Bruno found her out, he would bring her in front of the committee. They might consider her trial null, or even charge her with a criminal record. To be found out a thief would mean to let down all the women of Luceria, publicly. Oriana would rather die than allow that to happen. She could not fail.

To act as a compass in the Night, the object had to be a symbol of the smithy itself. Something small enough to be easily hidden, something important, but not so much so that its absence would be noticed. She considered a piece of coal, a chisel, some scrap metal, and a small hammer. However, all these objects could be found in any other smithy. Meanwhile, as she deliberated her choice and dusted the chimney, Bruno studied her. All morning he had been uncharacteristically quiet, keeping to his side of the forge. However, every time Oriana turned her back to him, she felt his eyes on her.

Riano was making big progress on his bending technique, curling an iron bar all on his own. Caught up in the joy of his success, he barely noticed the mounting tension between his sister and their master. When Bruno offered that Riano accompany him on an errand to the Dogana, leaving his sister behind in the smithy, the boy took it as a well-earned reward. Not that Oriana much minded, as it was the perfect opportunity to plunder her own prize.

Finally alone, she listened to the sound of Bruno's cart growing fainter in the distance. Then, with two bold strides she made for the tools' desk, where Bruno kept the forge's key ring. There were three copies of the keys, one belonging to her father, one to Bruno, and the spare. It was the easiest item to displace. She could use it in her dreams and bring it back before anyone noticed. She opened the drawer, pocketed the key ring, closed it, and picked up her broom.

When she looked up, Bruno was standing three steps away, the forge's door ajar behind him. His face brimmed with vindictive joy.

"I knew you were up to something," he said, smiling.

Before she could turn away, Bruno grabbed her.

"Don't you touch me!" she shrieked.

Bruno relented, his face tilted toward the open door.

"Give it to me, then," he said quietly, "and no one will get hurt."

"You wouldn't dare."

"You are quite right, I wouldn't. If you were daft enough

to pit your brother against me, I think he would trust your tale of violence before he would believe my story of theft. But then again, I am not sure the committee would be so gullible. What's it going to be, Oriana?"

Waves of fear set fire to her cheeks.

At last, she took out the keys and placed them in his hand.

"Good girl. Now, do you care to explain yourself?"

"I don't owe you an explanation."

"Oh, I beg to differ. You tried to steal property of the smithy while in training. This is a serious crime, one that could have you booted instantly from your apprenticeship. Talk."

"I—" she began, realizing that the only option was to tell the truth. "If you must know, I wanted to resume my training on my own, at Night."

Bruno was looking at her like she was made of glass. He sat on a stool.

"Am I to believe this load of steaming crap?" he asked.

"I am not lying! Since you don't seem to care whether I receive any training, I wanted to take things into my own hands, that's all."

"And come here on your own, at Night."

"Yes. I am not afraid of Them!"

She had told him the plain truth twice now, and she could see he was struggling to disbelieve her. But Oriana had been smeared by the colors of the Night, and the smith felt it.

"Very well," he said, standing up and walking to the tool's desk, "we'll see what the committee thinks of all this."

"But you said you wouldn't tell them!"

"Never said such a thing," he said, putting the keys back in the drawer.

"You . . . They'll kick me out of the challenge of peers."

"Quite certainly. I told you I would break you, didn't I?"

"And yet you didn't," she said, her rage flaring up, "for if you had, you wouldn't need the committee to back you up! And what if an inquiry is made, what if Riano testifies that you were harassing me? He did see me with a burned hand more than once."

"That was your doing, not mine."

"What if I convince him that it was yours."

Bruno's face was taut like the skin of a drum.

"Riano," he said quietly, "won't act against his own interests."

"But he is not the brightest, is he? And he is unpredictable and stubborn like a mule. Like *me*. Also, he is my father's only son. If I am able to convince Riano, what if Mastro Peppo listens to him and not to you? What would you do then, Bruno Bucci?"

Fear and fury took turns in Bruno's eyes. He closed the distance in two steps, pulling her hard by the arm.

"You think," he spat, his breath reeking of cheap wine, "you had it rough these past days? That was just the prelude, Oriana. From now on you will get *all* your tasks wrong, and you know what? That thick brother of yours will see it and think he is a genius, and you are a dimwit. He is already well on his way to believing that. You see, I won't just crush you, I will ruin him too. So that when he really becomes a smith, he'll be as incompetent as he is unintelligent."

Oriana shook like a child. All rational thought had been incinerated by Bruno's grip. She opened her mouth to speak, but nothing came out. The smith pulled her toward him in a yank and then shoved her away. She stumbled forward.

"Oriana Siliceo, you are dismissed."

Blind with panic, she grabbed her shawl and scampered outside.

With every step that pulled her away from the smithy, the tangle of her terror unraveled, her mind's clarity returning. Would Bruno tell the committee? Probably not. Would he make it impossible to steal even a nail? Most certainly so. Or worse, he could catch her in the act, this time with Riano as his witness, and all that it entailed. No, she could not risk taking anything else from the smithy, ever. Tears of rage cut her cheeks. Mostly she was angry at herself. A touch of Bruno's hand, and her mind had dissolved. He could have done anything to her and she wouldn't have raised a finger. The only deterrent that had worked against him was the threat of other men. She shuddered. Where was Riano when she needed him? Her eyes widened. There he was, standing in an alley by the Dogana. Her step froze. He wasn't alone.

Half-hidden by the smithy's cart was a girl her age, her face close to his. She walked straight toward them.

"Is that how you run Bruno's errands?!"

"Oriana," he said stepping back, his face flushed. "What happened?"

She tried to speak, but caught the girl's hair color, torch red, and lost her words. It was Angia. Her old friend glanced at her, eyes low and cheeks crimson.

"You," Oriana began, but could not finish.

"Me and Angia were . . . talking about the fire festival," he said, and then grew bolder, "but what happened? Did Bruno do something? Oriana?"

She could see his concern was genuine, and she could have told him. Instead, she shook her head.

"Not at all. I was just wondering where you were. See you at home."

She turned her back to them and walked away.

Shaking, half-blinded by emotions she could not even name, Oriana stumbled inside palazzo Nicastri. No one was there to notice—not her mother, who was at the Thursday market with Cetta, nor Villabianca, working at the archive. As she climbed the stairs, Donna Marisa, the gatekeeper, stuck her head out from the concierge's window.

"Miss, Mastro Peppo was here," she said.

Oriana froze.

"Father? He was?"

"Aye, he said he was on his way to Foggia for a king's commission. He brought three rolls of brocade cloth in the house and left to find Signor Merello."

"Did he leave a message?"

"Only that he will not be here for the Day of the Dead."

"I see. Grazie, Marisa."

Oriana pressed her lips into a line, considering that maybe he didn't come by the smithy because he was not allowed to by some regulation of the Guild. Or perhaps he didn't want to interrupt his children's training. By the time she had reached her room, her excuses had run out, leaving the simple truth that her father did not show up because he didn't care to. She sat down on her bed, massaging her wrist. Despite all his claims of support, Mastro Peppo had deserted her. For the first time since her childhood, Oriana felt the desperate need to cry. Yet the well of her pain was dry. She opened her palm and stared at it. She dared not call Scandar, fearing that it would alert the Duke. But as her agony surged, she wondered if she should in fact call for the Emistuchivio himself, and collect his Boon. A shadow leaped onto the mattress, landing next to her.

"W-what are you doing here?" she asked. "It's dangerous! If mother sees you . . ."

But she couldn't continue. She didn't want Growler to go away. The cat's muzzle traced an invisible line up her arm, grazing her skin with the faintest smack. She hugged him tight, burying her face in the warmth of his fur, her tears spilling freely. The cat's purring reached beyond the space of her pain. Finally, she pulled back.

"Thank you," she told Growler as he sat on the bed, tail a-flailing.

And then, through the veil of her tears, she saw past him. On her desk there was a parcel. She stood, the cat landing at her feet to follow, and opened the thick wrapping paper with fidgeting fingers, revealing an iron rose. Underneath it was a card, penned in childlike handwriting and uncertain spelling.

Made it for yor moder, to replace the paper one she throwed away.

A flush on her face, Oriana held the last item Mastro Peppo had made in his smithy, one forged as an act of love. She turned and presented it to Growler with both hands.

The cat bellowed in feline assent.

TWENTY-NINE

Sitting on the rooftop of Serapide's great black spire, Oriana stared down at the panorama of Lucerìa's that had never been. She knew that her body was still lying in bed, the cat asleep in her lap. They had reached Serapide's spire in their shared Dream by no little effort on Growler's part. The cat had cut through dreams like a knife to reach the fulcrum of the Second Night. And now, time was short. If they didn't return before the Hour of the Wolf, they could be stuck in Serapide's realm for good.

From her position she counted six different skies, all imperfectly concentric to one another, with more extending just beyond her line of sight. Crimson sky-rings brimmed with golden specks of ashes, azure shone in the silver reflections of a seaside town, and verdant heavens mirrored the Babylon-like gardens hanging from the rooftops. These sky-crowns orbited around the spire. And yet she noticed they were unstable. They advanced and retreated chaotically, and, in doing so, crashed into one another, a conflagration that left only one standing.

We should go before it gets worse.

Growler's one eye looked down at her. Perched on the spire's roof, the cat had taken on his giant form, taller than a bear.

"Can it get any worse?" she asked.

Indeed. These are the early stages of the Dreams that will blossom on the Day of the Dead. Their possibilities are still in an ebullient state, competing with one another. It will get worse before it gets better. Take out your compass.

She reached into her pocket and retrieved the iron rose. It was time to see if her intuition had been correct. At first, nothing happened. But then, beyond the sixth circle of sky, a red shimmer appeared, refracting the glowing wound of a twilight sky.

"There," she pointed eagerly. "There is our forge!"

Good. Hop on.

Holding the rose in her mouth, Oriana hugged the great cat's lowering neck.

Hold on tight, this will be quite a ride.

"As bad as before?" she asked, grabbing a tuft of his fur.

Worse.

Oriana's exhale turned to a half-scream as the cat leapt thrice in rapid succession, jumping across the tops of the spire's turrets. He landed on the street and sprinted forward, cutting through the concentric Dreams. An inferno of shops bursting in red-yellow flames ceded to a cool seaside sky echoing in the seagulls' cries, which gave away to a verdant city of hanging gardens and arboretums that grew behind closed windows.

As they passed through the latter, Oriana became aware of her growing curiosity. When she was eight, she had not given a thought to it, but: What was the real relationship between daydreaming and nightdreaming? Suddenly, Oriana felt the full weight of her responsibility. To be a dreamer in the face of the collective meant that she had inspired in others desires they didn't know they had. And yet what if she didn't win? What would happen to the women of Lucerìa then?

A roar snapped her from her daze.

The greenhouse turrets were being obliterated by a stone street suspended by two stout buildings—two dreams crashing into each other. A shower of debris rained on them.

"Growler!"

Ears forward, the dream-cat doubled his speed. A boulder the size of a cottage fell six steps in front of them, blasting the ground into a hole. Without missing a beat, the cat cleared it in an impossible leap. Torn apart by the town of highways, what was left of green Lucerìa were gardens in disarray, dilapidated statues, and a vivarium nestled within a half-crumbled tower. As they passed by the latter, Growler came to a halt, his muzzle up.

"Why are you stopping?"

We'll need a specific dream-plant. I just smelled it. It's here somewhere.

"What plant? What are you talking about?"

Miss, don't you want to remember your training when you wake?

"Of course!"

Then we need to find tarragon flowers. They only grow in certain dreams. Wait here; there might be Caruncoli around, dream-scavengers.

"You'll go nowhere without me."

As you wish.

As soon as she dismounted, Growler began shrinking. By the time they entered the toppled tower's gate, the cat had reverted to its normal cat size. They roamed through the ruin of shattered vases, some small as a fist, others tall as a man, and a mix of thorny flowers and sturdy palms. Growler sat still and wagged his tail.

Do you see those flowers growing in a pair? One deep yellow with a black heart, the other black with a yellow heart? Pluck a handful, but carefully, without damaging them.

Oriana followed his instructions artfully, but complained to the cat, "You could have taken the shape of a man and done that yourself."

With the right dream-token, maybe.

"If memory serves, you were good at making those."

I am not that cat anymore.

"But you liked it, I mean, to look like a man."

I did. I was not content with how cats lived. Food, reproduction, fights, it bored me witless, if you must know. I always wanted to be more than who I was. That is already not very catlike, you see. Cats are content. I was not.

"What happened?"

Six years of unending nightmares happened.

"I am so very sorry."

So you keep saying. Put those flowers away; we will need them soon.

They traversed another dream-town, and then another.

"So what are the flowers for?"

Growler still wore his normal cat-shape as he prowled by her side.

The yellow one, Remembrance, is to remember in the Day what you experienced in Serapide's realm.

"I've never had that problem before."

You were chaperoned by the agent of a powerful Night Saint. And now you intend to acquire, on your own, a skill in the Night to use in the Day. Major Ones wouldn't allow that.

"I see. What about the black one?"

That's Oblivion, for forgetting in the Day something that happened at Night, or vice versa. But look, I think your forge is close.

On the main street of this dream-Lucerìa there were hundreds of smithies. Some took over entire villas, some were tiny, others moving iron castles and bellowing great clouds of smoke. Oriana felt her lips curve into a smile. She held out the iron rose just like she would a compass. The rose guided her hand until it pointed at an oak door—her father's forge!

Oriana sprinted forward.

Miss! Growler's intent cracked after her like a whip, but she had already scampered to the door, lifted the crowbar, and slipped inside.

The door's crack dimly lit the main room's interior. It was larger than the original, with three anvils instead of one and two huge bellows, but it was definitely her smithy. Whirling around in delight, she met Growler's alert gaze as he slipped inside.

Danger.

She halted mid-spin. Slowly, she turned around and stared.

A noise of bones cracking, of feet shuffling, of chewing mouths.

There were three of them, crouched on the ground under the tool table, three thin women dressed in raggedy clothes, munching. They had long, wild hair that hung to the ground, obscuring their faces but not their necks. She took her time gulping down the knot in her throat. Their napes had mouths, vertical slits ripe with teeth. They used the black tendrils of their hair to pick bones off the ground and shove them inside those fat, red lips. Oriana's body instinctively crawled away, bumping into Growler, who had grown to the size of a big hound.

Make no sound and don't go near them.

W-what are they? Oriana replied using her own intent.

Grinners. Mothers who starved their own offspring to death. On the day of their children's passing, a wound blossomed on their necks. The only way for them to stop their pain is by feeding that wound with the flesh of others. I don't know what they are doing here. They don't see well, but if they hear us . . . I am sorry; we were unlucky. We must go back. Now.

After all we went through to get here?!

In dreams you do as I say; that was our deal.

So tell me, and be honest, is there any guarantee that we will find another smithy this similar to the one in the Day?

No.

Then I'm staying. I am not afraid of them.

You should be.

"We stay!" Oriana hissed, covering her mouth at once. She looked to the cat in horror.

The three Grinners were already getting up, their hair raised and swirling like algae pulled and tossed by invisible currents. They stepped forward in silence, their heads tilted to one side. Oriana and Growler backed away.

Miss, change me into a man.

"What?" she whispered, never taking her eyes off the approaching women. Their bodies swayed like pale corpses in dark waters.

I need to be your human champion if I am to beat them.

"Well, turn into a man, then!"

I can't.

"You said you didn't want to!"

I know what I said. I don't want to. And I can't.

"You . . ."

I lost that skill long ago. You must bestow upon me a dream-token, wish me into the best version of a man you can imagine, and then—attenta!

Oriana screamed. Something cold clutched her ankle. One of the Grinner's locks was crawling up her leg. A razor-like claw slashed, and the lock fell. Oriana watched aghast as it writhed on the floor. The Grinners turned to the cat, their hair rearing like cobras ready to strike. Head low, Growler backed away.

Miss, change me!

"I don't know how!"

Two Grinners blocked Growler's retreat, while the third stepped forward. Cornered, the cat receded into a rim of darkness. The deadly trio closed in.

Oriana's despair gave way to intuition, then a gesture. She clenched the iron rose tightly and threw it. The flower flew past the creatures, and a gloved hand caught it.

Clutching the rose, a figure stepped out of the shadows. The Venetian hat with three feathers, the green boots, and the Toledo blade were commanded by a face so familiar, yet so different. For the human-guised Growler wore the visage of an adult Riano Siliceo.

Sensing a new threat, the Grinners advanced, their long hair moving sinuously before striking. A blur of motion. Growler sidestepped the attack and countered with a swipe of his blade, only to be halted by a lash to the face. He stumbled back, blood on his cheek, as the second Grinner whipped him from the left. At once, the other two attacked with synchronized ferocity.

Growler spun and dodged a strike, then another, his rapier felling a lock. But the women's hair whipped against him relentlessly, across the chest, on the mouth, and wrapped around his left arm and his right leg. Growler cut the strands that held him down, but it wasn't enough. The Grinners' hair knitted together, weaving a cocoon around him. As they closed in Oriana could see the mouths on their napes drooling. They were going to crush him. Through the tangle she caught a glimpse of Growler's scared face. It looked so much like her brother's.

"Miss," he entreated, "run."

"Not a chance!"

A Grinner struck the man-cat from the flank, her hair coiling around his throat. Breathless, he kneeled on the ground, the iron rose falling from his hand.

"No!" Oriana cried.

She grabbed a stool from beneath the table and swung it against the closest Grinner's neck. At once, her portion of the web unraveled. Growler had an opening. His blade flashed, cutting the web that held him. He coughed on the ground beside her, but Oriana's full attention turned to the Grinner confronting her. Her face was hidden by a smooth cascade of black hair, and yet somehow Oriana thought she looked like her mother. She raised the stool as a shield, but the Grinner's tendrils snatched it from her hands. Beyond her own attacker Oriana glimpsed a dance of steel and hair. With a decisive thrust, the man-cat pierced his first assailant in the stomach. She didn't make a sound as she bent in two and tumbled over. When the second Grinner closed in, her attack was met with a swift repost and a thrust straight through her heart. Then the man-cat flashed his one eye.

"Oriana!"

Distracted, Oriana hadn't seen the Grinner coming. At the last second, the girl ducked, narrowly missing the silken wave whipping above her head. Stumbling, she fell hard on her back. She gritted her teeth as the Grinner drew near, her locks surging.

A spray of blood.

Oriana touched her face. But the blood wasn't hers. She blinked. Growler's blade protruded from the Grinner's sternum. As Oriana frantically backed away, the creature toppled over with a thud. When at last she lifted her face, Oriana's breath froze.

She had expected a demented smile, possibly even in the likeness of her mother, but what she saw was much worse. For the eyes that were looking at her were wide with horror, helpless, her cheeks slashed with tears. But the creature could not utter a sound, for she had no mouth.

Growler cleaned his sword's edge on the rim of his cloak.

Oriana stared at him blankly, incapable of stilling the furious beating of her heart.

Then the man with her brother's face swiped his three-plumed hat to the ground, and in a steady voice so much like Riano's said, "Miss, as promised, the smithy is yours."

THIRTY

For two weeks Oriana walked to Bruno's lessons alongside her brother.

While Bruno didn't boss or berate Oriana like he did before, he was constantly undermining her, always revealing her flaws and never her twin's. Moreover, his master's constant praise made Riano blind to the disparity in the way they were treated. As the twins learned to curve the fire poker's handle, Bruno had nothing but good words for Riano, and no words for Oriana at all. That is, when she was even allowed to touch a tool, which was seldom. Meanwhile she could feel Riano's ego bloating by the day, taking for granted that while he attended the "real work," she could sweep the smithy's floor.

"It's just business, Sis," he said. "Bruno needs a couple of pokers ready by midday, and I am quicker than you, is all."

After her daily toil ended, while the two walked back home, Riano strayed behind.

"You go on, Sis, I'll catch up. Tell Mother I won't be late."

Oriana nodded and walked on, ears burning. She didn't have to stay to know that, under a portico, Angia waited for him. Her old friend's betrayal burned more than her brother's. It felt like all the young women of Lucerìa had turned their backs on her. She didn't see much of Villabianca either, for her mother had Cetta ensured that she couldn't visit with the count unchaperoned. That her brother could do as he pleased with Angia ceased to surprise her. In the end, she didn't care anymore. While she endured their luncheons silently, listening to Riano brag about his successes, she looked out the windows at the darkening sky, her heart slowly filling with trepidation. For if the Days were his, the Night was all hers.

After midnight, everybody else in the Siliceos' house might as well have been dead. Oriana heard not a sound from any of the rooms, not from Cetta's, from her mother's, or even Riano's, as if the entire flat were submerged in the torpid currents of the Night. The only movement came from the corridor, where under the green vase's light, a black tail cut through the dark. Oriana had become quite fond of his visits. Growler could have visited her only in her dreams, but at the risk of being seen, he often skulked to her room. For the cat always felt when Oriana was most upset, and he'd spend hours on her lap before they passed together into Serapide's realm.

Every night she dreamed the same dream, of the two of them traveling through the Second Night to the smithy. Their passage through the dream-towns was always different, but without fail, the iron rose led them right to Mastro Peppo's forge. There the real work began.

First, she swallowed the golden tarragon flower so that she could remember in the Day what she learned. And sometimes, when she was upset by a particularly vicious remark by Bruno, she took the Oblivion, too, just to forget about it and concentrate on her task.

All the techniques Oriana observed during the Day, she now practiced in the Night. With Growler's help—looking like an exalted version of her brother, no less—she chiseled the hot iron bar and, using tongs to hold it in place, twisted the poker until it assumed its intended shape. She repeated this action hundreds of times, many more than she would have managed during the Day. She learned to judge the quality of a fire with just one look. Hammering became like breathing to her, a rhythm in her blood. What she loved most was seeing the iron take shape. For no matter how small the object she created, something of herself went in it. This was no shallow animism—it was simple truth. Every blow was a motion born in her will, passing through her arm, straight into the iron. As she had argued to that gentleman at the salon, the need to create with her hands was at the very core of her being.

Every morning she awoke in the same way, with Growler gone from her lap to the safety of the count's library, and her arms quivering with excitement.

A week before the Day of the Dead, the Guild members gathered at the smithy with Peruzzi to judge the second trial of the challenge.

This time, the bystanders were few. Only two dozen young women, Oriana's age or younger and dressed in black shawls to protect themselves from the drizzle, stood by the open doors. There were almost no urchins in the streets. Nonetheless, a pair of royal guards, the birri regii, were stationed outside to prevent another riot. The crowd's mood was different, though, their general sentiment being that Oriana couldn't possibly win.

Most of the curious were girls. When she didn't see Angia among them, she felt a stab to her heart. But then again maybe it was for the best. She would not be able to stand it if she saw her old friend cheering for Riano. Donna Lena's eyes pierced through the green halo of her hat. She, too, was sure this would be the end of it. In fact, even Villabianca, who waited on the sidelines in his coach, looked at her with the discomfort of pity.

Just as they stepped into the smithy, her brother whispered, "I'm sorry, Sis. You did deserve a chance."

Oriana wondered if he said that because he actually had noticed her ill-treatment or because he thought himself superior. It hardly mattered now. Bruno gave the signal and they started. They took shifts kindling the forge, removing the iron bars from the fire, drawing out their tips, and then hammering with the chisel to split it in two at the top. Though they completed these steps almost at the same time, as their work progressed, the crowd began to notice a difference between the two. For Oriana was not just quick, she was flawless. While Riano, looking more distraught by the minute, required six hammer blows to straighten the iron, she needed only four. And by the time her brother started chamfering the poker, Oriana had already finished.

Of course, this meant little, since the Guild members judged the results, not the speed. But, as became evident by their exclamations, Oriana's final product was nothing short of astonishing. In what little time she had taken, Oriana managed not only to create a perfect poker, but also to impress a signature pattern onto its handle. The judges took their time. The three old smiths looked at the two pokers over and over again as if trying to find their secret flaws, murmuring among themselves in somber tones. Then the trio pulled Peruzzi aside. The lawyer nodded reluctantly.

"By the power of this jury," he said, "I must announce that the winner of this challenge is Oriana Siliceo. Thus, the next challenge will be their last, resolving this legal controversy once and for all."

Bruno's eyes almost fell out of his head. Releasing a single scream, the young women hugged one another, crying, happy beyond all recognition. And then Oriana saw Angia. She had been there all along, probably keeping herself hidden so that Riano would not see her. But now her friend was dancing barefoot, her red hair loose. Pale, fists clenched, Riano stared at her in quiet shock.

Then Angia stopped and cried, "You showed them, Ori! You showed them who we are!"

Oriana closed her eyes. Her Moira had been set in motion. When she opened them, Bruno hovered a few inches away from her face, trembling in constrained rage.

"You cheated. Pray I never find out how."

That night, she rejoiced in her room alone with her feline friend, sharing her maccheroni with him. Her day had been a tour de force: the triumph at the smithy, Villabianca's embrace, Donna Lena's panicked look, Angia's barefoot dance. And yet not all her emotions had been happy ones. A letter from Caserta arrived saying that her father was still unable to come home. And of course she couldn't forget Riano's stare. It should have felt good to see his pride so rightfully chastised, but she felt the wedge between them growing. And in Riano's eyes, she had seen the same accusation as in Bruno's. Was it true? Had she cheated?

Don't you even think about it, Growler assured her one night. *What you accomplished at the trial just evened out your Fortune. After all, it was your mother who cheated Fate.*

And indeed, Donna Lena was not pleased. Oriana knew she was in danger when her mother began to treat her more kindly. She offered her sweets after dinner, invited her in front of the fire for some sewing, and asked how her work at the smithy was coming along. In short she was acting like a mother. It was only a pretense, of course, a ploy to learn her secret. Still the illusion was so convincing, and Oriana felt so alone, that she almost gave in.

Donna Lena even allowed her to go to the Thursday market with Cetta and visit Villabianca alone. This last liberty she took advantage of, for she missed her tutor very much. But she discovered that the two of them were never really left alone in the library; Mamma Emma was always dusting something just a few paces away. She wasn't the only one. In the days following the trial, Cetta tried many times to spark up a conversation about her ordeal, nervously clenching her hands. Oriana realized that she couldn't be sure that one or both of them weren't spying on behalf of her mother. From that moment on she didn't dare to talk about her challenge with anyone, including Villabianca. While she still trusted him, she didn't trust the very walls of his palazzo. And so though it broke her heart, Oriana had to stifle her enthusiasm and speak very cautiously, even with her dearest friend.

THIRTY-ONE

The last challenge, the one that would finally decide the ownership of the smithy, was a complex one. The Siliceo siblings would have to weld two iron bars together to form a perfect right angle. It was both the most critical forging technique and the hardest to master. It usually took an apprentice a full year to learn. It would be a miracle if they could get the two pieces to stick at all.

By then, Oriana's harassment at the smithy had reached its peak. Bruno resumed a more overt strategy, confident that Riano's feelings had turned him into an ally. In this he appeared correct, for Riano offered his sister nothing but sulking silences, allowing Bruno free rein. And he was nasty with her, sabotaging Oriana in the most dangerous ways. Her coals were often soaked in lamp oil, her tools all slightly dented, and when she tried to move the slack tub, she found that it'd been cracked, almost scorching her with its steaming brine. Yet somehow Oriana seemed able to anticipate them all: she replaced the oil-soaked coal, fixed her tools before using them, and dodged the flood of boiling hot liquid just in time.

Her intuition seemed preternatural, and it was. For this was why she had looked for the most faithful dream-copy of Mastro Peppo's forge. In her dreams all was revealed—the traps Bruno set, the location of her misplaced tools, the spirit-soaked aprons. And with Growler's help, she found them all, always ten steps ahead of Bruno.

Her young master had never been more desperate. The

possibility of Oriana inheriting the smithy and one day commanding him was becoming more likely by the day. So Bruno redirected his energies into instructing Riano to the best of his ability.

Truth be told, her brother had changed a great deal. Since his defeat, the quality of his work improved dramatically, and not only because of Bruno's attention. Riano was working hard, often with no interruption for lunch, and certainly with no time for any amorous encounter.

As for Oriana her victory had changed her too. The day she won she had bitten the fruit of self-reliance, and what a difference it made! She felt like her desires had been finally legitimized, that she was in her rightful place, doing what she ought to do. And while before she had only been concerned about the challenge, now she knew that she was not just adequate at forging: she was damn good at it too. New ideas formed at the tips of her fingers. With ease, in her dreams, she molded faces on doorknobs, making them look like Urchins or Wyrms.

Then one night, some ten days before the final confrontation, as Growler was putting fresh clippings of Remembrance and Oblivion into a vase, Oriana caught an expression not unlike one Riano sported while looking at something he was very fond of.

"What?" he asked.

"Nothing," she replied, hammering at her bar. "It's just that . . . sometimes you really look like him. I mean, fifteen years his senior and one-eyed, but still."

Oriana set the hammer down on the anvil and dried her hands on her apron. The welding finished, she had to wait until the iron cooled. The cat stared at her questioningly.

"Are you positive," he ventured, "that I look like your brother?"

"Well yes, who else would you look like?"

"You are twins, so I understand the confusion. But miss, this is a dream. Here, things are possible that would be inconceivable in the waking world."

"What are saying?"

"That I asked you to imagine your champion. Apparently, there is only one person who you can think of for that role: you."

"But you are a man!"

"And isn't that how you see yourself?"

She wet her lips, shook her head, and said, "No, I . . . you are making it up!"

Growler reared his head and burst out laughing.

Maybe, his intent said. And then out loud, "Our intents always tell the truth; they state things as we feel them. And how boring is that! What's the point of being able to speak if you don't challenge reality with words?"

"You mean lying," she said.

"Does it matter if what I said is real? I will make it real just by saying it."

"Nonsense."

"Not at all. Stories change reality. In Lucerìa more than anywhere else."

"If that was true, Growler, it would make no difference whether I was a girl or a boy, for I could change my gender just by speaking it."

And isn't that exactly what you've done, miss?

She stared blankly at the cat's smile.

"I see. Still, are you really a male version of me? I want the plain truth."

He made a conceding gesture and opened his mouth to say more, but then froze, his body shaking. A look of sudden horror crossed his face.

"Growler! What is it? Are you sick? What happened?"

Bent in two, choking, the man pointed at the vase.

Oblivion. Give it to me. Quick!

Oriana plucked the black flower and crouched down next to him.

"Here, take it!"

Growler snatched it from her hand and swallowed it.

"I choose to forget—"

Oriana blinked, and he was gone. She looked all around, but the fire's glow lit an empty room. What had just happened? The dream-cat looked so genuinely scared. Oriana plucked Remembrance from the vase, hesitated, then swallowed the flower.

She woke up in her bed, as usual. This time, however, it was not yet day. She was looking for her cat when someone in the house screamed. Oriana bolted out of bed and through the door of her room. Another scream sounded in the dark.

"It's all right, my dear, it's all right," Donna Lenna's voice soothed.

As she approached the kitchen, Oriana passed the emerald glow of the lantern under the image of the Madonna. Her mother, still in her nightgown, stood by the kitchen table. Sitting beside it, her face half-covered by her hands, was Cetta. It was she who had been screaming. Staring blankly at a bucket of water on the floor, the old maid was having one of those fits of hers, murmuring the names of her lost sons and daughters. Donna Lena, swathed in her loose hair, caressed her employee as if she were a small child and looked down at the bucket.

"Poor little thing," she said shaking her head. "I wonder how he got in there. Chasing mice, maybe. And who would've known we had a cat in the house."

Donna Lena put a hand inside the bucket and pulled something out.

It dripped water like a drenched mop. Slowly, she turned to her daughter, still gripping Growler by his tail, and grinned. Right then, Riano appeared in the hallway, staring first at the dead cat, then at his mother, then his sister. Fear flared in his eyes, and he fled.

Donna Lena's smile had not faded one bit. Walking toward her, Oriana grabbed something off the table and struck her mother's face with it. Cetta stood in a yelp as a red stream gushed from Donna Lena's split lower lip. The woman dropped the cat and doubled over in pain, hands pressed to her mouth. Her eyes were an emerald fire. Shuddering, Oriana looked down at the knife in her hands. At once, she let go; it clattered to the floor.

"Out," Donna Lena commanded Cetta in a muffled voice.

"But ma'am, the blood, let me—"

"I must speak to my daughter alone. Out."

Cetta shot a frantic look and hurried away. Donna Lena sat down at the table and removed her cuff to staunch the wound.

"You made this mess," she said to her daughter, "now you fix it. Light the fire in the stove and put that knife over it."

"W-why?"

"To cauterize the wound. I'll teach you. Now, move."

The smell of blood was so strong it made Oriana want to vomit. Worst of all was that wet lump on the floor, the black shape that had been her friend. But she did as she was told. With a paper cone and a stick of flint she lit the fire in the porcelain stove, feeding it with bits of wood until it grew high enough. The kitchen filled with the scent of burnt wood, slowly overpowering the reek of blood. Oriana picked the knife off the floor and held its blade against the flame. The blood that coated it sizzled and smoked black.

"Good girl," Donna Lena said, her face white as chalk. "When I remove my hands, you'll have to act fast. You put the hot blade directly on the raw wound, understood? If you miss, you could blind me, or worse. Good, I'm ready."

White-hot blade in hand, Oriana moved toward her mother. She halted just a couple of feet from her, hesitating.

"H-how did you learn to cauterize a wound."

"My dad, your grandfather, was an army officer, was he not? And so were four of my brothers. I helped my mother stich them up more times than I can count. Now, if you don't mind, I am in a lot of pain, titilla."

"I'm sorry, I—I—"

"Just do it, Oriana. Here, I'm going take my hands away."

The instant she did, blood began to stream down her chin, soaking her dress. At once, Oriana panicked and backed away, but Donna Lena's white hand gripped her by the wrist, her green eyes wide, demanding.

Finally, the girl pressed the blade against the wound.

In all the years she had yet to live, there were two sounds Oriana would never forget: the hiss of her mother's flesh as it blistered and burned, and the thud of her head on the table after she fainted. But the wound was closed, and no more blood dripped onto her dress. Oriana sat on the ground, buried her face in her elbow, and burst out crying. Her sorrow was a bottomless sea, and she cried not even knowing whether it was for Growler, her mother, herself, or something else entirely, the echo of a happiness she could not even remember.

When at last she raised her face, the light in the room had changed. From experience she knew that the Hour of the Wolf had passed and Dawn was fast approaching. Her mother's body stirred. In the penumbra Oriana could not make out her face, but she sensed her eyes: clear, unencumbered.

"Mamma," she sighed, tasting her own tears. She sat on the table, brushing her mother's cheek in long strokes. "My *Mamma*."

"Do you know," her mother croaked, "how much it cost me, to seek Them out?"

Oriana quivered, her hand frozen in place.

"Who?" she asked, quickly removing her hand.

"You know who. Them, who I despised. Them, who I still loathe. For three years I looked for a way to get to Them until that cat," she said, pointing at the black lump on the floor, "brought me to the market."

"If you sought Them out willingly . . . why did you forbid us from even saying their names!"

With effort, Donna Lena stood. Her face was streaked in tears and blood, her lips swollen, yet she looked more alive than Oriana had seen in years.

"You really think I didn't know what it would cost me? That I accepted their bargains blindly? I knew everything, Oriana, all that would happen to me. Including this! It is because of this scar that you gave me tonight that people in town will remember me as Lady Grin."

Oriana turned her face away, but Donna Lena grabbed her by her chin.

"Oh no, you stay here and listen. Do you know why I looked for Them?"

"To be rich and feared, as you yourself said."

"Yes, I won't deny it. Yet those desires came later, after the Dame showed me what I could have. But that's not why I searched for Them in the first place. It was because of you, sweet blood of mine. You see, I've seen Them since the day you were born. Garaudi. Mazapegul. Larvae. Even a Wyrm, once. Slithering in the streets at Twilight, coiling around chimneys at Dawn, jumping from one moon-shadow to the next, trying to speak to you. So I protected you. I saw them but pretended not to. That's the reason I went looking for Them, to try to swap places with you. You see, if somebody in this family had to be Night-touched and Night-bound, then it would be me. Not you, not Riano, *me*. So you can hurt me, Oriana, and hate me, and curse me to Hell, for all I care. I did what I had to."

They remained face-to-face, mother and daughter, until a gust of wind stoked the green lantern's wick and it flamed, casting emerald shadows around the room.

Donna Lena quickly kissed Oriana's cheek, just like she used to, then strode away. Alone in the half-dark kitchen, Oriana touched her wet cheek, then put two fingers in her mouth.

They tasted like her own blood.

THIRTY-TWO

The cat's death marked the end of her apprenticeship. For without Growler, she could not find the dream-smithy, and without the dream-smithy, she could not train.

Worse still was what her mother had told her that night. Oriana didn't know if she could trust Donna Lena's words, but she could not forget her last kiss. Her mother's wound had not healed properly. And now, whenever she smiled, her lips made her look as if she were grinning with all the seething hunger of her dark green heart.

The remaining days at the smithy were unspeakably dreadful. Oriana had lost the will to resist Bruno's torment, and Riano wouldn't even look at her. She knew her brother blamed her for her mother's scar, but she also sensed that he felt guilty about the cat's death. In fact, rather than Cetta or Mamma Emma, it could have been him who told their mother about Growler. It hardly mattered. The cat was gone, and no investigation would offer her the peace she longed for.

For nights on end Oriana tossed in her bed thinking about Growler. She missed him more than ever, especially now that she needed his counsel. What should she do? Would she dare call for Scandar or the Duke? She was too ashamed to face Scandar and too afraid of what the Emistuchivio would do to her once their deal was done. And so her mind spun in endless circles. Then, one night, she had a strange dream.

In it she walked through crooked alleys, moonlit streets, and silent piazzas, looking for her smithy. Iron rose in hand, she searched for signs to show her the way and followed a throng of farmers to a crowded square. This place felt different somehow. The area buzzed with vendors peddling a vast array of goods ranging from trinkets to towering statues. In the way of dreams it didn't strike her as odd that the entire square was filled with the chill of their silence. Oriana herself was one of the silent ones, clutching the iron rose as she surveyed the stalls' vendors—shadows with faces that flickered intermittently in the shimmer of the lamps—emerald-green, crimson-red, amber, and argent.

Finally, something in a small wooden stall caught her attention: a battered old chisel, the only object for sale. As she approached, Oriana felt that it was the most precious thing in existence. Emperors' crowns, kings' necklaces, popes' rings, they were all nothing compared to this item. She asked the vendor for its price. Its answer didn't faze her. She would have to sell her womanhood, the Reality of it. In turn she would become a great artisan, praised for decades. But she would live and be remembered as a man.

Oriana shrugged. She cared not for femininity and didn't want to marry, this by now she knew. And yet something held her back—a foretaste of regret and shame.

"Or would you rather have this in exchange?" she said to the vendor.

Crimson eyes gleamed in the shadows.

What are you selling me, little one?

"A rose," she stammered. "I—I can't recall exactly what it was for, only that it holds no value to me now. Would you trade it for that chisel?"

An aged, calloused hand emerged from the dark to collect the rose—the hand of a blacksmith. Oriana peered at the shadow's face, realizing that it belonged to an elderly woman, one who exuded a peculiar sense of familiarity.

Give the rose to me, and our deal is sealed.

Her glimmering eyes looked so sad when she said it. Oriana looked down at the rose in her hand, suddenly noticing a wound on her palm. Was that the thorns' doing? Then the wound's lips parted, and a familiar voice whispered:

"Milady, wake up."

Oriana bolted upright, her heart racing. The Duomo's bell tolled twice. A jack-o'-lantern flickered in her windowsill. It was two o'clock in the Second Night, on the Night of the Dead, when the silent people returned to their homes and Lucerìa dreamed strange dreams. And so did she. For she was certain that she had dreamt of the Secret Market. Had she sealed the deal with the vendor, she would have gotten a Moira in return, just like Donna Lena's, maybe even stronger than hers. Only, she wouldn't have been Oriana anymore, but someone else's shadow.

She opened her palm to whisper Scandar's name into it when a terrible spasm seized her abdomen. She yelped and squeezed her knees to her chest in an attempt to lessen the cramp. When the sharp pain gave way to a dull throbbing, she noticed that the blanket between her legs was damp and sticky. She had been expecting it for some time now, and there it was, the womanhood she had refused to renounce. Later, after her cramps subsided, she looked for her iron rose. But though she tried, she could not find it.

On the eve of her last challenge, as she passed through the courtyard to find Villabianca, Oriana stopped in her tracks, hearing muffled sobs coming from the staircase.

Warily she looked under the arch, only to discover—to her surprise—that it was Riano. Her brother was sitting on the steps that went down to the cellar, looking more dejected than she had ever seen him. As soon as he heard her, he sprang up, wiping his tears with his sleeve.

"A bit too late for that," Oriana said, "though Cetta would make a good proverb out of it: *It's no use crying over the dead cat.*"

"W-what in the name of Christ are you talking about?"

"Oh, don't fret, I won't tell anyone that I saw you crying. Wouldn't want to threaten you by acknowledging that you do possess a range of human emotions."

Riano stared at her with an ashen face.

"You have no idea, do you?" he said.

"That you told Mother about Growler and now are feeling guilty about it?"

"No. About Father."

Her mouth dry, she felt blood rushing to fill the vacuum of her heart. "Is he hurt? Is he all right?"

"Yeah. He's all right and happy."

"Happy?" she repeated, confused.

"I have—I know a boy our age, a carpenter's son who often travels with his uncle to Caserta. He told me Father has a woman there."

"A woman?" Oriana repeated again.

"They aren't married, of course, but he says it's like they are. The woman has a son and a daughter. She claims they are from her previous marriage, but everyone says they look like us."

"Everyone?"

"Everybody knows. Even Cetta."

"And Mother?"

"*Of course* Mother knows. That's what she wanted in the first place. To get rid of him, to do as she pleases in his house! And he can't raise a finger against her, or she'll denounce him for . . . what's it called?"

"Bigamy."

"Yes, bigamy. She got everything she wanted in the end, just like she always does."

He leaned against the wall, clutching his own arms. Oriana thought of her mother's blood-kiss, of her words in the kitchen. No one, not Riano nor their father, would ever know what Donna Lena had done. But what if Oriana had just done the same? She still hadn't been able to find the iron rose, the one Mastro Peppo wanted her mother to have. Oriana must have given it away in the market. What else did she give away with it? Her father's Reality? No, she decided: it was the idea of the four of them ever being a family again.

"He's not coming back," continued Riano. "He never will. And you know what? I don't blame him. I only wish it hadn't ended up this way."

At a loss for words, Oriana simply nodded.

"Sorella," he said, "I didn't want any of this to come between us. The challenge, I mean, all of it. If only he had talked to me that night. Yes, I was there, just outside the door. I heard you together. That's why I told Mother about your Sanctum. I was jealous. I didn't . . . I'm sorry. And I did see Marfisio in your room, but I swear I didn't—"

"Stop it."

"But I want to explain! Remember when I told you that you were trapped? Well, I was also talking about myself. I'm trapped too. I know that everyone thinks I am a good-for-nothing; I had made peace with it. But then, our challenge . . . it made me proud. At the start, I just wanted the smithy so that you couldn't have it. But now . . . now I think I can do it, I really do. So, whatever happens tomorrow, I wanted to say that without you, I—I . . ."

Riano trailed off and hid his face in his elbow, like a child would. His sister held him tight, his cheek hot against hers. It was the last time Oriana would hug her brother for decades to come.

THIRTY-THREE

Half of Lucerìa crowded into the streets adjacent to the smithy. Street vendors profited by selling salted nuts, fresh fruit, and water. And from their blazoned coaches, countesses and dukes sent their servants as envoys to the front to keep them constantly updated. One could glimpse the tête de mouton of Alfonsina Vernarecci through her coach's window. She sported fashionable binoculars, like the ones taken to the San Carlo opera house in Naples, and used them to scry beyond the solid wall of spectators. Most of the artisans' and farmers' wives stood on the outskirts of the crowd, forming a solid dike of scorn. Any bystander cheering for the Siliceo strumpet was subjected to their piercing contempt.

Finally, the carriage carrying the Siliceo women slithered through the crowd and arrived at the smithy door. As soon as Oriana stepped out, the young women in the street let out feral screams. Angia, Rosetta, Teresina, and all the other girls of her old contrada were there. To them she was vengeance made flesh, a promise to their sex and class. After her came the Emerald Dame herself. Never had she looked so ladylike and imposing. She wore her scarred lips like a medal of disdain, something to be proud of. Her hair defied gravity in a turret of green ribbons, a perfect contrast to Oriana's shorn head.

Guarding the workshop were four birri armed with rifles to prevent the crowd from entering. Inside, Lombardi sat in a corner by the tool table with an open notebook and a quill to record the event for "scientific purposes." Villabianca was there, too, having convinced Peruzzi that he needed to be there to represent the legal interests of his prospective wife. Finally, the Guild members entered, followed by Bruno. The young master was quite obviously in a terrible mood, as betrayed by the sorry state of his clothes. Two pairs of iron bars were brought in. And this time, two anvils were stationed by the forge so that the siblings could work simultaneously. As soon as Peruzzi gave the signal, a roar rose from the crowd. The two contestants began to kindle the hearth. In his corner, Lombardi removed his wig and dried his bald head with a silk kerchief.

As the siblings lifted their bars to put in the fire, Oriana stopped, turned to the jury, and cried, "My bar's scarf is too deep!"

The smiths approached. Signorina Siliceo was right. Her bar's scarf, that is, the sloping edge that would be welded to the other piece, was uneven. Had she gone ahead, the result would have been nothing short of disastrous. While the judges tried to assess the situation, the crowd outside made up its mind: Oriana had been cheated. The uproar that ensued almost threatened to overrun the jury and Master Bruno, who was white with rage and fear. The four birri exerted all their authority to keep the craftswomen out.

Angia pushed forward with all the strength of her long arms.

"Cheaters! Give her a good bar, or we'll take your life!"

Finally, the Guild members found two new scarfed bars. Oriana was given one, and the challenge resumed. As soon as the bars' ends began to sparkle, the Siliceo twins retrieved them from the forge, doused them in carbon powder, and brought them over to the anvil. Two Guild members helped them each to keep the bars in place, flat against the anvil, since the tiniest of angles would render the weld uneven. And then the two siblings started to hammer.

Unlike the other tests, this process was a quick one. It took less than five minutes for the bars to cool. And while the apprentices would have to keep hammering, their outcome was all but decided in those first blows. As they hammered, Riano and Oriana's faces were streaked with sweat; it trickled down their noses, though neither dreamt of stopping to wipe it away. Then the hammering stopped. The challenge was completed.

Outside, the crowd was wild with expectation. Heads swayed and nodded at the flimsiest of rumors. Was it true that Signorina Siliceo fainted? And Bruno, that bastard, it was him who tampered with the bars, wasn't it? As the judging went on, the crowd's murmuring rose in volume until it bubbled over in an outpouring of shouts, cries, and screams of protest.

And yet the verdict didn't come. Never had the Guild members disagreed more or quarreled with such alacrity. Villabianca lost his temper. But they couldn't choose a winner, for the siblings' work was impressively similar—the same solid weld, each with the same strengths and the same flaws.

A man wearing an expensive cloak and a tricorne hat made his way to the door. He seemed to be from out of town, maybe a Neapolitan, for he walked with the self-satisfied stride of people from the Capital. With a courteous bow, the man addressed the jury. In a loud and clear voice, he announced that the challenge had resulted in a draw. The two siblings were equally matched. When Oriana heard the voice, she looked up, beaming.

Mastro Peppo was almost unrecognizable. Underneath his new cloak, her father wore a silk shirt and a flannel cassock that made him look a bit like an archpriest, except with a silver brooch, the king's sigil, pinned to his collar. His eyes, too, were different, as they belonged to a sated man. But when they rested on Oriana, they grew self-conscious. *He knows that we know*, she thought.

Peruzzi gestured to the birri to let him in. The smith entered, trailing in a small crowd behind him that included Donna Lena, an effigy of hair and pride.

"As far as I'm concerned, both my son and daughter have earned the right to become first apprentice. So, if my son agrees, I will grant them both full ownership of my smithy."

All eyes were on Riano now. Villabianca, Peruzzi, Bruno, Lombardi, and Donna Lena stared at him. Oriana watched him closely too. But her brother's eyes were fixed on his father, and their look was not a kind one. For the first time since the trial began, Oriana empathized fully with her brother. If he accepted his father's proposal, from this day onward, he would be forever second. Bruno, his noble friends as well as the lazzari, they all would view him as someone who had lost his rightful place to a girl. But Riano's face changed, his expression of hatred unraveled, revealing a completely different emotion. Pride. The young man advanced a few steps and touched his father's arm, not pleading, but asking for acknowledgment.

"I accept."

In a heartbeat, astonishment turned to celebration.

Angia and the other craftsmen's daughters stomped their feet, Mastro Peppo embraced his son, Donna Lena stood frozen in scorn. Riano, at once submissive and proud, smiled, his eyes shining. As for Oriana, she found tears in her eyes, too; tears of rage. For now, Riano would be accepted as the unofficial true heir of the smithy, the prodigal son who embraced his destiny. It was she who would be forever second. Whatever work she accomplished in that smithy would be credited to Riano, simply because he was a man, just like her great-grandfather had claimed his wife's achievements. The Duke of the Under-earth himself had asked her to be his apprentice. She fought monsters, outwitted a Major One. Why should she be second?

"I do not accept my father's proposal," she said.

At once, the cheers around her chilled. Faces frozen in stupor stared at her. Both Riano and her father, still locked in an embrace, looked at her in disbelief. There was deep hurt in their faces, especially in Mastro Peppo's. For the smith sensed that his compromise had been spat back in his face as a rebuke of his duplicity. It was precisely at that moment that Oriana realized that she hated him, fiercely. For Donna Lena's pact with the Emerald Dame was born out of a desire to protect her children. Even her ambition, Oriana could understand. But Mastro Peppo had abandoned them for no other reason than the comfort of another woman and work well-paid. This she would never forget and never forgive. The only person still smiling was Donna Lena, steeped in the forge's shadows and yet with a green glint in her eyes. She strode closer to her daughter, brushing a hand over her naked arm.

"Well done. Don't accept anything they hand you. It's either all or nothing," she whispered, and walked away.

Riano disentangled himself from his father's grasp and came straight at Oriana, his fists clenched. He didn't say a word, nor did he need to. For a moment, her determination wavered, but she wouldn't take her words back. And anyway, it was too late now. Signor Peruzzi and the other master smiths crowded together to discuss how the challenge would proceed. Oriana looked around and saw that only a few of her most fervent supporters would still meet her gaze, among them Angia, Rosetta, and Villabianca, of course.

The contract stipulated that it was the right of the challenged apprentice to set a new, tiebreaking task. It had to be something simple, that could be performed right then and there using what little training they had received. Bruno pulled Riano aside. As the smith whispered to him, Riano's lips curved into a mischievous smile.

"I have the new task," he said. The silence from inside the smithy extended outside it. "I dare my dear sister to wield the Beast and use it to strike the anvil."

This was no test of skill! It was a feat of strength! But as Bruno quietly explained to those who protested, by the rules of the Guild, any work using any tool in the forge was considered fit for a challenge. Even Lombardi had to agree. The Beast was taken off the rack and handed to Riano. It was the biggest and heaviest sledgehammer in the smithy, one that new masters used to strike the anvil as a good omen. To use it well took a full-grown man two years of practice, but for their purposes, it would be sufficient to lift it off the ground and swing it against the anvil.

Oriana tried to stifle her arm's tremor. Perhaps when they started their apprenticeship, she and her brother possessed almost the same physical strength. But since then, their training had taken drastically different paths. Riano performed his tasks in the forge, while his sister had learned what she knew in a dream. Now his strength far superseded hers.

Riano doused his hands with chalk powder and gripped the handle of the Beast. He was given three attempts. He wasted his first by not raising the Beast high enough, missing the anvil entirely. The second attempt was better. With one violent heave, he managed to raise it over his head, but then lost his balance and fell backward. Someone in the crowd cackled and was harshly silenced. Donna Lena looked at her son with such an intensity that, for a moment, Oriana imagined that the entire smithy was an underwater cave, hazy with a green glow. Then Riano howled and raised the Beast over his head and landed his blow.

Everyone in the smithy covered their ears, except for Donna Lena. The ringing of the hammer was still echoing when a member of the Guild handed the Beast to Oriana. She took it as if in a nightmare she had no power to stop. The crowd was perfectly quiet. They hadn't even cheered when Riano struck the anvil, for they knew that this was the moment everything would be decided. She absorbed her brother's fear, Bruno's crooked smile, Mastro Peppo's regretful stare, Lombardi's scientific curiosity, Villabianca's kindness, and her mother's impatient triumph, then seized the handle of the Beast and heaved upward. The hammer didn't move an inch. She tried a second time, and then a third, summoning all the strength in her legs, trying to wrest it from the ground. But the Beast wouldn't budge.

When it was clear to everyone that Oriana had lost the challenge, an awful din came from outside. Young women protested loudly, but the cheering and jeering of Riano's supporters drowned out the other voices. Lombardi closed his notebook with a smile; his scientific inquiry was over. The Guild members complimented Riano, who shook their hands heartily. Very few dared to look at his sister, among them Mastro Peppo. Oriana could read in his eyes the profundity of her defeat. He could do nothing to save her now. Had she kept a low profile, she might have found her way to the smithy somehow, eventually. But not after she had caused such a public spectacle. She'd never be a smith. Villabianca approached her with a coat.

"Let's go, dear. My coach awaits outside."

But Oriana didn't take his coat, nor his arm. Instead, she closed her eyes.

"Two challenges in a row," she said.

Barely audible, her words seized those assembled in a tight grip of stillness.

"Two challenges in a row," she repeated, louder, "that's what the contract says. My brother has won one. I still have another chance."

A mutinous cacophony of voices erupted at the back of

the smithy as Peruzzi retrieved the contract, reading it frantically above his glasses.

"Is this true, Signor Peruzzi?" croaked Riano.

"Well, it is not exactly clear but—"

"Is this true or not?"

"I—I think it can be interpreted that way, yes."

Rosetta, Angia, and the rest of Oriana's young supporters crashed against the birri. Such was the violence of their protestation that it was clear if the Siliceo girl was not given her chance, the Mayor of Lucerìa would have a riot on his hands before sunrise.

"So what is your proposed challenge, Signorina Siliceo?" sighed Peruzzi.

"It is to be completed by tomorrow night, at this same hour," she began.

"Well, it needs to be settled today as it's—"

Oriana stared at him until—slowly—Signor Peruzzi backed off.

"It is for tomorrow," she explained, "because it's not a simple task. If he completes it, then I will renounce my legal rights to the smithy."

Bruno couldn't contain himself any longer.

"What is it, then! By the Madonna, spit it out!"

Oriana surveyed the faces around her, wondering if this is what it felt like to create a new destiny for yourself.

"I dare my brother to forge a ring made of water."

Oriana took in the crowd's emotions: first shock, then surprise, despair, and fear. This last sentiment lingered, perfectly etched on the bystanders' faces, even in the women who had thus far steadfastly supported her. Angia's face betrayed the same dread as it did on the day her tongue turned blue, for Oriana's last words contained a touch of Night, that nocturnal madness none dared speak of in the Day.

Donna Lena's laughter shattered the quiet. It was a howl so at odds with her countenance that it looked as if she were possessed. She walked to the door, the crowd parting, and then, just as she stepped outside, she turned sharply.

"Mad! I've driven you mad! Oh, what a fantastic pair you'll be!"

THIRTY-FOUR

Villabianca's coach shook along the uneven country road. Oriana had not stirred an inch, her fists on her temples. Each of the count's attempts to comfort her had failed miserably, her mind lost in some furious activity she would not share. The coach slowed, and Oriana felt the slightest pull of gravity. They were climbing up an incline. She leaned to face the window.

"This isn't the road home," she said.

"No, it's not. We're going to the countryside."

"What?"

"I do still have a country villa, if you recollect. It's all that's left of my mother's land and, in fact, hardly a manor, but suitable enough for our needs. There you can relax, read, write, and not a moment too soon. We'll reach it before dawn."

"Why?"

"You don't really think you can stay in Lucerìa after tonight? Clearly you need rest, some fresh air, and certainly—"

"Turn the coach around."

"Oriana, don't—"

"Turn the coach around, you fool!"

Her scream froze a spasm of pain in his face.

"Of course," she sighed. "You, too, think I'm mad."

"My sweet, anyone who went through what you went through tonight would feel shaken. Anyone. I know how hard this challenge has been on you. You haven't told me much, but I can guess. They cheated you. They mistreated you. And that's all the more reason why you need to leave this town. We'll think of a new strategy. Unlikely as it may seem, I do have some friends in the administration of the municipality. I'm sure there is some other loophole. Not all hope is lost, not until—" He paused. "What is it?"

"You are very kind, Villabianca, you always have been. But if you don't halt this coach right now, I swear to God I'll jump out."

The count stood to rap on the wooden slit of the driver's cabin.

"Francesco, stop the coach," he said. The coach slowly came to a halt. Then to Oriana, he said, "Would you listen to me for once? What's the use of staying in Lucerìa now?"

"I need to forge the ring. If I don't produce it by tomorrow, I'll lose."

This time, Villabianca could not hide his disconcert.

"Oriana," he sighed. "I don't think you're completely yourself right now."

"Oh, but I am. In fact, I've never been more myself in my entire life. *A destiny denied is twice a destiny.* He told me so from the start, and I didn't listen. I can't become a smith any other way, not in this town, not in this time, not in this body. Don't you see I have no other choice?"

"We always have a choice."

"You think I should have accepted my father's offer. That I was an idiot, that it was all my fault."

Villabianca leaned forward and took her hands in his.

"Oriana, do you really think I'm so old that I've forgotten what it feels like to be young? You were cheated, threatened, and insulted, and by your own blood. It didn't surprise me that you acted the way you did. Well, maybe a little, but not much. You wanted to shine, to show them what you are made of."

"Thank you," she said, smiling, biting her lip to stop her mounting tears.

"For what?"

"Because you *know*, Fernando, you really know what it feels like to be trapped. That's why I bonded with you so much, because we are similar in so many ways. But this is also our doom. For she knows it too. Even your present kindness is part of her Moira. Can't you see? By bringing me to the countryside you are making me fail my challenge! And if the challenge is lost, then I would marry you, because there would be nothing else for me to do."

"Indeed, a most dreadful fate . . ." Villabianca muttered.

"No, no it's not, Fernando, because I do love you. Yes, I love you, my sweet old fool. But my love is not the affection a man would want from a woman, for I would never be the mother of your children, or your wife in anything but name. I'm married to the forge. That's the way it is. That's how it always will be. If I married you, we'd both go mad. Didn't you hear what she said? *What a fantastic pair you'll be!*"

"Oriana, my bird, if what you just said is true . . ." Villabianca's voice trembled.

"It's true, you always knew it was. That's why it is so difficult for me to do what I must do now. But she's left me no choice."

"What is that?"

"I'm going to ask the Duke of the Under-earth to grant me his Boon."

Villabianca froze. There was concern in his eyes, but something else too. Fear. For it was one thing to spurn the existence of the Night Saints in broad daylight, but quite another to do so in the middle of a night road.

"Where are we?" she asked, peering outside.

"I'm not sure. I think we're close to the crossroad for Troja."

"Of course. It couldn't be otherwise. You see, I have a Moira now, one that is entirely my own. And so you've led me to exactly where I need to be."

"I don't understand you, Oriana, I swear I don't."

"That's why you are so precious to me. For even if you don't know what's best for me, you always do right by me."

Oriana leaned over and kissed her tutor on the lips. The count was so taken aback that he literally jumped from his seat, hitting the coach's roof and bouncing back down. He had no sooner righted himself when Oriana opened the door and fled from the coach.

Villabianca began three actions at once: knocking on the coachman's window, leaping out to pursue his fiancé, and remaining completely still. Finally, the count stepped out of the coach, finding himself in the middle of a country road bordering a thick beech wood.

Hands cupped around his mouth, he shouted his pupil's name in all four directions, Francesco by his side doing the same. But as much as they shouted that night, they didn't see Oriana Siliceo again.

PART III
THE CRUCIBLE

THIRTY-FIVE

Long before Oriana ceased to hear the two men, she knew she was lost. Lost to the Day, lost to her family, lost to the only man she had ever loved. There was no turning back now. She couldn't return to Lucerìa until she had forged a ring out of water.

Standing at the edge of the beech wood, she looked out at the distant hills of Selvapiana. If memory served, she was halfway to the fork in the road that led to Troja, not far from the ancient mound that housed an entrance to the Under-earth.

Oriana set off apace.

She had never visited the mound, but she remembered the path that led to it, a remnant of an old Roman road that ended in a broken bridge. There, her father told her, the Duke of the Under-earth built his first forge. On the quietest nights, farmers said they could hear the echoes of his hammering like distant thunder. With long decisive strides, she approached the tree line, where darkness thickened into a wall of obscurity. This was not the partial blackness of dark alleys; this was Night at its wildest, at its core, for darkness belongs to nature, not to man.

Oriana stopped. She had never meant to reach the mound all by herself. Slowly, she opened her left hand and whispered Scandar's name. Nothing happened. She repeated her call twice, louder each time. The wind flew through the high branches, stirring their leaves. But no one came. A flash of fear quivered down her spine. She considered returning to the coach. But what then? There was no way she could convince Villabianca she spoke the truth. Or the people of Lucerìa.

And so she entered the wood alone.

While it wasn't her first time entering the Night, before she had always been invited, escorted by one who knew it well. A thousand stories flooded her mind. She thought of Old Ermia, who was said to have been kissed by a Mazapegul in her youth, her face a horror to behold forever after. Or Zi' Pasquale, whose right hand had been turned to stone by a Basilisk. And Mad Pettino, who giggled and screamed at every Fullmoon. Whether by the brightening of her surroundings or the adjusting of her eyes, Oriana could just barely distinguish shapes within the beech trees. She was blind yet *seen*. Was that a wrinkled face watching her?

Then, the wood opened. Oriana's blood pounded when she saw that rising just behind the distant hills of Selvapiana was the full moon. Hadn't it just been a half-moon? It didn't make sense. She tried to remember what little she knew of the Fullmoon's Major One, Briace, Lord of were-creatures and lunatics. Her eyes widened. What if she was in fact mad? Maybe there had been no Cats' Parliament, no Secret Market, no dream-smithy, only her lunacy. Maybe she had come back from Foggia's spring fair with a brain fever. Wasn't that the reason her mother had locked her up for months? It was tempting, to go down that road. And yet Oriana was too rational, too practical to discard her experiences as delusions. So she kept walking, out of the wood and in the direction of the Roman bridge.

On the edge of a steep stone slope, she came into view of an abandoned farmhouse. It was two stories high and shrouded by thorny briars and ivy, its white stones glistening under the moonlight. A fence, no less battered than the house, circled the property. Beyond it stood the Roman bridge. Farther still, she could make out the dark shape of the mound.

Her tread grew lighter, quicker, but as she reached the fence, a movement caught her eye.

She stopped. There was a fox sitting on one of its pickets. It looked at her with its head tilted to one side, its tail raised. The moonlight defined the strands of its fur perfectly; she could feel their rough grain just from looking at them. Instinctively, Oriana stretched out her arm. The fox didn't retreat. It was so warm to the touch, and she could feel it breathing steadily under her fingers. Then the fox opened its mouth.

You are beautiful. I think I will marry you.

Swiftly, she snapped her hand away. The fox had spoken with his intent, but the voice in her head seemed the real voice of a young man, a man *yearning* for her.

I'm a good husband; you can ask my other wives, the fox pressed.

With its snout, he pointed beyond Oriana. Slowly, she turned to face the farmhouse. It was five stories high now, more mansion than cottage, still decaying and wrapped in vines; yet its tall windows glowed with lamplight. Laughter and voices poured from them.

"It is a wedding party," rang out a voice behind her, "ours."

Oriana turned back, but the fox was gone. In its place stood a tall, handsome man with red hair and a purple waistcoat. When he smiled, she saw that his teeth were pitch-black.

"Come, it's not polite to keep them waiting."

Oriana nodded. But when the red-haired man reached for her arm, she pushed him hard. The man cried out, but Oriana had already sprinted away. She didn't dare look back, just kept running. When she stopped to catch her breath, looking upward, the moon filled nearly half the sky. It was so vast that she could discern its craters.

When she looked down, she realized she was exactly where she had started: the farmhouse-mansion not behind her but in front, the gentleman smiling as he climbed the hill to meet her. He did so leisurely, as if he had all the time in the world. He probably did.

She wouldn't be able to escape him until she left Fullmoon. Somehow, she had stumbled right into it, as in the wood all the phases of the Night existed simultaneously. So instead of running from the man-fox, she decided to run toward him. Meanwhile, she imagined the fence as the border between Fullmoon and Second Night. Oriana's move took the red-haired man by surprise, but when he saw her heading for the fence, he fell on all fours and raced after her like a dog. Oriana quickened as she heard the Nocturnal snarling behind her. Then, she jumped over the fence. She landed with a thud and buried her face in the high grass.

She held her breath, but no claw or fang reached out. Bit by bit, she raised her head. The nocturnal hills were shrouded in half darkness, a half-moon dangling in the sky. Slowly, she stood and resumed walking down to the bottom of the hill.

THIRTY-SIX

When at last she saw the shape of the old bridge, it seemed like only moments had passed since she left the fence. The bridge itself was miraculously functional, though half dismantled by time, a skeleton of what it once had been. Millennia ago, a river ran under it, now an overgrown thicket smelling of rot and decay. Oriana was about to cross when she heard a faint moan. It came from the middle of the bridge, where three large figures sat. She could barely make them out but saw something sparkling near them, perhaps a fire. Oriana pondered. If she went around the bridge, she could avoid them but would lose precious time. Besides, the thicket was so deep that she could easily end up trapped within it. She walked on.

By the time she was halfway across the bridge, she realized that the sparkles rose up from the figures themselves. Three men with spears on their shoulders, sentinels of some sort, shimmered like they were made of fireflies.

"Here comes another one," a deep, rumbling voice announced.

Oriana's heart pounded. The Garaudi didn't turn as she approached them. They didn't need to, for they could already see her with their cloaks.

"What do you want?" another asked.

"I—I wish to pass the bridge," she said, stopping dead.

"And why would you do that?"

"To talk to your master."

On their cloaks eyes blazed in surprise.

"Has it occurred to you, young mistress, that he might not wish to talk to you?"

"I think he does. Pray, guide me to him."

Slowly, the three creatures stood up. Oriana recoiled. They were taller than humans, their skin paler than a corpse's. Eyeless, of course, but this lack was generously compensated for by an abundance of other organs. One of them had three mouths, another two noses, and the last several ears attached to his forehead and cheeks. They also each had more than two arms, and, under their cloaks were probably more than two legs too. They couldn't be the same kind as Scandar. The Nocturnals sensed her disgust and basked in it.

"So," sneered the tallest, its three mouths speaking in a grotesque echo, "you sure you came here for the Duke? Wouldn't you rather have one of our Riddles?"

"I like her eyes," said the second to the third, "and her nose too. It's cute."

"Greedy," admonished the third. "You've got three. I'll take it."

"No, it's mine!"

"Will you two just shut up?" hissed the tall one. The others sulked in silence. "So again, what about a nice wee Riddle? Answer it and you can have one of our eyes."

"That's a very kind offer, but no thank you."

"Are you sure?" asked the second, putting a hand over his cloak and removing one of its eyes. At once, it changed into a diamond, reflecting the light of the moon in a dazzling fire. Oriana gaped. One would be enough to buy a palace in Naples. A large one.

"Thank you, but I'd still rather talk to the Duke."

The tall one turned to the other two and shrugged.

"She's no fun," he sighed. "I'm bored."

"Well, two in one night would have been too much to ask for."

"Oh, he was a precious one, wasn't he?"

"He was. We should have made him last longer."

"There's still some of him left."

"I wish you would have taken his mouth, though. It unnerves me."

At that, the moan resumed. She looked down. On the pavement was a body, or rather, what was left of it. What had once been a tall, strong man dressed in a miller's coat now lay motionless and dismembered, though not completely. His head and torso were still intact, as was a leg and an arm. His face was eyeless, earless, and noseless, but not mouthless. Oriana covered her ears with her hands, to block out the sound that came from the thin mouth.

"Dreadful, isn't it?"

"What are your names?" she whispered.

"We. Beg. Your. Pardon?" they said in unison.

"Tell me your names so that when I speak to your master, I can tell him how poorly you've treated his guest."

The three creatures looked at one another and burst out laughing.

"And what slaves would we be if we still had names! Our master keeps them, and with them our liberty!"

"You know, I think," said the first, "that it was quite rude of you to ask."

"Very." The second nodded.

"And she is a trespasser," added the third.

"Good, then. I get the head."

"No, *I* get the head!"

"You had the head before!"

As they quarreled, Oriana turned and sprinted.

She knew she'd hear them coming any second, but when

she didn't, she halted, turned in time to see the trio aiming their spears at her.

Instinctively, she whispered, "Scandar."

A thunderclap.

Scandar stood in front of her, his hand on her shoulder. The spears were shattered on the ground, a few inches from his back. There was a movement in the Night and Oriana found herself in front of her three assailants. They looked baffled at Scandar, who was tiny compared to them. Still, his presence was like a silent roar.

"We didn't know she was yours," the first Garaude pleaded.

"Didn't she say she was a guest of our master?" Scandar said.

"Diurnals lie," said the second uncomfortably.

"Not this one," Scandar replied.

Slowly, painfully, the three Nocturnals knelt, heads bowed.

"Please don't tell the Duke," they said.

The Nocturnal gestured for Oriana to follow him across the bridge.

When they arrived on the other side, he whispered to her, "Don't let anyone suspect that you know my name, or I will be lost. I'm sorry I couldn't come before."

Oriana looked up, a thousand questions on her lips. Scander looked shorter than she remembered. And then she realized—he was the same; *she* had grown up. Yet Oriana was so happy that he was finally there, not a memory, not a dream, not a voice listening in the dark, but flesh. And yet how little she knew about him! His features were so different from the three misshapen faces of the other Garaudi that it was hard to imagine they belonged to the same species. Even his name was a mystery, that and the way his kind regarded him with respect, but also fear. Who was he really? *A Riddle*, she thought, *for real this time.*

"Master Garaude," she said, "is it true what my mother told me? That I was the reason she went to the market in the first place, to protect me against the Night-Ones?"

"You believed her?"

"So, she *was* lying."

"Lying is a Diurnal concept. Your mother is almost one of us now, even though she is still alive. Maybe she did go to the Market to protect you from us. And maybe she didn't and used you as an excuse to pursue her lust for power. But this is not the real matter."

"What is, then?"

"That she said what she needed to achieve the desired effect in you."

"And what . . . Oh, I see," Oriana replied.

Though she wasn't quite sure, for what had Donna Lena achieved? In the end, she pushed her straight into the Night's arms, hardly what she had wanted for her. Maybe her mother just wanted to be seen, like Scandar had always seen her.

She was silent for six strides, then she asked, "Master Garaude, if I may, who am I to you? Why are you looking out for me? Did your master order you to?"

"I would lie if I said he didn't."

"I thought lying was a concept only Diurnals had."

"Ah, indeed, milady, indeed. But I was a Diurnal once, like you."

"This is becoming like a game of chess. Why do you care, Garaude? Or is this just another game? Is that why you look more human than your brothers? So that you could interact with me and earn my trust?"

He didn't answer straightaway but made a quick gesture with his hand. An eye detached from his cloak and grew a mouth where its iris had been. It buzzed its finlike eyelash wings, hovering close to Oriana's ear.

"I didn't have to give you my name," the eye whispered.

"Do you regret that you did?" she whispered back.

"Not at all, but my life is on the tip of your tongue."

"Why?"

"If my master were to learn that I gave you my name, he would annihilate me."

"I—I am sorry to hear that, but . . . why did you give it to me?"

Scandar slowed down.

"You trusted me," said the eye. "And so I trust you, Oriana Siliceo."

"But why! Who am I to you?"

"You . . . remind me of someone. From when I was alive. Someone who trusted me totally, whom I repaid very poorly. And so I trusted you with my life."

They spoke no more.

It was hard to tell for how long they had been walking. Time shrank and stretched all around them. Suddenly, she found herself in front of a low, squat hill surrounded by tall white stones. On its side was an opening like a wound in the earth. There stood a dolmen-like arch, vibrating with antiquity, and beyond it a darkness so deep that Oriana felt blinded just looking at it.

As they entered, Oriana felt a distant pounding, a thunder that belonged to the earth instead of the sky. It was quite warm for the season, but in an oddly discomforting way. Images of being buried alive crowded her mind. Her dread intensified, and after a while, she had to stop, her legs as stiff as stone. Scandar leaned toward her.

"What you're feeling," explained the Nocturnal, "is the pull of the Under-earth. Few Diurnals can resist it once they've entered. You're one of them."

Oriana shuddered, but the paralysis in her legs loosened its grip. They resumed walking in the dark. Little by little her vision crystalized. From the soft glow of the Garaude's cloak, she could see the outline of the long, tall tunnel that they traversed into the bowels of the hill. It smelled of roots and upturned earth, exuding a peculiar electrical sensation. The farther inside she traveled, the more energized she felt. Finally, she saw a stone arch, illuminated by a flickering light. As they got closer, Oriana's excitement grew. The Duke's smithy was reputed to be the biggest there ever was, so vast that no man could explore it fully in his lifetime. So, it was with a pang of disappointment that, when at last they passed through the arch, she found herself in a room scarcely larger than the parlor in her house.

She first noted the fireplace—a small, black, ugly thing—and the candles flickering inside stony niches. It was familiar, though she couldn't say why. Not until her eyes landed on the two figures bent over the worktable—a man-dwarf and a goblin working together on a music box—was she certain that she was in the right place. It was *that* box. Only, the ballerina didn't have a finger bone for a torso anymore, but a regular piece of porcelain that Gobbo finished inserting using a pincer. Time stood still. It was almost the same scene she had stumbled upon at the spring fair in Foggia when she was just a child.

"My Lord, Oriana Siliceo is here," Scandar announced.

The man-dwarf kept painting the tiny dancer's torso with a most delicate brush, scarcely thicker that an eyelash. As soon as he heard Scandar, though, Gobbo raised his ugly head and screamed, eyes sparkling with joy. Oriana shuddered. Finally, the Duke turned. His face was a blackened root with small flickering flames for eyes.

"Are you here to become my apprentice?" he asked in an inhuman voice.

Oriana shivered, curtseyed, and replied, "No, your Lordship, I'm afraid not."

The Night Saint wiped his hands with a piece of fabric.

"What do you want, then? As you can see, I'm busy."

"I—I came to collect my Boon, my Lord."

He scowled, and in doing so his face regained a semblance of his former humanity. Then, noticing the four Garaudi shuffling uncomfortably around the room, he commanded, "Out, all of you! Yes, that includes you as well."

Scandar hesitated as if to warn Oriana, then bowed and went out with the others. The Duke motioned for Gobbo to fetch a stool and he obeyed, his face drooling in adoration.

"Sit down."

Oriana sat. From this vantage the forge seemed rather bigger than she'd thought. To begin with, she realized now that she couldn't see its ceiling. Tiny geckos darted across the wall, though when she looked at them closely, their shapes began to change.

"Well? I don't have all Night."

Oriana smiled politely at the pun. In fact, she felt more anxious than ever.

"I'd like to learn how to forge a ring out of water."

"That would be considered an apprenticeship, I'm afraid."

"Which is why I'm asking for this lesson as a Boon. I only want to learn this one skill. You said the Deep Red Hammer could do it."

"Yes yes yes, I know perfectly well what I said."

He fell silent, his eyes lost in thought.

"It's a complex task. It will take—"

"It has to be done in just one night—this night," Oriana interrupted.

"Have you any idea what you are asking? These secrets mustn't leave this forge, ever. What if you taught others how to forge water? It could change human history, all for a girl's stupid whim!"

Oriana felt her anger swelling.

"I swear on the Grim King that I'll never reveal how it is done. Besides, wouldn't you need the Hammer to do it?"

"The Hammer can be stolen," he grunted, "as you well know."

"This is the Boon I want, my Lord."

The Emistuchivio considered her.

"Maybe I was hasty in granting it to you. But then again, you did help me to make peace with my sister," he said. In unison they looked at the music box. "Serapide would never have accepted my apologies and her trinket without your involvement."

She wet her lips. Was it a coincidence that he had been fixing the box's ballerina on their first meeting or had it been part of his plan all along? As he walked over to the fireplace, the Duke stopped and glared at her.

"So?" he called. "Have you changed your mind or what?"

"No! I— Wait . . . are you . . ."

"Follow me before I change my mind."

Oriana stood up, cheeks flushed.

"Oh, my Lord, thank you, thank you so much!"

Up close the hearth was bigger than it appeared, as large as her father's. Somehow the walls had vanished, and she could hear the faraway ding of a hammer pounding an anvil. The Night Saint reached into the fire and retrieved what at first seemed to be a poker. As he touched it, it morphed into the Hammer itself. It was even more exquisite than she remembered, its horse head reflecting the fire's glow in traceried silver. The Duke beckoned her closer.

"Most of what you'll need is stored within the Hammer itself. It knows exactly how to shape water into a ring. That is, if you know how to use a smith's hammer, which I know you do. The hard part is finding the right water and bringing it to welding temperature."

"It won't turn to steam?"

"Not if you use the right water and the right fire. There are three steps you must perform to make a ring of water. But even with the Hammer, the process is dangerous. It could kill you."

"I'm not afraid of dying doing what I love."

The scowl on his root-face loosened like a knot.

"That's all very well, Signorina Siliceo, but as you know by now, there are quite a few fates worse than death. The Deep Red Hammer is not a human tool. It doesn't just forge things, it forges the smith as well. You yourself may change as you complete your task."

"I don't care," she said defiantly.

"Good, then. One more thing. Be very careful of what you think and feel while using it, for whatever comes into your mind will flow through the Hammer into the ring. And now, Oriana Siliceo, I welcome you to my forge," he said, making a grand gesture, as if opening an imaginary curtain.

As he did, the darkness finally parted, and she could see the true vastness of the place in which she stood. Above her were ancient arches of unimaginable proportions, and beneath them stone staircases that led to hundreds of different landings, all supported by enormous caryatids, metal statues of Garaudi, Basilisks, Earth Wyrms, Wiccae, Gale Riders, Grinners, and Gowls. Each landing had its own furnace, over whose fire monk-like creatures hammered, welded, and chiseled, bending every alloy known to man, and many of those unknown.

As she watched them work, Oriana felt tears streaking down her face. For this was her Sanctum made real, the only place she knew she could ever call home.

THIRTY-SEVEN

Oriana's awareness came and went. She climbed down the endless stairs hewn in the rock, leaving the din of constant hammering high above her. Oriana's understanding of her surroundings faltered. Sometimes it felt like she was having a conversation with someone, only to realize it was just a memory. Was she alone? A cloud of eyes illuminated her way as she descended lower and lower into the depths of the Under-earth. There was in fact someone guiding her. It wasn't Scandar, as she had hoped, but moon-faced Gobbo, leering at her. The monkey scurried ahead, waiting for her under every arch until the floating eyes caught up with them. Finally, Oriana heard the rustling of fresh water. At the noise, Oriana startled.

They were standing in the largest cave she'd ever seen. The limestone ceiling glistened with glowworms' silk threads like an underground starry sky. The cavern floor descended in concentric terraces, almost like a shallow, inverted cone. At its bottom was a pool of the purest blue, reflecting the faint light from above. As they approached, Gobbo produced a flask from his belt and handed it to her. She took it unquestioningly. The pool was about the size of a small square, and yet its presence loomed so large that Oriana felt the urge to kneel.

"What is it?"

She hadn't expected an answer and was startled when the Goblin said, "This is the first water that appeared on earth over a million of million years ago. It is said that water cannot hold memory, and for the same reason it cannot remember shape. But this water *is* memory. Like blood is the memory of a species, she is the memory of Earth."

His voice sounded like a grinding of stone against stone. And yet she didn't suspect he could be so eloquent. Oriana stared at him.

"Gobbo, who are you? *What* are you?"

The creature grinned, but its face was slowly overcome by a deep yearning.

"I am a nameless slave. I am a broken promise. I am a Riddle," he replied, his usual fierce mask replaced by a look of such longing that Oriana felt her heart ache. The Goblin pointed at the flask, then at the water. "If you drink it, you'll die. Yet only in the body can it be kept."

Warily, she placed the flask in the blue water.

As soon as her hand touched the liquid, an electric freshness galvanized her body. And yet the flask had not filled at all. Had Gobbo given her a leaking one? Oriana placed the flask in a rocky niche and, using her hands, scooped the sapphire water. But when she tried to pour it into the flask, it streamed away like quicksilver. The monkey leered at her.

"Damn! Can't you help me instead of just standing there?" Oriana complained.

Gobbo's sneer grew wider. In the blink of an eye, he shoved her into the pool. Oriana released a sharp scream, for she didn't know how to swim. But the pool was so shallow that she faced a greater risk of drowning in her bathtub back home. While her body absorbed the shock, something seeped out of her. All her fatigue, all the dark recriminations of her mind dissolved. She felt fresh, a child reborn, her mind clear as crystal. She picked up the flask, but no matter how many times she put it under the surface, it didn't fill up. And then, in a flash of intuition, she knew what had to be done.

She crouched down in the water and took in a good mouthful, careful not to swallow. As soon as she closed her lips, the battle began, for that water wanted desperately to be swallowed, to be absorbed by her body. But Oriana understood that if she did, she herself would dissolve into the pool. It was tempting, for she would be one with the memory of Earth, and know no anguish, fear, pain, past, nor future. With a quivering hand, Oriana Siliceo opened the metal flask and spit the water into it, careful not to waste a single drop. Gobbo applauded with his tiny hands, eyes ablaze in delight.

For her second task they climbed even farther down to the Duke's most ancient coal mines. In a short outburst of loquacity, Gobbo explained to her that she had to select a single piece of coal, a fossil from the first forest that covered the earth. This piece alone could spark the enchanted fire she needed to forge the water she'd collected. Still vibrating with energy, Oriana followed her guide through caverns whose stalactites spiraled down at them like wisteria. But when at last she spotted the mine and understood what was being asked of her, she shook.

It wasn't a cave at all but a bottomless pit, a large, cavernous crack on a vast, sloping surface. At its top, monk-like creatures used harnesses and ropes to lower themselves into the depths by means of an ingenious pulley system. While suspended in that perpetual void, they dug into the walls. Oriana's task was even worse than theirs, for she had to travel to the coal bottom of the pit, and there, with her bare hands, dig out the heart of the most ancient forest. While the tiny-eyed, lizard-tailed creatures strapped her in a web of sturdy leather ropes, cinching her waist, Oriana looked pleadingly at the Goblin.

The idea of descending alone into that living darkness

was unbearable. To her astonishment, Gobbo jumped on her shoulders.

"We'll go in together," he croaked.

And so the creatures lowered them down, Gobbo's and Oriana's bodies spinning in the black void. One by one, they passed the dangling monks with their lanterns, until even the memory of light faded. And yet Gobbo was always with her, whispering with his broken voice that soon they'd reach the bottom, where she would have to fight the Flesh of the earth to tear out its living heart. His words should have scared her, but somehow they had the opposite effect, for hearing any voice in that darkness was a solace.

At last, their descent stopped. She looked up, then down. Darkness above, darkness below. As the monkey left her shoulders, holding on to the rope, Oriana screamed.

"For the love of God, don't leave me here!"

"You must jump down. The coal will absorb your fall."

"Jump? But then how will I come back up?"

"The only way back is forward. Jump or give up!"

Oriana thought of Villabianca, of Riano, of her father, of Bruno, and her mother. She tried to picture their pity, their scorn, their disappointment, and their triumph as she came back to Lucerìa empty-handed, Night-touched, and untouchable. But even her hunger for vengeance, even her fear of failure wasn't enough. She just couldn't let herself fall. Then an image filled her mind: the market, with its silent stalls and hopeless customers. In time, she would become like them, with no great love or great adventure, no true talent, just the endless drabness of the Day. She untied her harness at the waist, removing the last strap with one strong pull, and fell.

Her drop was short-lived, for at once a soft darkness embraced her.

It filled her mind as well as her nose, mouth, and eyes. This was the ancient Flesh of the earth, coal that had once been trees and animals, long before man. It sucked her in, burying her alive. With utter terror, she realized that she would become coal herself. What was the use of fighting? Every living creature would end up like this, in the end, even Nocturnals, no matter how long-lived.

But then, just as she was about to give in, she felt a throb through the dark soil. There was its heart, beating in the depths, calling to her. It spoke the same language of her blood, the tongue of unrelinquished Desire. The struggle started in earnest, Oriana pulling and shoving, the Flesh at first opposing her but then—little by little—giving way. A scream on her lips, Oriana stretched her arm toward the throbbing pulse until she felt her fingers close around that black heart, a piece of the first tree from the first forest.

As soon as she grabbed it, the blackness surged like a wave, pushing her upward with an earthly tide, until Oriana felt the joy of fresh air and a little hand, pulling her the rest of the way and helping her to untie the rope around her waist.

Time shifted, streamed, pooled, started all over again.

She looked up. Scandar was at her side, filling the forge with dry wood.

She was outside, under a black starry sky. On the top of the hill she could see for miles in every direction. If she squinted her eyes, she could even make out the dark shape of Lucerìa. The Duke had moved his forge above ground. Oriana inspected her hands. They were jet-black with soot. She made for the water basin, but the Garaude's hand stopped her.

"No, don't wash it off. The Flesh will protect you."

"From what?"

"You'll see." He smiled.

Gobbo handed her the Deep Red Hammer. As soon as she grabbed its handle, all the different phases of the water forging were made clear in her mind. First, she took the metal flask and poured its contents over a stone slab. Then she reached for her pocket, where she had stored the Flesh's heart. Her clothes were as blackened as her hands.

"Mother will kill me," she muttered absentmindedly.

Her peal of laughter startled the crowd that had gathered—clouds of gleaming eyes, lumbering shapes, hooded monk-like creatures, willowy crones, a knight wearing a cloak of thorns, three bodiless heads. Oriana looked at them in shock. She didn't realize that she had attracted an audience. And what an audience! She could see no end to them.

"Word has spread," said the Duke from behind her. "It is quite an occasion for them to see a Diurnal wield my Hammer."

Thousands sat in a hemicycle around the Duke's mound, like members of a secret jury. The exact count proved elusive, for their forms shifted, morphing in accordance with Oriana's perceptions. Garaudi turned into clouds of fireflies, coalescing in unison into a cloak of shimmering eyes. Serpentine figures undulated up and down the slope, only to transform, upon second glance, into winding trails of stones scattered across the tall grass. Earth Wyrms, most likely. Many she recognized from the Vigils, others from Cetta's tales. That boulder growing a tree sapling could only be the bulky head of a Giancano, an underground behemoth, and that solitary hair the source of all his might. But quite a few she didn't recognize at all: robins with flaming crowns over their heads, foxes who casted man-shaped shadows, goats made of scrap metal who screeched at one another, and a woman with scissors around her neck and one bloodied eye on her forehead. Their shapes shifted, changed, and shimmered under the half-moon. In whichever form they took Oriana sensed their curiosity, vibrant like the smell of jasmine in summer. She realized that for a Night-One to see a Diurnal in their midst was no less miraculous than for her to see a Night Saint at midday.

"I can send them away, if it bothers you," offered the Duke.

"No, it's fine."

But it wasn't just fine; she basked in their attention. Cautiously, she removed the coal-black heart from her pocket. She knew now why she needed the Flesh's protection.

She turned to the crowd and said, "Stand back."

They obeyed. Even the Duke took a step backward. But just as she walked toward the fire, Gobbo hurriedly returned, a small black cap in his clawed hands.

"For your head. The Flesh don't stick on hair."

Oriana smiled and put on the cap, then threw the Flesh's heart into the fire. The flames leapt up, bright yellow and all-consuming, sweeping over the top of the hill with a terrible blast. She felt it on her face, her eyebrows singeing to the root, but not a mark on her skin. And yet it wasn't enough. This forge had no bellows, and now she knew why. Tightening her grip on the Hammer, she called for the winds. First the East Wind, then the Scirocco from the desert, then the Bora from the far North. They came at once, feeding the fire with their strength until the top of the mound burned like an inferno. What would the farmers of Lucerìa see from the distant hills?

The water sizzled on the stone slab, not steaming but changing color like welding iron. When it had reached a deep ocean-blue, Oriana began hammering. In her father's forge it would have been useless to try hammering flat metal into a circle. But the earth's water was no metal and her Hammer was no human tool. As soon as the water started to cool, it curled, slowly taking the shape Oriana channeled into the Hammer. What resulted was still much bigger than a ring, more like a wide bracelet, but Oriana knew that was no problem for the instrument she wielded.

She had to be careful not to let the water cool too much, for if it did, if it lost the memory of its shape, it would immediately steam. She would not be given a second chance. So Oriana kept hammering, calling the winds to feed the flames every time the water dropped in temperature. The flames leapt at her command, engulfing her body and her instruments in its yellow-white sheets. Air and fire, water and earth—her forging was a crucible.

When she needed strength, she asked the Hammer. And the Hammer gave to her the power of rivers and ancient roots. When she felt exhaustion taking over, she asked for stamina. And the Hammer gave her the hardness of stone and the piercing vigor of dripping water. And when she felt her vision clouding, again she asked the Hammer. And the Hammer gave it to her, offering the searing clarity of flames that burn deep and are never extinguished.

In the living crucible Oriana had become, thoughts and emotions merged. She had started forging to show Riano and the Lucerini that she could accomplish the impossible. But as her work proceeded, that thought melted away, revealing the emotion that lay at her core. For Oriana loved her twin brother like she loved herself. And since in the end a ring is nothing else but the link of a chain, that sentiment became so imprinted in its shape that no one, not even the Emistuchivio himself, could undo one without the other.

Finally, the Deep Red Hammer gave a slight pull. She stopped, letting the form on the slab rest. As it cooled, it shrunk, changing shape. Breathing deeply, she reached for it. It was a ring indeed, yet wet to the touch, shifting like water—a paradox made real. And it was hers. She had made it, and no one else. Oriana raised it overhead, a tiny crown to coronate her success.

The Nocturnal crowd stood in unison. They didn't scream, they didn't clap, they didn't stomp their feet or shout her name. They just stood there, the Wyrms and the Wiccae, the Garaudi and the Urchins, and stared, yet Oriana felt that they would never forget her, not till the Night lay over the hills of Lucerìa.

THIRTY-EIGHT

Scandar left her just inside the city gates. His handsome face was stiff with reverence and another emotion that Oriana couldn't name. Their goodbye was brisk, as if their parting were to be short-lived. Only, Oriana looked at his sky-patterned figure and knew that long years would pass before they met again. She examined his masklike face. Who was he really? She would never know, she reckoned, at least not while she lived in the Day. But that was also why she loved the Night, for not everything had to be explained, and so not everything was.

She walked away, propelled by the urge to show the ring to her brother, to Bruno and Donna Lena, to prove to them that she had achieved the unachievable. Brazenly, she walked toward the smithy. The streets were mostly deserted, a thin layer of sleet covering the cobblestones. Oriana had lost Villabianca's coat but wasn't cold. In fact, she felt so full of energy that she had to stop herself from breaking into a run. Then the Duomo's bell tolled ten times. Oriana frowned. She was almost an hour late. What a fool she had been, relying on a Nocturnal's sense of time! She hastened through the sleepy streets.

When she was just one street away from the smithy, she slowed down her pace.

The alleys were *too* silent. No cheering crowd awaited her, no collective triumph for her to savor. They had probably given up on the challenge. She didn't care. All she needed were the members of the Guild and Riano. But when she finally came into view of the smithy's door, her heart stopped. It was shut, locked by a chain. They hadn't waited for her. Anger swelled in her. It wouldn't have been hard for Bruno or her mother to convince the Guild masters of her madness, persuading them to move on. But she had the ring. She could still prove she had completed the challenge and won. She sprinted so fast that she had to hold her cap in place on top of her head.

Via de Nicastri was dark, barely illuminated by the half-moon and a few old jack-o'-lanterns. The palazzo's blinds were all shut. She pounded on the main gate.

"Aprite! Let me in or I'll smash the door!" she yelled.

In her fervor she didn't notice that the doors came unhinged, unable to withstand the battering of her blows. When at last someone stirred inside, asking who she was, Oriana shouted, "It's me! Open up!"

She heard a fumbling of keys, and when the door opened, Oriana barged in. Donna Marisa, the gatekeeper, stared at her in fright, a swaying lantern in her hand.

"W-what do you want?" she asked.

"Wake them up! I have the ring and by God I will own the smithy!"

Donna Marisa whimpered but didn't move. Oriana began to shake her when she saw someone coming down the stairs. A boy. It was clear he had just woken up, barefoot as he was and yawning, eyes still puffy with sleep. He stopped when he saw her.

"Ah, there you are!" cried Oriana in triumph. "Look, I've done it! Here is my ring. Where is yours? Let me see it."

The boy looked down at Oriana's open palm and then at her face.

"Who are you?" he asked.

"Enough with the tricks! The contract was clear. If you couldn't do what I've done, then you've lost the challenge. Now, look!"

"W-what is it?" the boy asked.

"It's the ring made of water, you dimwit! Touch it, feel it, it's real."

He cautiously brushed it with his finger.

"It's . . . wet."

"Of course it's wet! It's supposed—"

She was interrupted by the three people on the landing staring at her. One was her mother, her hair done up even in the middle of the night. The second, a young man in his twenties. And then there was Cetta, though all her hair had turned white.

"What happened to her?" said Oriana in a whisper.

By then, the young man had climbed down the steps to meet her. Muscular, broad-shouldered, with a hint of stubble on his cheeks, he held a walking stick with both hands, half raised as if to defend himself. He stared at her wide-eyed.

"I don't know who you are, but you will leave my family alone," he said.

"*Your* family? And who the hell are you?"

The young man was about to come forward when a red-haired woman in a nightgown rushed down to the stairs, a baby in her arms.

"Riano, keep away from her!" she said.

"Riano?" Oriana asked.

Her head ringing, she turned to look at the barefoot boy. He was not her twin brother. She could see it now in the different angle of his jaw and hawklike nose. Oriana felt the floor slowly pulling away from her.

"You're Tato," she said. The boy nodded and smiled. "B-but you're only six!"

"I'll be thirteen this coming summer."

"Who is she?" the brawny young man asked Tato.

"Our dead sister, back from the grave."

At that, both Cetta and Donna Marisa recoiled, making a

gesture to ward against the Evil Eye. Oriana grabbed her own shoulders to hold them steady.

"I'm not dead," she corrected, almost pleadingly.

"How come you're black as obsidian, then?" Tato asked curiously.

The Flesh! She had forgotten to wash it off. But as she tried to rub it away with her fingers, she found that the inky blackness didn't come off. While she frantically tried to remove it, she saw two other people approaching from the courtyard, lanterns in their hands—Mamma Emma and the count. As soon as she saw Villabianca, Oriana raised her hands to her cheeks. He had aged, too, his hair streaked with silver. He gaped at her, pale as a soft cheese.

"You fled from my coach that night," he said. "You fled, and I couldn't find you. I thought I'd never see you again."

"That was last night," Oriana replied.

"That was seven years ago!"

Gradually, Oriana sank down onto the steps.

"I'm sorry," she said. "I didn't know. I should have, but I didn't."

She felt a tentative hand rest on her shoulder.

"Ori, is it really you?"

She nodded without looking up at her twin brother.

"What happened? Where have you been all these years?" Riano asked.

"I went to the Under-earth to forge a ring out of water."

If ever there had been a chance that she could return to the world of Day, those words shattered it. She felt their shock and her own. At last, she was beginning to see herself as they did—a stranger with skin as black as Night, speaking of secrets unknown to the living.

"What ring?" Riano asked.

She looked up.

"The water ring. Our final challenge to become first apprentice."

A memory lit up his eyes, like when a man recollects a childhood tale. That, she realized, was what she had become to them: a tale told at the Vigils.

"I became master smith last month," he said uncomfortably.

"Bruno?"

"Dead. Killed in a quarrel over a girl, in Foggia."

"Typical." She smirked.

He smiled, too, a familiar grin on a stranger's face.

"Father?"

"Gone. Never came back," he said. "But you can stay if you want. The smithy is big enough for two."

"Would you really do that?" she questioned, searching his eyes.

"Yes," he said, stiffening.

She rushed over to hug him. Immediately, she felt his horror as he shrank back. In that moment, Oriana realized how strong she'd become. Not only could she lift him easily, but she could also crack him in two if she wanted. She gasped and let go. Riano staggered back, fear and shame in his eyes. An awkward silence fell over the courtyard. Oriana could feel their eyes scorching her new skin. Struggling to regain his composure, Riano looked to his wife.

"Oriana, I think you remember Angia."

The woman walked over warily, shielding the sleeping baby on her breast, and stopped two paces away. Oriana tried to smile, breaking inside. For it was indeed her childhood friend. No longer the promise of a woman but a woman in her own right, her face slightly swollen, circles under her eyes. Her red hair was held captive under a cuff, yet she looked happy, mature, at peace. Looking at her, Oriana realized what she herself might have been, had she stayed. In addition to her otherworldly sheen, Oriana still had the body of a fifteen-year-old girl, and she knew that this was how she would always be.

"Ori," Angia said, "I'm sorry I didn't recognize you."

"Nor I you," she said.

Her eyes were drawn to the baby, still rosily asleep in its mother's arms. Small as it was, Oriana could see that it had her brother's face and Angia's red hair. As Oriana looked at the baby, her smile became less forced.

"This is my third," Angia said proudly.

"What's his name?" Oriana asked.

"Giuseppe." She smiled.

Oriana looked first at her brother, then back at the baby. With her black fingers, she brushed the newborn's forehead, where a few wisps of red hair grew. Sensing her otherworldliness, the baby opened his eyes, then burst into a squall.

Instinctively, Angia shielded the baby and retreated, as if to protect her son from harm. Oriana's anguish escaped from her lips in a moan, pushing everyone else away from her. Seeing their reactions, she let out a short, dry cackle.

"See, Mother! See what you've done to me!"

Oriana grabbed her cap and tore it off. A cascade of shiny black curls fell down her shoulders and back, almost to the floor. It was quite simply the most beautiful hair anyone in Lucerìa had seen in a thousand years. This, she realized, they would add to her story at the Vigils.

Donna Lena descended the steps, the others making way, as if they didn't dare to brush against her. As she approached, Oriana saw that she had aged as well. Some of her locks had turned white, but it was her mouth that looked the most changed, as if it held an echo of love.

"I thought I had lost you. That the Night had swallowed you," Donna Lena said. "That all I did had been in vain."

She had expected almost anything from her mother, but not this. Her mother brushed her hand against her daughter's jet-black cheek and smiled. Not the Emerald Dame's smile, but her own.

"Look at you," Donna Lena said, proud. "Just look at you, my titilla."

Oriana held her mother's hand against her cheek and shut her eyes. This is what it meant to be seen, if only for a moment. She wanted this moment to outlast time, but already she could sense the Night moving away, calling out to her with a yearning deeper than any known to man. Donna Lena understood, for she pecked her daughter on the cheek.

"If you have to go, go. Farewell, daughter of mine," she whispered in her ear.

Oriana opened her eyes. They stood around her like statues, petrified by her silence. Finally, she turned to her brother. Ignoring his flinch, she placed the water ring in his hand.

"I made it for you. Keep it and remember me. All of you."

She beheld her mother, Tato, Cetta, Angia, and Giuseppe, Donna Marisa, Mamma Emma, and finally, Villabianca. Unable to find words to offer him, she walked up and caressed his cheek. Instantly, his tears solidified into crystals. He flashed a most innocent smile, one in which fear and awe merged in equal measure. And then he laughed, the earthy laugh of a child.

Oriana walked out the door, into the streets of Lucerìa, and ran. And she kept on running, faster and faster, her shoes coming undone, leaving her barefoot. She raced past the sleepy night guards, and the city gates, through the woods, and up the hill, never stopping to catch her breath, for she didn't need to. At the top she reached a clearing. Lucerìa lay below her, asleep in the dark currents of the Night, and yet she could see it perfectly, as if it were midday.

She was not alone. Two figures joined by her side, the

taller one hooded in a cloak of stars and the shorter smoking a thin clay-pipe.

She turned to the Garaude.

"You knew," she said.

"I told you," he said, his face impenetrable like a mask, "not to trust me."

"And bloody fool that I was, I didn't believe you."

"He only did what he was told," said the Duke.

"And you!" she said, surprised at her own fury. "You tricked me!"

"Indeed. That's what masters do. They trick their pupils into doing what's best for them, for they don't know any better."

"But why? You could've forced me into your apprenticeship from the start, thirteen years ago! All that I endured in Lucerìa, the challenge of peers, my battles, it was all for nothing!"

The Emistuchivio frowned, his pipe blazing.

"That shows how little you know of us, still. We're living stories, Oriana Siliceo. You say that all your struggles have been for nothing, but it's precisely because of your struggles that you've become who you are now. They've been telling tales about you and your challenge of peers for the last seven years. And yet it was only tonight that you gave them what was needed to turn you into a Nocturnal: a glimpse of what cannot possibly be explained. For in mystery alone are stories truly alive."

She remained silent for a while, her irises glistening in the blackness.

"But this isn't what I wanted. I wished to work in the real world, for real people, creating work that would be an inspiration for all."

"Aye. And that's why I searched so long for you."

"Y-you were looking for me?"

"From the very start. What did I tell you when we first met?"

"That you were looking for your Deep Red Hammer."

"No. I told you that I was looking for my most precious tool. It's you that I sought at the Market of the Dead, you that I helped to forge and create. And yet as much as I helped, the forging and the creation was all your own. You are your own masterpiece, Oriana Siliceo, and you should be proud."

"But I didn't choose this. It was supposed to be *my* path, but I didn't choose it!"

The Duke's eyes blazed in amusement.

"You didn't? Tell me then, daughter of the Day, when your brother offered to share the smithy with you, why did you refuse?"

She didn't answer, her fingers playing with her locks of black hair.

"You had won, and yet you didn't collect your prize. Why?"

"Pride," she answered uncertainly.

"Maybe. But what kind of pride? Pride in creating something. Even better, in *becoming* something. You see, I couldn't really trick you into becoming someone you are not, that is not how a Moira works, the wanting had to be all yours. And it was."

Oriana touched her face, expecting to find tears, but there were none. Her pain was someone else's, a shadow's. She saw in her mind, just as she had when she was a child, the silhouette of the Duke striking the anvil with his hammer, and by his side a woman with long black hair and eyes which reflected the forge's fire. Through Time and Desire, she recognized her own recognition and knew herself.

"So, I will never see them again," she said in a shudder.

The Duke's eyes softened.

"What do you think we do in my forge? We inspire them with our work. Everything that was ever built and forged throughout the centuries by mankind was first dreamed of in my hearth. We create the impossible, so that the possible might exist. And you will need them, Oriana, for why create anything at all, if you didn't have someone to dazzle with your creations? So, no, this is not the last they will see of you, for your ring is a link in a chain that cannot be broken. But be warned, all your creations must stay in my smithy. I permitted you to give away the water ring because it was part of the story that made you change, but there will be no more exceptions. And should you one day forget this and give away something you are not meant to give, then you will cease to be my hand, and become my slave, just like this one here. For the beauty of the unseen, that deep mystery, should not be touched by a human hand, not until the last day of mankind. Now come, my apprentice, for Dawn is approaching and we have much work to do."

He stretched out his hand.

She hesitated for the span of a breath, then took it. As she did the entire hill shook, the earth opened under their feet, and it swallowed them in one sonorous crash of thunder. Silence coiled over the dark hills like a black-scaled Wyrm, as the Night yielded. And far away, across the black expanse, the sun started to climb into the sky.

ACKNOWLEDGMENTS

For this story to reach you, I had to cast my voice through another language and another culture. Acknowledging all the people who helped means recognizing all those who believed this story could cross linguistic and cultural boundaries. It's not just about the book you are reading, the Night it carries, and its Nocturnals, but all the people who—through the years—had faith in them.

I will start with Paolo Guerrieri, my mate. Paolo read the first installments of what would become Lucerìa and its nocturnal world fifteen years ago. His affection and enthusiasm were the foundations that made this project possible. A special thanks also goes to Anne Woodall, whose contribution was essential in helping me ferry this paper boat. Yael Artom was also of great support: my first colleague at school to read it and give feedback. Emil Van Zuylen, of course; this book is born out of our conversations on folklore. I miss those chats, Emil, very much. I hope my thanks reach you wherever you are. Een hartelijke dank, mijn vriend.

I will always be indebted to CLARION—fellow writer Jaymee Goh was one of my first international readers—and to all my peers and tutors, especially Delia Sherman, whose support for the first draft was vital. An agradecimiento especial goes to Arianna and Dani, who let me stay in their magic bosquedeto, and whose Extremaduran folklore informed the last versions of Serapide's festival.

A heartfelt thanks goes to—whom else?—Paul Lucas, my agent, who believed in Lucerìa for the longest time, showing an unwavering kindness, the likes of which I have never seen in this business. Paul, you were and are a treasure; may the Duke of the Under-earth keep you. Last but not least, to all the people at SAGA, and most of all Sareena, who believed this story could resonate with an American audience and fought for it with a tenacity Oriana would have greatly admired.

To all of you, un grazie di cuore.

ABOUT THE AUTHOR

GIOVANNI DE FEO is a fabulist, novelist, and comic book writer. He previously taught literature at International Baccalaureate schools in England and Holland. Currently, he lives in Bologna, Italy, where he is also a performing storyteller with a repertoire of Italian folktales.